PENGUIN BOOKS

ALL THIS CO

Sarah Thankam Mathews grew up ___ ___ing to the United States at seventeen. He ___ ___ ___erican *Short Stories* and she is a recipien ___ ___ ___erican Writers' Workshop and the Iowa Writers' Workshop. In 2020, she founded the mutual aid group Bed-Stuy Strong. *All This Could Be Different*, a 2022 finalist for the National Book Award for Fiction, is her first novel.

★ ★ ★

Praise for *All This Could Be Different*

"Wholly original . . . [Written] with such mordant wit, insight, and specificity, it feels like watching a new literary star being born in real time."
—*Entertainment Weekly*

"Darkly witty and finely wrought . . . *All This Could Be Different* illuminates the hardships of immigrant life, the elusiveness of lasting romantic love—and ultimately the joy and belonging that can come from a 'family' of friends."
—*People*

"Bold and wide-ranging . . . Mathews expertly captures and elevates the position of being a young queer person in the postrecession US."   —*Vogue*

"Mathews has a big heart and a sharp tongue . . . [and] a wonderful eye for the things that make friendship and community just as valuable as romance."
—*The New York Times Book Review* (Editors' Choice)

"Easily a contender for Book of the Year."   —*The Observer*

"Both lyrical and page-turning . . . *All This Could Be Different*, in which the lives of a group of millennials become fascinatingly entangled . . . offers us a panoramic view of mingled desires, fears, and joys that will be familiar to readers of Eliot and Austen, but [Mathews] does them one better: her novel is about an underrepresented first-generation immigrant, and it's incredibly gay."
—*Los Angeles Review of Books*

"Radiant . . . Mathews's writing is daring, sharp, and authoritative. She's a master in building rich characters who are imperfect and complicated, charismatic and lovable. At times, the prose felt luxurious and welcoming in the way

that the scent of your favorite candle might slowly fill up an ever-expanding room."
—*Vox*

"A novel so good I was torn by the incompatible desires to never set it down and never finish it . . . [Mathews's] skillful alternating between lush imagery and straightforward, plain language makes *All This Could Be Different* pulsate. . . . A masterclass in character development . . . It is perhaps the greatest depiction of what *chosen family* really means without ever explicitly using those words."
—Kayla Kumari Upadhyaya, *Autostraddle*

"A beautiful, authentic rendition of the brown queer experience and immigrant dynamics, *All This Could Be Different* is a love letter to these communities. It is a novel of possibilities, and a novel bound to steal your heart."
—*Electric Literature*

"Perhaps it's too soon to say which books we'll look back on in fifty years as the ones that defined a generation, but [*All This Could Be Different*], a close-to-perfect coming-of-age romp, is surely a contender. Bitingly funny and sweetly earnest, it's one of those rare novels that feels just like life. . . . [Mathews] captures some unnamable, essential thing about being a twentysomething struggling through work and love and late-stage capitalism. . . . In the manner of books that stay with you forever, *All This Could Be Different* is a singular story that extends beyond itself. . . . [A] funny, vibrant, heartbreaking book."
—*BookPage* (starred review)

"A bildungsroman, an immigrant story, a hero's journey not to be missed."
—*Lit Hub*

"[Written] with tenderness and exhilaration."
—*Elle*

"Dazzling . . . An epic and beautiful first novel from a writer to watch."
—*Them*

"Wholly original . . . Mathews convinces the reader that yes, maybe all this could be different after all."
—*Vulture*

"[What] initially blew me away was the clarity of Mathews's writing and the accuracy with which she describes experiences I'd previously taken for granted. Her writing is funny, incisive. . . . This book gave me a lot to ponder, but ultimately left me hopeful."
—David Vogel, *BuzzFeed*

"Engrossing . . . A moving immigrant's story and a heartfelt queer love story that tackles socioeconomic issues with nuance."   —*Rolling Stone*

"Sneha's equally vulnerable and cutting narration . . . captures the queer, immigrant experience unlike any other."   —*Harper's Bazaar*

"Funny [and] poignant."   —*Shondaland*

"Captivating . . . [*All This Could Be Different*] will sneak up on you and grab your heart."   —*San Francisco Bay Times*

"Sarah Thankam Mathews's tender and beautiful prose renders the story unforgettable."   —*The Millions*

"Moving . . . A searing portrait of the joys and pains of being a young adult in turbulent times."   —*Debutiful*

"I deeply appreciated Mathews's *choices* in this book—toward nuance, toward lyricism that elevates queer emotions, toward being present in the complex reality of straddling cultural expectations between family and community. . . . Mathews is a great writer and does the complexities justice."
    —S. Bear Bergman, *Xtra Magazine*

"Mathews achieves what so often seems to be impossible: a deeply felt 'novel of ideas.' . . . Beautifully written, lusciously felt, and marvelously envisioned. Resplendent with intelligence, wit, and feeling."
    —*Kirkus Reviews* (starred review)

"Sneha is a magnetic teller of her tale of finding love, growing up, and summoning the power to change—and choose—her life. . . . This novel burrows deep."   —*Booklist* (starred review)

"Everything about this novel is perfect. It's about friendship and work, two things that so rarely get treated with such nuance and care in fiction. Sneha's narrative voice is both snarky and warm. Every scene comes alive. If you're looking for your next great queer millennial read, this is it."   —*Book Riot*

"Poignant and illuminating."   —*Publishers Weekly*

"*All This Could Be Different* is spiny and delicate, scathingly funny and wildly moving. Sarah Thankam Mathews is a brilliant writer, one whose every ringing sentence holds both bite and heart."   —Lauren Groff, author of *Matrix*

"Some books are merely luminous. This one is iridescent—with joy and pain, isolation and communion, solemnity and irreverent humor. *All This Could Be Different* is a declaration, an electrifying act of resistance."
                                         —Susan Choi, author of *Trust Exercise*

"Battle cry and love song both, *All This Could Be Different* is an ode—tender, sexy, and smart—to coming of age in turbulent times. Sarah Thankam Mathews writes like a blaze, and this book will remind you what it is to be young and powerfully alive."
                          —C Pam Zhang, author of *How Much of These Hills Is Gold*

"Sarah Thankam Mathews's prose is undeniable."
                                         —Raven Leilani, author of *Luster*

"Sarah Thankam Mathews's *All This Could Be Different* is quietly epic, breathtaking in its beauty, and profound in its meaning. Mathews captures the complexities, contradictions, and dissonances of life with astounding aplomb and care."   —Robert Jones, Jr., author of *The Prophets*

"Sharply observed and deeply empathetic, *All This Could Be Different* is a gorgeous story of dreaming and daring against the odds. I loved these flawed, funny friends and I rooted for them, and as I raced toward the end I felt an ache in my chest, missing them already."
                          —Dawnie Walton, author of *The Final Revival of Opal & Nev*

"Exquisite. Mathews's is a completely original voice that is, by turns, fierce, witty, musical, poignant, and, yes, deeply sexy. [*All This Could Be Different*] is the kind of book one should read not only to be entertained or impressed but to feel less alone."   —Sanjena Sathian, author of *Gold Diggers*

Penguin Reading Group Discussion Guide available
online at penguinrandomhouse.com

ALL

THIS

COULD

BE

DIFFERENT

Sarah Thankam Mathews

PENGUIN BOOKS

PENGUIN BOOKS
An imprint of Penguin Random House LLC
penguinrandomhouse.com

First published in the United States of America by Viking,
an imprint of Penguin Random House LLC, 2022
Published in Penguin Books 2023

Grateful acknowledgment is made for permission to reprint lines from the poem
"Catastrophe Is Next to Godliness" by Franny Choi.

ISBN 9780593489147 (paperback)

THE LIBRARY OF CONGRESS HAS CATALOGED THE HARDCOVER EDITION AS FOLLOWS:
Names: Mathews, Sarah Thankam, author.
Title: All this could be different / Sarah Thankam Mathews.
Description: [New York] : Viking, [2022]
Identifiers: LCCN 2021052494 (print) | LCCN 2021052495 (ebook) |
ISBN 9780593489123 (hardcover) | ISBN 9780593489130 (ebook) |
ISBN 9780593493502 (international edition)
Subjects: LCGFT: Bildungsromans. | Novels.
Classification: LCC PS3613.A8274 A78 2022 (print) |
LCC PS3613.A8274 (ebook) | DDC 813/.6—dc23/eng/20211029
LC record available at https://lccn.loc.gov/2021052494
LC ebook record available at https://lccn.loc.gov/2021052495

Printed in the United States of America
3rd Printing

BOOK DESIGN BY LUCIA BERNARD

for Shireen and for Phil

Lord, I confess I want the clarity of catastrophe but not the catastrophe.
Like everyone else, I want a storm I can dance in.
I want an excuse to change my life.

—FRANNY CHOI

We wanted a chance for every human being
to be strong and live a life of happiness.

—EMIL SEIDEL

I

I would like to tell a story of a different time. I was twenty-two. A teak switch of a girl. I had finished college. There were not many jobs. The economy had punctured like a tire. Obama had won a second term. He said jobs healthcare national healing; he said, Trayvon Martin could have been my son. I was moved by this, thought that sort of imaginative exercise bravery. I would listen to his speeches on NPR as I dressed for work.

I had found a job. This set me apart from my college friends. I was a consultant, or going to be. This despite my arty degree. A consultant in training. Three toddlers hiding in a suit.

I did not consider myself a sellout. What I felt was that I had been saved from drowning. My classmates without jobs had moved in with their parents, were working unpaid internships at noble nonprofits. I wished them well. My parents were not with me, had left me to make my way in the new country. I was glad they did not, for now, need me to send them money. They had before.

My client was a baobab of a corporation. Fortune 500. They made car seats, heating units, pedometers, batteries. My boss demanded I wear pantyhose. You are a contractor, he told me, no benefits. Women who work for me wear makeup, that is how it is. My men wear suits. You must dress better than the clients, always. That is how they know we work for them. We get the client to their definition of success. People only want to hire a guy when they want to be him, a little. Remember that. Try some makeup. Just a little. Nothing tarty.

I listened dutifully. The pay was only okay. Billable contractor's wages, this despite the fifty-hour weeks. I had to file self-employment taxes. But my boss liked me. Early on he called me his rock star. This was funny to me, since in actuality rock stars get onstage, perform, fuck many girls, wreck the hotel room. I, meanwhile, sweated competence, a hungry efficiency. Waxed my arms, radiated deference, never met a Gantt chart I didn't like.

He had first offered me nineteen dollars an hour. His firm was tiny, only nine people. I said, Thank you, I will think on it. I walked to a good restaurant in my college town and drank a full glass of white wine in the middle of the afternoon. I called him back. I said, Hello, Peter. I have another offer but I want to work with you. Would you consider thirty. In the space between the gin bottles, the mirrored bar showed me a soft-featured girl, skin the color of Hennessy, eyes vacant with fear.

My boss said, like a god granting a boon: Twenty-three an hour. You'll relocate to Milwaukee, where your client is. I will pay for your apartment.

That sounds great, I said, may have added, I'm honored to get to work for you. All nonsense. Once I hung up I punched the air and yelled. I remember the restaurant as deserted, but it may not have been. This is not a story about work or precarity. I am trying, late in the evening, to say something about love, which for many of us is not separable from the other shit. As the summer began, I moved to Milwaukee, a rusted city where I had nobody, parents two oceans away, I lay on the sun-warmed wood floor of my paid-for apartment and decided I would be a slut.

Thomas Zwick was a compact bear of a boy a few months older than me. In college we had settled into an instinctive comradeship. Half Italian, half pure Germanic Sconnie, Thom had disliked me at first. Then mysteriously decided I was good. Could be one of his boys.

I had been very shy then around his girlfriend, who had dark wisps of hair and a beautiful face, as soft and malleable as a baby's. This, paired with an alarming kindness, left me barely able to speak. Thom I was comfortable with. At some basal level of emotion we were alike, even though Thom was a spiky version of what we called a bro, a man who would not veer from a masculinity at once laid-back and entrenched. He lived in sweats. Listened to death metal when he was not listening to yacht rock. Lifted weights daily to a podcast on Engels. Managed, with good humor, the flares of his irritable bowel syndrome. He gave good hugs. He called me his dude. I loved that.

In July, Peter said that we needed a new junior consultant on the project. Another me. I forwarded his email on. Thom was unemployed then. Still living ninety minutes away in our college town. Going to free concerts at the Terrace, taking meandering bike rides around Madison's lakes. His inability to find a job startled me. He was the smartest person I knew. I comprehended at a technical level what a recession was, but not what it meant, truly meant, for the people tumbling into its maw. Some half of my generation never recovered.

thx my dude. will think on it, Thom replied, and I, in my sparsely furnished apartment, felt my anger flare.

I'd reached out in a bid to cement friendship beyond graduation and one-dollar drinks at bars and burgers at the Plaza. In remembered fondness, knowing he needed the job and that he was from around here. He, like me, unlike our most forceful, savvy friends, did not seem ready yet to flee Wisco for the coasts.

cool, I wrote back. you do that.

So far being a slut had returned mixed results, and I suspected that, like swimmers with small feet or curvy ballerinas, I was not built for the championship leagues. There was some part of me too sensitive for it and I was not yet confident I wanted that to die. At the same time I had an opposing instinct, this counterweight of anxious hunger. Like a timepiece, ticking always.

I made myself a dinner of saaru and box-origin idli. I masturbated for hours.

Then I walked an aimless zigzag around the apartment, avoiding the open question of a shower. I had bought a stack of books on the history of Milwaukee, thinking they would help me unlock this stocky city with its emptied streets. These I had not opened. I looked through the introduction of one door-stopper tome, turned some pages, and impatiently thumped it down beside me on the floor.

On my phone I read an article about how, in certain cultures, there are no separate words for the color green and the color blue, and if you showed someone a grass-hued paint swatch next to one the color of summer sky, they would say these were the same. Different shades of one thing.

My phone buzzed. A green (?) bubble hung from its ceiling. It said, Amy Downstairs.

Amy was the property manager of the apartment Peter was putting me up in. She lived, as noted, below me. When I had moved in, she had stood outside and watched me struggle alone. She had an asymmetric haircut, one half razored close to her scalp. The other a dark red swoosh. Maroon comma ending at her jutting chin. A frowning face. Thin grooves in it.

The haircut made me feel strangely hopeful. I walked over, said, Hello, I'm—

Yes, Amy had said flatly, cutting me off. I should tell you right now. We don't like noise. I work at home and I need quiet. We don't tolerate any parties. I'm the property manager. I'll be checking out all the maintenance and collecting your half of utilities promptly. It's a great neighborhood. Quiet, clean, full of—she took a breath before the word—grown-ups.

This was so needlessly hostile I almost laughed. Nevertheless I said something gracious and conciliatory, casting around for empathy. Perhaps she'd had bad experiences with younger tenants before. Maybe college kids had lived above her, doing keg stands, screaming obscenities. Mocking Amy when she pleaded for consideration. She could not be that old herself. In her waning thirties at the latest.

Amy said she would show me the washing machine in the basement. She nodded at a shadowy figure leading a large dog, up on the screened porch above us.

That's my fiancé. Tim. He'll install your air-conditioning. If you want that.

She had emphasized the word *fiancé*, said it in a fashion that meant, Stay away. So I'd read the haircut wrong.

Before I relate the text in question, I should pause to say that so far, all this has been me casting fishing line into memory's river, reeling in what bites. The truth is I remember every single thing this woman wrote to me. Close my eyes and I can see it still: ovaloid gray, lime green.

(Some people might have called it blue; it all depends on your frame of reference.)

What the text said was,

what is wrong with u. be QUIET

I held the phone with both hands as though it might detonate.

Excuse me? I wrote back. I haven't made a sound. Think you must mean someone / something else?

There was no response. Many minutes passed. I allowed myself to move from the middle of the kitchen, where my feet had frozen me.

I brushed my teeth, running the water at the quietest trickle.

Sweat on my palms, drying now. It was impossible that she had intended this for me. I had not been blasting loud music or moving furniture. I'd been padding around the empty apartment in bare feet.

She must be perishing with embarrassment. Must have texted me this utterly butterly paagal thing meaning to send it to a family member, to her big lunk of a fiancé. Thinking this induced sympathy on my part. I ate a creamy bowl of yogurt and made a plan for how to while away the evening, which stretched too long ahead of me.

By the time I set out the night felt like something cooling from an oven. My hair wet and clean. I did not have a car and was not able to drive one. I calculated the blocks ahead of me, having left my phone behind, and walked to Brady Street alone.

Do you know if the hardware store is around here, I asked a young man with a long, horsey face.

Two blocks farther, then one block over, he said. Just past the pink awning, you see it, says Sneha Dry Goods, a block west after that.

You pronounce it SNAY-hah, I said. He'd replaced the *e* with an *i*. But already he had returned headphones to his small pink ears.

A clock, that was what I wanted. I would put it on the yellow kitchen wall. Its face would watch me as I moved through time.

As I stood in the checkout line I noticed her.

A woman in a hurry. Almost vibrating. Darting through the aisles. Drill in one hand, still in its red box. Surge protector in the other. She was wrapping its pale cord around her wrist, staring up at something on a high shelf.

She wasn't my type. Blond hair almost white. A Virginia Woolf nose. Her skin was somewhere between henna and marigold, came straight from a sunbed. Still, something about her stopped my breath. I did not want to stare, and I had no other option besides. I paid, counting out my cash. The store was crowded, harshly lit. Against the warm soft night I walked back home.

Distant fireworks that celebrated the country's independence shot off as I worked to hang the clock. Wobbling violently on the folding chair I stood on, I yelped and clutched the wall I'd hammered a nail into moments ago. I dropped the clock. Half the glass of it smashed outward. Seconds later, coming up through the floorboards toward me, a loud cry of rage.

In college I had not known how to get women. Not in person. In secret I'd posted on Craigslist in the sleepless reaches of the night, replied to a personal ad or two. These assignations had given me a degree of confidence. Were bulwark against the terror of total inexperience. Now I had moved to a new city and wanted the real thing.

Some damp July night, I walked an hour to a bar I had heard was right. I was wearing the makeup from work and a filmy blouse. It showed my body's clean lines. My hair fell to my collarbone.

It all gave the wrong idea. Dykes in hiking boots and windbreakers took one look at me, and the few that did not prefer white girls in that wordless unexamined way made a beeline.

No no no, I wanted to say, not you. We could be friends. Move together in a pack. I shrugged off the tall butch in her brown vest who was bearing down on me, thumbing the curve of my waist. As bad as any man.

I crossed toward the girl who'd just walked in. A white little face set against dark hair, a *Pulp Fiction* bob. An uncertainty in her eyes that made her soft. She was at the bar, drinking wine out of a doubles glass. I looked down at her red, bitten mouth and felt my clit jump.

I smiled a wolf's smile with my eyes. In the past I had tried to be suave, elaborate, and things had gone a mediocre route. This time I simply said, hello. When she laughed, leaned close to me, I looked for the aging woman in the brown vest. Our eyes met and she looked so sour. In her mind Pulp Fiction and I both should have been hers. My lips twitched.

Washed-up old dyke. I knew how beautiful I was in that moment, felt it burned into me, a brand. This is how I felt: alone and powerful. This is what I felt: the shock of how your life's longing can sometimes be smoothly realized, without great strain or cost, easy as buying a clock.

In undergrad I had been required to study a near-unreadable German novel about a young man who runs away from home to escape the pressure of his family's desires for him. For years he roams around, joins a theater troupe, gathers the friends that become the extension of his family, but by the end he chooses his destiny, chooses the staid sensible life that his parents wanted, finds a wife, all of his own free will. That's what a true adulthood had come to signify for me, a bowing down before the inevitable. For the lucky, this could be preceded by a period of freedom, the latitude of youth.

That's what I have right now, I thought, tracing the outline of my debit card, leaning my elbows against the cold dark acetate of the bar.

As we crossed the bar windows, when I was sure Brown Vest would be looking, I gathered Pulp Fiction to me, kissed her. This is what I remember, even now. Pulp Fiction. Who meant nothing to me. There was a safety in this nothing, a gate around me. Black glossy hair. A vacant smile. Her lips softly parting for mine, her tender little throat exposed. Streetlights turned the night the dark orange of a bee's thorax. A slow delicious violence rose in me. I gathered the crown of her dark bob tight in my fist.

August turned ripe as a fruit. Sneezeweed and tansy brightened the sidewalks and my mother called to say my uncle had died.

Acute pancreatitis and cirrhosis of the liver. In the last year his eyes had turned the color of old urine, his calves swelled to balloons. They were keeping the body refrigerated until every possible ammai and achayan, from Dubai to Brampton, Kolkata to Scotland, could fly back to put him in the cemetery. The timing of my uncle's croaking was notable. Right during our harvest feast. His funeral falling on its most auspicious day. If I had been there still, I would have taken a great and malicious pleasure in eating the sadhya as though the day held only something to celebrate. Would have shoveled red matta rice and coconut parippu and beans thoren into my mouth like a greedy little boy. Asked for seconds of sweet creamy payasam over the wails of the mourners.

To my mother, I said stiffly, I see. Sorry to hear this. I did not offer to come home, to support my parents. To support her.

My mother was crying. You are a very cold person, she said to me in our language.

His whole life my uncle had bullied her. Once in a drunken tantrum he had slapped her in front of my father, who summarily threw him into the rhododendron bushes. After that my uncle decided that I was a more strategic target. He was fond of me, in his way. An affection emulsified with something dark and rancid.

The memories tumbled back to me, rolled into each other like socks.

My uncle waiting by the elementary school's iron gate. How I would run to him, my schoolbag flapping up and down against my thin back. To the person who paid me the most attention, who laughed at my every joke, who said he loved me. A darting creature with huge eyes, Monchayan was. Wispy hurricane of hair circling the bare eye of his scalp. He would play Legos with me, then stamp on the house I had built. When he was especially jobless he would take me on his long ambling walks and pinch my nipple hard if I dawdled. There were other things, and I did not wish for a second to dwell on them.

And here my mother was, weeping for this useless man.

In the background I could hear the opening music of the Kannada serial my grandfather liked to watch from the bed. Thank god I was now far away, from the people who had hurt or overlooked me, the neighbors and cousins who had lionized my parents when they achieved a modicum of success and visibly scorned them when it had been taken away. I would never, if I could help it, live there again.

Yes, I said acidly to my mother, you are correct, very astute of you.

Once the phone went quiet I felt a wicked pang. Thinking of my parents, living two oceans away, with their slackening bodies, their private burdens.

In silence I wiped the kitchen counters, wrung the rag out in the sink.

The hands of the clock had stayed where they had been upon its fall. This seemed like a metaphor for how people were. Impulsively I had left it on display, propped up on a kitchen shelf. The nail it was supposed to go on angled upward in the drywall, bare and alone.

I longed for a friend. Thom had accepted Peter's offer, would be starting in September. He did not so much as thank me. He'd left Madison, was now in Wauwatosa at his mother's house, which he felt shame about, a shame I did not consider fully legitimate, given that where I originated, children stayed in the parental abode well into adulthood.

But how did one meet friends in Milwaukee? Anywhere? I was irritated with the one person I knew near the city. Work did not seem like fertile ground for socialization, unless I wished to go to wine nights with portly middle-aged Republicans named Susan.

And even if a certain perverse part of me did, the Susans treated me as if I did not exist. My own specific Susan, the project manager at the battery-making conglomerate, referred to me as the—I believe the term was—resource. To my face.

I wanted a friend. I wanted, too, a woman. I did not know if these longings were separate. Someone who would roll with me. A laughing woman, dapper, with a car.

Pulp Fiction had, after only a few weeks, abandoned me for greener pastures, pastures I sensed she enjoyed tantalizing me with in sporadic late-night texts. Returning to the bar, walking the hour there and back, I had not been able to replicate my success. I looked on Craigslist. Every poster appeared mentally unstable or a very expensive cab ride away.

I was already sick of taking the two buses to the Fortune 500 company's HQ. Sixty-five minutes of commute, of waiting as SUVs—American cars that looked like they had been bred with trucks—sped past.

Sweat on my skin. I stared at the air-conditioning unit collecting dust in the corner of the paid-for apartment. Without specifying a timeframe, I wondered what would happen to me.

Work left me a wrung-out mop. The hours were long and brutal. I found it difficult to talk to the people on my teams, all much older. Few of them spoke normal English. I was grateful for Thom's addition, his texting me jokes, his offers to pick me up and drop me off.

The IT man seated in the cubicle next to mine never stopped talking, continually droning on about his open tickets and his bowling league and workflow optimization and the sticky key on his keyboard. Each week a senior consultant who resembled an apprentice Santa Claus bought donut holes for the whole floor. Red-cheeked and jovial, that was Keith La-Marchese. He lived on a private island off the coast of Florida, ran his own one-man firm. He flew in Mondays, flew out Thursdays, was put up in better hotels than Peter. In the break room he caught me looking at the watch on his chubby wrist and said, only sunshine and amiability in his jokester's voice, Rolex means more sex, let the ladies know.

Always I was aware of my own melanin. I say this without self-pity. Some people look at your skin as if they are preoccupied with how best to scrub it without being rude. Thom, who was disgusted by Keith La-Marchese, did suggest that I was imagining this. I suggested he sit on his thumb.

The word *complexion* has its origin in the Old French *complession*. A combination of humors. Temperament, character. It borrows from the Latinate *complexus* (surrounding, encompassing), which has as its past

participle *complecti*: encircled, embraced. The specific present-day meaning (color or hue of the skin of the face) developed by the fifteenth century. This was something I'd happened upon when writing a paper in
college, clicking through OED links in a dim recess of the library. When
I walked into the bathroom, the forgotten brownness of my own features
shocked me. Sent my heart rate soaring.

What would remain of the things I had learned about history and science and literature, come four or five years, I did not know. What was the
point of knowing anything, of learning how to think, that favorite
phrase of my American teachers, if all it did was burnish my contempt for
the mentally negligible project managers and associate division directors
all around me? I should have majored in Microsoft Excel.

On days he was happy with me, Peter would still refer to me as his
rock star. This had less to do with talent than with the willingness to be
first in, last out, reply to every email within five minutes of receipt, to
say as I did, like some insistent heartbeat: *yes yes yes*.

From two cubicles down, Thom texted a photo he'd snuck of me.
Grim of face, nearly cross-eyed, staring at the luminous rectangle ahead.

dat sweet sweet cortisol glow of adult life, the green (?) bubble under
the picture said.

If you put this online I will end you, I texted back.

come here bruh, he wrote, ive a superabundance of rum in my desk.

We poured the pale spiced liquid into our Nalgenes, clicked them together, resumed our spreadsheet ministry. He drove me home, the car
weaving slightly.

I went for evening walks, signed up for a class on Portuguese that I attended four sessions of, then abandoned. Began to keep a journal in a
yellow leather notebook, noting down meals and the minor events of
each day. Work did not seem worth capturing in detail. From YouTube
I learned to give myself a bikini wax. I potted a four-dollar basil plant

from the hardware store in a Cento can that previously housed crushed tomatoes, where it promptly died of overwatering.

I joined an online dating website.

These were newish, these bright-colored interfaces with clean lettering, intended to signal a stripping away of the illicit. Still, writing it out, making bald my desires, my preferences mundane and not, was for me unavoidably scented with shame.

The truth is I was so lonely. Thom spent his evenings Skypeing with his girlfriend, who had stayed back in our college town, or drinking great quantities of beer at Y-Not II. If I kept up with him I would not fit into my pencil skirts, my mandated pantyhose, and then where would we be? I made a profile, feeling a pale thrill. A vague pain.

World traveler, I wrote, thinking of the rained-on orange footpath of my parents' home overseas. Of the two nights I had spent in Frankfurt on a layover.

For hours I scrolled through the selection available, sending messages, appraising faces and bodies, attempting to extrapolate personalities from stray lines of text, and then.

I saw the woman from the hardware store. A name attached to her. Marina, 27.

I touched my laptop's screen. The display dimpled against the pressure.

A long, tender face. Tombstone-white teeth. Something arresting in her eyes, which appeared to lean green: seawater stirred with a weight of sand.

She was a dance teacher and choreographer. She liked to read. Her favorite book was *White Oleander*, which I'd read as a teenager and loved; she liked, also, the collected poems of Rumi. She had not listed the college she had gone to. Under her profile's Looking For section, it said: Casual Fun, Dating, A Relationship.

Blues and pinks and palest grays filled the screen before me. I felt eager, buzzing with a light electricity, and a little ashamed. Biting my lip in concentration, I clicked the message icon. Began to write.

In summertime Milwaukee is six-packs in parks, listening to free jazz, festival everything, gastropubs with the young and hip foaming out of them, home repairs, grilling out. All neighborliness, sweet like a laugh.

The city is a clenched hand as it grows colder, its people chapped and flaking. Hunkered down. Shoulders stooped against the freeze rolling out from the north, barely tempered by Lake Michigan.

It was fall when I first messaged Marina, those early days of cold, and she did not reply.

My pride was burned, and by this person I'd never met. No matter, I thought, and found other beds to lie in. Took refuge in ordering furniture from the Internet. I was tired of living merely with a bed, a table, and a couple of folding chairs, so I overcorrected. This is built into adulthood, like one of those wall-mounted ironing boards in old houses. Somewhere in their twenties, people like me become far too horny for interior design.

My paid-for apartment was in Brewers Hill. Once this had been the American dream. Perched on bluffs overlooking the Milwaukee River's valley, the neighborhood housed hundreds drawn to the foundries, mills, and tanneries that lined the riverbank. Foremen and owners lived next door to immigrant laborers with callused palms, and tight-crocheted workers' cottages hemmed grand Greek revival and Italianate houses on large lots. Neighbors knew each other. Their children played free.

Postwar decline gutted the neighborhood. Smoked it, cased it, cured it for another day. Businesses left the valley. City officials demolished vacant dwellings in resignation, one by one. In the seventies and eighties, spared the redlined segregation of neighborhoods directly to its north, Brewers Hill began to see people trickle back in, steady, slow. Modest condos popped up on demolished lots. Factories converted into coteries of apartment lofts.

The pretty rows of colonials house Neighborhood-Watching mothers and fiancées, who peer through blind slats and email the Hill Listserv when they see young Black men from five blocks north cross the sight lines of their porches. *Suspicious character*, the Amys type, pulses pleasurably heightened, eyes darting window to screen. Older people in their front yards nod at you, offer flower cuttings, suggest you shrink-wrap the windows when winter sets in.

I use the present tense, but I mean, that's the way I remember it, and these are the things I learned about it, later, and the two combined have formed my truth of a place. We all have our truth of a place. There is no universal narrative of any city that is also real. Only marketing.

A late-October storm blew through the city, pelting it with freezing rain. It caught me outside in a gray woolen dress. I let it soak me to indecency. Inside again I toweled off. Stripped to nakedness. I went on the dating website and shot off messages to the women whose pictures inspired gritted-teeth lust in me.

	A	B
1	Brianne	hey
2	Emily	hey gorgeous
3	Wanda	hey (:
4	Ashley	my doctor told me I need some Vitamin U

	A	B
5	Kayleigh	sup
6	Carlene	omg frank ocean! got me through college
7	Tanvi	hey! always great to see another queer brown lady here. how are you?

My attempts ranged from awful to lazy.

Some of the women replied, but the ones who did seemed unable to sustain a conversation, seemed too dull to live. My lack of high-performance results left me self-conscious. I thought of jokes people had made in college about men who came from where I did, men who would message girls and ask to be shown boobs and vagina, spelled *bobs* and *vagene*.

I checked the tracking numbers of the furniture items I'd bought. The pieces—dressers and tufted sleeper sofas and leaner mirrors—were lodged in the belly of the country, moving slowly, implacably, toward me.

You've totally lost your old accent, Thom told me, somewhat accusingly.

Worry about yourself, I replied, my throat constricting for reasons I did not quite have a handle on. We had gone out for a martini lunch. Six toddlers hiding in two suits. This was at a Bar Louie near the client. There were decorative gourds on our table, a quarter sheet announcing fall specials: a pumpkin spice tiramisu, apple cider hot toddies.

My martini was pineapple elderflower. Thom's was clear and burny, only a red-stuffed olive anchoring it.

He told me I should never order a girly drink like that again, unless I was alone.

Dudes like women who drink like men, he said.

What makes you think I care what *dudes* like?

My homie. It's so clear you want men to admire you. Or fear you. One of the two.

So clear. Right. Got it.

Stay away from the froufy booze. Or don't. It doesn't matter to me.

It doesn't. Right.

We're in competition, really. Too bad I like you. Will our loyalty survive capitalism? Da-da-dum.

Don't assume anything about my loyalty, I said. Less because I meant it, more to sink nails into the power of being cold.

When our waitress brought us our checks, mine was missing a $10.99

pineapple martini. I noted this aloud. Brilliant, Thom said, you've scored one puny shot against the man. Let's roll, broseph.

I shook my head. I liked feeling holier than someone. It happened so rarely. I waved over the waitress, who had some kind of uncomfortable-looking growth on the left side of her nose.

It's been taken care of, she said.

Pardon?

She got it.

What?

She gestured over to the back of Bar Louie. A swishy-haired blond woman with no breasts was playing pool. Surrounding her tiny form was this cluster of laughing androgynes. Cropped of hair. Suspendered. Some of them wore T-shirts that read STRIVE DANCE.

The woman's face was heart-shaped, a bow tie nestled at its point. She leaned over the red-felt table and took her shot.

She looked up straight at me.

I thrust my eyeballs down, fumbled at my wallet. Face flaming.

Ayyy. You have a *fan*, Thom said, licking his lip in a parody of male grossness.

She ghosted me on a dating app. It's not a come-on. It's an apology. Like, politeness. Come, we're going to be late for our check-in.

Wait wait wait. Are you a—are you dating? Are you dating *girls*?

Let's go, Thomas.

How many years have we been friends, bruh?

Like, not that many, actually.

I tell you about my sexploits down to the queef. I told you about the time Isabel threw up on my dick, and she literally swore me to secrecy. Here I was thinking you were some Indian chick zealously guarding her virginity. Meanwhile you're Gertrude Steining all over the Ill Mil, apparently. I'm hurt, my dude.

Fuck off. Here's cash, you can pay me back. Let's *go*.

Do you not want to thank your *polite* friend?

I am not going to be chewed up by Peter and Susan because we show up late and stinking of gin.

Agenda item tabled, Thom said, smiling ominously, for now.

We walked out of Bar Louie, buttoning our coats against the chill, and I did not glance back. It's truthful, this cliché: my heart was pounding.

Messaging Marina in the days after should have been simple enough.

But when I summoned the courage to go into the app's inbox, the late morning after many pitchers of Coors at Y-Not II, my conversation with her picture had turned a curious kind of blank. My message—long, chivalrous, more thoughtful than the ones I typically sent—now appeared to have been lobbed over to the gray outline of a head. A mannequin's mug shot.

She'd blocked me. Or deactivated. Had she actually *blocked* me? That would make no sense. What kind of person would ignore a great message from someone good-looking, send a pineapple martini across a restaurant, and then block its recipient online on the only portal where contact could be made? A nonsense person. A falthoo person.

A person not worth my time.

I opened cans of channa in a fury.

When I sliced through the heel of my hand the color of my own blood astonished me. Orange as the rained-upon footpath of my parents' home. Blood left me helpless. I remember fainting once on seeing it as a child. In adulthood, I had grown to tolerate it only in menses.

For my chickpeas the oven had been set to 400 degrees, and my ancient stove could not contain the heat that roared from it. The blood from my palm had dripped onto the stovetop, and was slowly, it appeared, being cooked. This seemed both funny and disgusting. I did not have the right supplies. I took a length of paper towel and a bottle of whiskey. Upended the bottle onto the balled fist of Brawny. Pressed the boozy plug hard into my hand.

The sting of it against my little gash, a time machine. Arnica on my cuts, my mother holding me aloft by a single thin brown arm while I wailed. Light coming in through dusty curtains over the bed that my grandparents would, years later, lie in and never leave. Dettol in the small hospital in Kerala. I had gone to have my wisdom teeth taken out mid-university; it made no sense, my mother said, to pay American highway robber prices. I thought of how in childhood I would fold into my mother after tantrums and punishments, how she would envelop me. Stiff bright fabric, soft ropy arms.

My mother's smell. Fennel seeds. Sandal soap.

When I stopped crying into my hands, I could hear Amy's raised speech, muffled by floorboards. Another voice responded to the snarl of sound—a man's. The Fiancé.

I wiped my streaming nose with the whiskey compress. Then, moved by curiosity, sank my head to the floor.

Most words stayed indistinct, but I heard, again and again: I am a nice person! I am a nice person!

Well, if you had to *say* it.

A silence. The Fiancé appeared to have stormed out. Their front door swung, let out its metal groan.

My entrance was through a west-facing side door through which you could access both the basement and the absurdly narrow set of stairs that took you to my paid-for apartment. Theirs was the front of the house. At the highest part of Brewers Hill. From there you could see the Milwaukee skyline, squat and glassy.

Before I raised myself from the floor, I heard the Fiancé's voice so loudly present in my stairwell, it was as if he were speaking and invisible next to me.

Amy, it's been open all friggin' night, the voice said.

He meant the side door. My apartment door was bolted, chained. I felt glad for this, with this awful male boom on the door's outer side. Last night I had been out with Thom and his roommates. Had returned at 3 a.m. I must not have let the key turn all the way.

The Fiancé's stomps retreated. In my stomach I felt the storm coming.

I took my chickpeas, dusted them with turmeric and cumin. Salted heavily, covered them with ketchup.

Resting the bowl between my breasts, I lay naked in bed. Mashed and ate with my right hand, taking care to avoid my cut. My breath fast and shallow. Curried ketchup smeared under my nails. With my left I tapped at my keyboard. Began to nudge and change my profile.

I wanted friends. I wished to have adventures. I did not want a relationship. That is what I set down.

I messaged back Carlene, who seemed pretty and sweet and dumb, appeared unable to distinguish between *you're* and *your*, and we made plans to go on a date. I chose the bar closest to my apartment. Can't wait, she wrote, added a kissy face.

Still, part of me felt unsatisfied.

Staring at the conversation that had once been with Marina, not the anonymous gray outline of a woman's head, rage broke again in me, quick and nasty as a dropped egg. How unbearable it is to desire what another person can deny you.

I closed the laptop. Wiped my hands haphazardly. Pulling the covers over my head, I put the corner of a pillow in my mouth. Shut my eyes.

I began to knead and whisk myself, summoning the froth of lust. When I came I cried out loud.

My phone dinged. I knew that it would be nothing good. For now, it felt like I had lain in a patch of sun and eaten something luscious. I smiled. Rolled over. I needed, I knew, to hold on to this.

At work we moved into Phase Two of our Organizational Change Management Process (OCMP). It was imperative that we continue to present good appearances to the client. Peter said this in a brightly lit meeting room full of modular gray seating. He stared pointedly at Thom's belly, where shirt buttons were beginning to strain against the aftermath of libations at Y-Not II.

I recrossed my legs, becoming aware once again of the stubble growing under my pantyhose. Imagined myself a spider catching flies in a corner of the conference room. Squinting against fluorescence.

It was almost 7:30 p.m. I had to be at LuLu in Bay View by eight. We were in the far north of the city, where my client's sprawling corporate campus unfurled. This would involve catching three buses, waiting a total of twenty minutes, arriving nearly at nine. My face must have signaled desperation. Peter asked me if I had a train to catch.

Oh, I have an appointment at eight, but I can *totally* cancel it, I said, in the most servile of tones. I added, This is important to me.

Peter, seeming mollified, let his people go.

Thom and I raced to the parking garage, letting out a shared whoop once we left the client's lobby. We had walked our dress shoes decorously past its pop-art mural of Wisconsin landscape, woods and lakes and farmland, with batteries, car seats, heating units erupting like boils from grassy knolls and forested enclaves. Now we were children freed. The parking garage was November-cold, emptied. Thom tucked himself into the car, lifted a cheek, and let out a ripe trumpet of wind several minutes long. I swatted at him, groaning, laughing.

Thomas, good god, I'm gonna suffocate—

Sorry, bruh, had to hold it in all day, it got potent up in there.

Why don't you use the bathroom at work? I mean honestly, this can't be healthy—

So I can blow ass in earshot of Peter and the division managers and AVPs who I owe cleaned-up spreadsheets to? You get a ride, you gotta smell a fart now and then. Call it the ass tax. The gas tax.

Hey, can you not drop me off at my place?

Yeah, for sure, homie. Where you need to go?

LuLu, it's on, uh, let me look it up—

Bay View or Brady?

Uh, Bay View. Thank you. Really.

Coo, coo. Thanks for telling me exactly one minute before the exit.

Sorry. Sorry.

One day you'll drive and then you'll understand.

You sound like my mother. Since I was born she's like, When I Die, Then You Will Understand.

Moms be crazy. Universal truth. So who's at LuLu?

It's not like, a date—

Oh, this old song.

Shut up. I'm meeting this woman called Tig.

And how did you meet Ms. Tig? Old friend?

Fuck off. We met online, but I changed my profile. It says now I'm looking for friends and adventures. She messaged me and said she wants the same. Burned out on dating. She seems cool, though not my type, but yeah. Friend date.

Friends and adventures! Why is she not your type.

We absolutely don't have to discuss this.

It's the tax, my dude. Price of the ride. The 411 fee. C'mon, give me something good. The fuck, that fucker just completely cut me off. You have a death wish, asshole?

I don't know. She seems a little on the fat side? But I haven't met her. What is *your* type?

I like very soft women. Like I like the idea of every part of a woman being like a breast. Just a walking collection of breasts conjoined. Just like, soft. Squeezable. Also have a thing for big eyes, wide mouths. And brains, *of course*.

I'm dead right now. Okay, take this right. You are outrageous.

Dog, you asked.

Wide mouths explains Isabel.

Don't talk any shit about my girl. Off-limits.

I was not. I think the world of young Isabel. She just indisputably has a wide—all right, this is it. Thank you thank you thank you.

Get your not-date to drive you home. It's too far and cold to walk and I do not intend to retrieve your ass.

LuLu was beautiful in the way that my favorite American restaurants are beautiful. Tin ceiling. Real wood tables, buzzing with noise. Buttery light. The host was bosomy, with broad soft lips. I glanced down while I spoke to her, trying not to grin or blush.

Tig had texted me, its packed. they got heat lamps outside, let me know if that's not okay.

I meandered to the back patio.

A curious face, mobile and energetic, unselfconsciously looking up for me. A strapping woman. Dark honey skin, nearly the same shade as my own. Hair in tiny braids. Her smile showed unflossed teeth. Still, there was something magisterial about her. She stood up and took my hand. In the chill of the Edison-bulb-strung patio she was wearing no coat, only a sweater.

It's nice to meet you. I'm Antigone. Antigone Clay.

Good god, I thought.

She added, Most call me Tig.

I'll call you whatever you need me to, I said, hunching over a menu, smiling slightly.

Do you want to sit inside?

Ah, I'm okay.

The waiter arrived. Antigone smiled broadly. Not once glancing at a menu. Said, Give us two glasses of your favorite red wine. And she'll pick the food.

I was startled but made the calls. Blistered shishito peppers, which I had never heard of but sounded sophisticated. Gnocchi with brown butter and crisped sage leaves. Corn and zucchini fritters with labneh.

Tig was twenty-seven. Five years older than me. She loved talking and she loved listening, drew you out with questions and commentary, and this made her a rare pleasure to speak with. She owned a softer voice than I expected. Had a big vase of a laugh, one that seemed large enough to hold my own. I let mine ring out more often when speaking to her. She was tired of dating, she told me, had been in a series of fruitless flings in the past year, her most recent girlfriend so controlling she'd made Tig share her location at all times on Find My Friends. I was struck by the easy revelation of this detail.

Tig had grown up in Milwaukee, in North Division. When she was my age she'd left. Driven down to Disney World and found a job. Stayed for years. She'd been a greeter, a clerk, a cast member, and by the time she left, an unofficial apprentice to a ride mechanic.

Why'd you come back? I asked.

Antigone dragged the tines of her fork through the labneh, speared the gnocchi. Closed her eyes to take the flavor in.

Weird, was her pronouncement, and then she did it again. I waited for my answer. Her attention had a curious, roving quality.

She had family drama. A sister giving trouble. She'd also wanted to go back to school, she said, which is where she was now. Studying philosophy at Alverno. A women's college. Her professors were these radical wonderful broads, she said. But tuition was high. She had many loans. She lived in Bay View, with a Turkish roommate she called, strangely, Turk.

I asked Tig who her favorite philosopher was.

This week, she said, it's Kant. But it changes every week. And we have only just started reading Kant.

I ate the final shishito. It was hotter than the rest. Sour, pepper-bright.

So what was the high point of your week? Tig asked, sensing me draw into myself. What was the low point?

I considered the question.

	A	B
1	High Point, Week of November 11	Completing the massive Gantt chart showing the phase sequencing over the weeks and months for the Organizational Change Management Process (OCMP), getting it to output successfully on the client's massive printer, sticking it up on the glass walls of the conference room with deep blue/green tape, all the while fighting the clock, all the while misting with sweat given various curt emails from Susan and Peter. Looking at the Gantt chart, seeing the work already done, the work yet to do, the language in it barely English, a language you had no real fluency in before this, full of phrases like *stakeholder engagement*, *resource onboarding*, *bottomlining*, *sprints*, *86ing*, *train the trainer*, *green belt*, *go/no-go*. Looking at it and thinking, You make money, you work in an office with people in suits, Peter will sponsor you for a green card if he continues being pleased with you, you have money for back home and to go to a nice restaurant if you want and to buy a tufted sofa if you want, you are safe, you are safe.

	A	B
2	Low Point, Week of November 11	Staring at a phone screen and taking in long bloated cells of text, many entirely capitalized, from Amy. The crux of the content was the leaving of the side door unlocked, though various alarming intimations had been made that Amy and the Fiancé had been tracking your movements in and out of the house each day and could report you to the landlord for having left a door open and "left them in danger" for "upwards of twenty-four hours."

Tig reached a hand across the table, lightly touched mine.

You've gone far away, she said. Laughed gently.

I had a pretty bruising week at work, I explained. So the high point is just being done with it. The low point? Probably getting into it with my property manager, who lives below me and hates my guts.

Who could ever hate you?

You don't know me, I said, pleasantly enough. By now I was shivering. Tig picked up her coat and put it over mine, over me.

Do you want to come drink wine at my place? she asked. I live five minutes away.

I had considered this possibility and was alert to its dangers. Liked this woman but did not want to bed her. I've an early morning tomorrow, I said. She nodded, grinned. Unfazed.

What did your property manager say?

I passed my phone over. She squinted at it, appearing to not want to read too long.

It's a lot, was all she said. She added, perhaps sensing my disappointment, Landlords are the worst.

I regretted this overture. We talked about my first impressions of Milwaukee. Antigone asked if I'd been scared. To move to a new city where I knew nobody, parents far away. To come to live in a place where I had never been.

The fact is I had come here once before. Amit, my friend and briefly my boyfriend in college, had grown up first in tony Brookfield, then lived in Bay View. His family was in Shorewood now. Junior year I had been invited to his parents' Thanksgiving, rather than stay in the dorms alone. We'd eaten a tandoori turkey. We'd been put in different rooms to sleep. When he snuck in to go down on me, I thought, despite marshalling every neuron available to block this comparison, of the half-blind family dog, who'd licked my shin repeatedly during dinner. It had been a hot minute since I had spoken to Amit, who was one of the rare people who I felt understood me, even if we were dreadfully mismatched in the romance lane. He was now printing money in San Francisco.

I should text that boy sometime, I thought. See how he is.

It was *fine*, I said to Tig. Honestly, like fine in the context of the other moves I've had to make, much larger ones. This was like nothing—in the abstract.

Antigone only nodded, but I felt, suddenly, a little better seen.

The check arrived. I put my debit card down. Antigone made to protest. I held up my hand.

You're a grad student, I said. You can get the next one.

To be generous felt like the best thing you could be.

Tig flashed yellow teeth. When my card came back, she picked it up. Looked hard at it.

My bank has fraud protection on, I said, only half joking.

Thank you for dinner, she said. I've been trying this whole meal to find out your name.

A laugh began to bubble in me. The absurdity of this whole interaction. I had forgotten. My display name on the apps only said *S*.

It's pretty, she said.

I hate my name, I said. I've hated it all my life.

Say more.

Nothing to say.

All right. Let me drive you home, ma'am, she said. You can tell me more about this property manager of yours.

As she pulled up to my curb I turned to her. A large clot of warmth in my chest. I was happy to be spared having to ask for a ride, or to walk two miles glazed in cold.

I like you lots. I want to be your friend, I said.

I felt abashed and earnest and yearning and very very young. It was the truth.

Tig touched my cheek.

Friendship is work, she said. Friendship is work, and a commitment, and a practice. I don't know if you share that view.

I think I do? To like, the extent I've thought about it.

Damn, would you look at that; it's snowing. Year's first snow.

I made to touch the windshield of the tiny car, where small pale flakes were dying. The sight of it, even after years in this country, left me drenched in wonder.

I like you too, Tig said. I want to feel things out. Let's go on an actual adventure next.

All right.

Have a good night, babe.

And she was off. When I walked toward the entrance, I noticed the flick of Amy's blinds.

I told my parents I would not fly back for Christmas. We celebrated it only loosely, in any case. A rickety tree of green plastic, a paper star on the veranda lit from within. Peter had informed us we could not all take vacation at the same time during an ongoing project, or it would look less than ideal to the client. He suggested I go during the client's division retreat instead. I sent the WhatsApp messages as I was waiting between buses. Snow driving down. My fingers full of heat and pain. I said to them: Sorry Mummy and Papa. I have to work. I will send money now. I will come in February.

My bank account, courtesy of the paid-for apartment, had crossed fourteen thousand dollars. An obscene amount, bringing to mind bathtubs of cash, videos where money rained down on women's bodies.

I set aside four thousand to pay my self-employment taxes, wired two grand home. To help with the house, buying food, medicines for my grandparents. The house required roof repairs, and a new door for the guest bedroom.

The original construction had only two rooms for sleeping. Until the age of fourteen I had slept on the trundle bed beside my grandmother, and this seemed the goal that justified our great migration, to cross two oceans and arrive at a land that appeared to constitutionally guarantee each person their own room. When my father's new business in the States had begun to make money, they had built new additions back home. A third bedroom, with real tiles for the floors, and painted walls instead of limewash.

To send my parents the transfer to replace the roof and the damp-rotted door was easier than saying, I think of you always. Than asking, why did you leave me.

Life by now had settled into habit. Workdays Thom picked me up at 7 a.m. and we would drive the thirty minutes to the client's campus, groggy with sleep, listening to podcasts, saying little. Thom decided to go paleo. Quit eating tumorous cranberry muffins with me in the client's giant cafeteria. He braised fatty pork nightly, made pancakes only of mashed bananas and egg, went to the butcher to buy bones for pho. The inside of the car those cold early mornings smelled like meat broth and pine sap, and this, day after day, began to seem a comfort. We would drive past Y-Not II some mornings and marvel at the people already sitting in there, nursing their beers as the sun rose. Wisconsin is dark-sided, Thom said. Thinking of the quiet wife-slapper drunks I had known as a child, I began to say, Boy, so is everywhere. Then I looked at the electric chair salvaged from a bygone time, displayed in the pink neon window of Y-Not II, and something in me froze shut like a door. I didn't know everywhere. I knew the place that spawned me, which, based on visits past, already was mutating beyond my recognition. I knew our college town, the way someone still essentially a child could learn a place. One day maybe I would know Milwaukee.

Weekends I called my parents, bought Antigone dinner, went on a date here and there, sometimes texting Pulp Fiction late into the night. She was hung up on a man. Some open-married doctor in her college town. If I thought too much about it, it drove me mad. To distract myself I went on other dates, most functional and forgettable. Some Thursdays I'd go to shows with Thom, who was, in college and now, a concert obsessive. Isabel had now moved to Milwaukee, but she rarely joined us out. To Cactus Club and Mad Planet and Fire on Water we went and, like the rest of the crowd, bobbed from side to side like graceless buoys. We saw Foxygen and Poliça, Peter Wolf Crier and Atmosphere. Sometimes we went local. Painted Caves, Tay Gutta, Volcano Choir. Thom dragged me to Born of Osiris at Wisconsin Metalfest. Our ears ringing for days.

It was at the Poliça show that I saw Amy. Thom and Isabel were pawing at each other. Away from them I floated, washing up against the stage's left. Sound moaned through me in loops. Red light bathed my face and all I saw. At the other side of the stage, a woman was crying, hand on chest, looking up at the singer. Her features twisting, transported. A spoon of hair cradling her face. The Fiancé nowhere in sight.

For minutes I stared at her, feeling the hot dark flush of the voyeur. To me this woman was a pestilence. At best she had anger management issues. But watching her cry, I had to consider that she had a private life that I knew nothing about. Don't get me wrong: I did not care to. As I saw her wipe her nose, I took in one last view of her softened face. With the requisite muttered apologies I pushed through the crowd to the back of the dark hall. When I went to use the wet-floored bathroom, the edge of my boot tapped a syringe—equal parts clear and orange, lying in a mess of wadded toilet paper. Into the next stall I kicked it in disgust.

Tig and I, at her repeated requests for adventure, took a Saturday. Went to a place called Devil's Lake. A state park. In cheap wool gloves and coats we clambered over boulders until we were gasping and sweaty. Tig exclaimed at the view. I thought it was nice enough. For me, going to restaurants and ordering food rich Americans ate was the true adventure. Tig told me names of plants her dad had taught her. Wild parsnip, poison ivy, nettles. Oak denuded of most leaves. She stripped down to a T-shirt, whooped through cupped hands. Attempting to make an echo. I watched her face, trying to decide if I found a beauty in it. Her arms were darker than the rest of her. Their hands dimpled, sweetly pudgy. We drove back to the city, warbling along to "Stay" by Rihanna, off one of Tig's infinite unmarked CDs. She skipped to Robyn. "Dancehall Queen."

Tig's boldness moved through other people. I stuck my head out of the Honda Fit's moonroof and sang its refrain into the cold evening air.

After dinner at Balzac that night she ferried me home, the center of her lips purpled from wine. Are you okay driving? I asked, and she said with a laugh, This is Wisconsin, baby.

Still, she stiffened when she drove past a police car on Water Street. Asked me twice if she was weaving. Was she too far to the right of the lane?

That means you're over the white line? I asked, and she hooted derisively.

I never knew someone could be so smart while knowing almost nothing, she said.

Oh, happy to expand your horizons.

We were laughing when she pulled over to my curb. In one fluid motion, Tig killed the engine, leaned over, and kissed me.

Like a dead thing I stiffened. Imagined Amy's eyes boring a hole into my neck from the porch. Tig's tongue in my mouth, wet and hungry. My lips had parted. The rest of me was still and cool as a lake-bed pebble. It was not nice of me but I did not want a woman like her. A woman bigger than me, brown like me.

I wanted a white girl. Thin-limbed, with pert full breasts and lips. Pink in all the right places. Wanted someone like the dancer who'd rejected me. I knew that my thoughts were impolitic and ugly. Desire, though, burst through the word *should*, water breaking down a flimsy dam.

I touched Tig's face with genuine tenderness and shook my head.

Clientside, things were newly harried, with additional firms added to the project, with angry emails sent full of errant grammar and chaotic capitalization, with twice-daily tense-jawed meetings between managers and senior consultants. The timeline was delayed. Thom and I kept obedient noses in our double monitors, wondering if we would join the growing list of axed consultants. Peter pulled me to take notes in a phase reorientation meeting with Susan, with the senior consultants from the three other firms on this project. Susan got into it with Keith LaMarchese, who, it appeared, had been slacking, giving his other clients more attention. LaMarchese screamed back at her. His cheeks filling with blood. Keep your eyes down, I instructed myself. I typed polite and euphemistic transcriptions of their actual speech into the Word document in front of me.

Then something hit my arm.

A stuffed leather chair. Its soft parts bounced off me, its shiny wheels scuffing the boardroom wall. LaMarchese had thrown the chair as he exited the room in fury. He had aimed for nobody, but it had hit me.

Pain danced down to my elbow. I bit the inside of my cheek as hard as I was able. Typed on.

Susan appeared calmer after the throwing of the chair. She smiled, smoothed down her dark curls. In her face you could see it: she had won.

No one said a word to me. An example of how not to behave in front of clients, was all Peter muttered as we left the conference room.

Stress had me dizzy. I said nothing. I reached a hand to the avocado-hued walls, let them steady me.

In two weeks, email blasts would start to go out to segments of the client's two hundred thousand employees, letting them know their software was going to change, how to package their email, folders, data so things could migrate over effectively. That's what all this work was for, this project with the consultants from four different firms. A yearlong project, costing a little over a million dollars.

No way, Tig said when I explained this. She was laughing now, full-throated. No way. To change a software program? Like some Microsoft Outlook to Gmail shit?

We were at BelAir. Busy eating two-dollar tacos we'd waited two hours to be seated for. Tig had appeared strangely impervious to my rejection, continuing to text me often in good humor, making jokes, telling me about new dates. My mouth closed around the BelAir special, priced extravagantly at five dollars. The softest flour tortilla cradling a chunk of lobster flesh. Doused in tomatillo sauce, flecked with cotija and charred maize. Tig had gone traditional: chicken, carnitas, veggie.

I got you one better, I said. They're switching to Microsoft Outlook. From Lotus Notes.

What even is that? Some eighties shit? Why are they switching to *Microsoft* in this day and age? Why does it take a whole year and ten million zillion dollars for this whole change management thing?

Because the larger and more complex a system is, the harder it is to change from the top down.

Tig sucked her teeth. Isn't that the problem, she said. That the change is top-down. Everywhere.

What would it look like, an uprising of battery sales specialists, demanding to use Google products? Listen to me, I'm trying to explain this shit. This is the gist of change management, okay? If my client employed fifty people, this would be done in a month. But they employ like a hundred ninety thousand people in like ten countries, and people will be super super mad if the process isn't managed well. They'll come in to work and be like, Wait what, you're changing my email in a week? My email where I need to do all my work? And odds are it won't be managed well, and that's why there are consultants.

Huh.

Ya. It makes the firing easy, when it's not managed well. My title sounds fancy, but it just means that I do the work without being an employee with benefits. Susan gets the healthcare and the retirement match and the HR.

Tig ate the last bit of her carnitas slowly, chewing it like she did an idea. I like your mind, she offered. You see through things, even if you don't always question them.

Just because I don't speak every question out loud doesn't mean I don't have questions!

I'm a philosopher, s'all I'm saying. My job to question everything.

I guess we both have our *jobs*.

Bitch—

We laughed together, sound ringing out over the hushing restaurant. She ordered a pitcher of sangria without a glance at the menu. It was Tig's confidence, I thought, that left her serene in the face of rejection, that allowed her openness to possibility. I sensed that the confidence was hard-won, the world being what it is, and I admired it.

Meeting Tig had made my own life slow and thicken, seem for the first time worth noticing. For the first time I felt as though I had stories to tell, once I had her to tell them to. It was a change from flapping between the fluorescence of work and the yeasty darkness of the dive bar like some perpetually camouflaged moth.

She showed me pictures of the redheaded woman she had gone on two dates with, someone in an open marriage. The redhead's husband, too, had expressed interest in Tig. The wife was all heavy softness. He was skinny and tattooed, with dark blond locs and a cat's teeth. A knitting needle to her ball of yarn.

You look so horrified, babe, Tig said. I'm not going to sleep with him. Not my type.

Surprised, I guess, that he's anyone's type.

Do you not like men at all?

I considered offering my view that an open marriage seemed cheap and disgusting. But it originated somewhere instinctive in my belly, not my brain, and knowing Tig, she would want to debate this. Instead, I said, Mostly no, and mentioned Amit. Tig seemed only minimally curious, beyond asking if he'd gone to high school in Milwaukee.

Yeah, Rufus King, I think it was.

My sister—she's my half sister, we're real different—and I both went there. But I wouldn't have met him. Y'all too young. Also I sometimes have a hard time telling Indian people apart from each other anyway.

Das racist.

That's me, she said, giggling. No, no more sangs. I gotta drive us.

Tig asked me if I'd been seeing anyone.

I took a deep swig of my drink.

I had loose plans to see Pulp Fiction the next evening. I had, late at night, turned my LinkedIn to private and found Marina.

She worked at a dance studio in a rich suburb of Milwaukee. Strive, which explained the T-shirts. In addition, she was the "assistant CEO," a nonsense title if I ever heard one, for Shamar, a dance intensive company. Whatever that was. She had once worked as lackey to a reasonably well-known TV actress in L.A.

Marina looked less beautiful on LinkedIn, her smile forced, her pale hair in a silly bump above her forehead.

Nah, I said. Too busy.

Too busy managing change.

Always.

Isn't this place rad? she said as she signed the check. Our sangria was on the house. Tig's charms.

I looked around. I was drunk and happy. Wide-smiling at my friend.

Yes, I said. It's rad.

Milwaukee was my education, in a hundred different ways. For me at twenty-two BelAir was pure discovery. I had chewed the lobster taco with my whole face. I'd never tasted this sort of meat before, and it was sweet and creamy but still of the sea, retaining the essence of its origin. That seemed beautiful to me, and haunting too.

Tig ferried me toward Brewers Hill past banks of snow.

Look at that one, she said, pointing to a cloud-pink mansion in need of a paint job, surrounded by weeping willows. We had gone on a drive around the city—by McKinley Park, where she pointed out the banh mi stall run by a handsome polyamorist, past the backpacked UWM students on the Upper East Side. Up into Shorewood, where I marveled at the grand houses.

It's been empty forever, she said. It's a perfect location—close to the beach, close to the city, enough land around it. If I ever make it big, I'm going to live there.

The pink house was enormous. A frosted cake. Admiration stirred in me. I would never have thought to imagine a place like that for a home.

Celebrity Philosopher Antigone Clay Buys Million-Dollar Baby-Pink Mansion, I said. I can see the headline.

Yessss, bitch. Except we're definitely talking over two milli for the Pink House. It has like twenty rooms. I looked that shit up.

Start selling those books.

Tig checked her phone at a stop. Some message from some girl. Black hair, tattooed arms, a very young face.

I thought about how best to ask the question.

Do you ever worry about matching with your students on the apps?

My what?

Oh. Don't you teach?

Tig gave me a funny look, confusion cut with something else. We were pulling up the hill. No one on the sidewalks. Mummified city.

No, Tig said, frowning, I don't teach. I don't think other students in my program do either.

Aren't you doing a master's? I asked, wondering if I was vaguely crazy.

Ohh. *No.* I'll get my BA in two years.

This was a shock to me, and I tried to hide that.

I must have done a poor job. Tig killed the engine, cleared her throat.

I want to tell you something about me, she said, but you have to, first, tell me something real about you.

What?

I just want this to be fair. You tell me very little that's meaningful about your life.

I—wasn't aware this was all getting put on the scales and weighed.

It's not, babe. But friendship is work.

I glared at her. Within me thoughts hummed like flies. I did want to know whatever she was offering up, hiding behind her back like a child trying to bargain for a toy.

But she could not get to have this kind of power over me.

I need to use the bathroom, I said. Turning my voice soft and cold, I added, You shouldn't feel like you have to *divulge* anything you don't want to tell me freely. Thank you for the ride.

Her eyes turned enormous and stricken; the sight of them pierced me, even as I closed the car door with petulant force, moved toward the apartment. The noise of her car's exit in my teeth. Generous Tig would forgive this, could forgive more. In the morning I would apologize, she would brush it off. Still, I knew it right away: I had made a mistake.

Winter appeared in earnest, moved in rudely. Something deadening in every morning, everywhere I looked shorn of color and beauty. Getting out of bed froze me. In a strange burst of kindness, Amy offered to help me weatherize my windows. With her hair dryer, 3M plastic film, and a tube of caulk, we worked through my flat. She chatted with me as though we'd never in our lives had a disagreement. She laughed and smiled. Good night, she called in her reedy voice. My head spinning. I would never understand this woman.

Susan asked Thom to set up a series of precisely configured pivot tables to track the moving parts of the Stakeholder Engagement spreadsheet, make them digestible for the status update slides for each day, and he, knowing only the most basic and Googleable aspects of a pivot table, muffed it, and got it hard from Peter, who was pulled in to clean up his work. The gush of consultants and firms from the project seemed to have been stanched at least for now, though some days you could sense the blood from the night before on the boardroom walls.

Tig had a new job. At the Lush Cosmetics near UWM. Sometimes she would give me a bath bomb, a little sample of shower jelly. I stored the bath bombs in a shoebox. They were of little use in my shower, a narrow vertical casket. The bombs and jellies seemed sweet and childlike in their novelty, extravagantly scented. I had never been to a Lush. From Tig's stories I imagined it a Wonka factory of toiletries, where foaming colored liquids poured from ceiling faucets and attendees grabbed and soaped customers' hands with glittery medallions. She was discussing unionizing the store employees with her coworker Jervai. She had crushes on everyone. Everyone had crushes on her. Her hands smelled like ylang-ylang all the day long.

I explained what a bath bomb was to my mother on WhatsApp, how if you dropped it in water it would fizz, turn the tub water bright colors, scent the air, and she just said, Okay.

She and my father took baths using large metal buckets, bailing the water out, splashing it upon their bodies with red plastic mugs. Their house did not have a shower. The lime-scaled pipes let out water at a trickle. Easier to use the well. My father's parents got sponge baths, towels covering their bodies in sections.

My mother attended to them while dramatic Kannada serials played, offering distraction.

This is what would be in wait for me, come February.

One Saturday Isabel texted me that she hadn't seen me in ages, and did I want to come with them to Allium.

Isabel had good taste. This was what separated her from Thom. Allium was like Europe in Milwaukee—small and dark inside, every detail chosen with care, the ingredients good, no American excess in the portions. The three of us perched on heated seats, crafty benches with cushions placed over ventilation grates. We ordered pricey cocktails, the white pizza, something with mushrooms, something with sausages, and settled in.

What got me upset was the talk of landlords.

Thom had been blabbing about Engels, growing louder with every new Belgian beer. Now he was getting into how he didn't think much of Obama. Imagine Obama's actions from a white dude, no one would be impressed with him, he scoffed, and Isabel nodded seriously and obediently.

To me it seemed possible that most people other than fancy-college types would love Obama way more if he were white, and it seemed explicitly because he was not that people were asking him to move heaven and earth. But I did not really follow politics.

Somehow from there we were talking about Amy. I was glad for the chance to vent, but Thom would not permit me. Landlords are the scum of the earth, he said, again and again. We needed to seize their assets, he said, and give them to the people. Housing, he said, should be something you should pay for only to eventually own, not a way for rich people to make an investment off of other people's precarity.

Yes, well, Amy is a *property manager*, I explained again through gritted teeth.

Property managers are cops. The police of the ruling class. Landlords are part of the ruling class.

It seemed to me that my good friend Thomas, while working in the stultifying fluorescent light of our client boardrooms, was slowly becoming some species of shaggy radical. Which was fine, I supposed, but for me he was near impossible to follow. For me a landlord was like a shopkeeper. They sold something people wanted. And as much as Amy was a demon out of hell, even my parents rented out a modest flat my mother had inherited in the city close to them, and this, given my father's unemployment, was their primary income source. They had done this because the money helped, because the alternative was to leave the property empty and let it fall into disrepair, or—while he was still alive—have my sodden creep of an uncle reside there, which would ultimately produce the same outcome.

I tried to say a gentle and reasonable version of this.

It was the first time I had mentioned my parents to him in years. Thom had once asked lazily, jovially, in some college bar with a tree growing in the middle of it, where they were, what they did. I said they had returned to India to take care of my grandparents. That my father did accounting and business things in the States but had not been able to find a new job. My mother was a nurse, worked at our town's small clinic. My face, I think, had grown dark and troubled, because I looked up and saw Thom watching it closely. In a total betrayal, my eyes slicked with tears.

This was years ago. We had been waiting for our drinks. When they arrived—big pint glasses with columns of jointy ice still spinning from energetic stirs—he put down cash for both of us, patted me on the shoulder, and then walked back to his boys. Left me behind.

If your parents are landlords, your parents are part of the ruling class,

Thom repeated now, with the fervor of Pentecostals or saffron-robed men with oiled plaits yelling Har Har Mahadeva.

Just like Peter is, he continued. Fuck, Peter is probs a landlord *and* a boss. I know that type. Collecting paychecks, handing out paychecks.

A flicker of discomfort crossed Isabel's face. Her mother was vice president of something or the other company in Minnesota. She demurred slightly. Thom doubled down.

When the revolution comes, he said at monologue's end, every cop and landlord, every boss and capitalist, will be going about their business. On the phone, in the bath, sipping something pricey at a vineyard, watching a good show in the fuckin' home theater. They won't even know how big the powder keg will have gotten. They won't know until the first brick is thrown through the first window.

And in that moment, he said, voice dropping to a whisper from its great decibel height, *everything* will change.

Thom was faded. His eyes red. This was not how he talked normally, this spouting and grandstanding. Somewhere in me I sensed that intellectually he believed these things, or was coming to believe these things, but the anger did not arise from what he was describing; it rose from an expectation for a much better life than the one he owned.

My mother's face swam before me. As did my father's eyes: large and intelligent, with great capacity for laughter and fear. How afraid they had looked when the knock came on the door. How defeated my parents sounded when they asked me how I was each week, a grainy Reliance call across oceans. The mechanics of a wire transfer, the constant mental conversion of dollars to rupees. In a history class I'd taken, the room flooded by the fluorescence that would prepare us for the light of our office cubicles, a graying woman in a kimono coat had lectured in a strangely little-girl voice on the Chinese Land Reform Movement. Listening to her I had remembered my father, the knock at the door and the flashing lights outside. My mind floated into a corner of the room like a balloon a child let loose. It had bobbed there, with a helium blankness, until the ringing bell punctured it, announced the lecture's end.

I was willing to believe that Keith LaMarchese—Rolex means more sex, let the ladies know—was a dues-paying member of the so-called ruling class. I knew at a cellular level that my father was not. And neither, horrible as she was, was Amy.

I've never asked, I suppose, I said, my voice sounding choked and ghostly to me, what your mother and father do, like what they do for money.

Thom looked discomfited for the first time. He shrugged. They work in medicine, he said.

My mom works in medicine. Lots of different ways to work in medicine. What do they do?

Thom ate a sausage with violent chews. Isabel said, Let's change the subject, pals, it's a Saturday night—

Do they work in insurance or something nefariously embarrassing to you? I asked.

Fuck no. I'd disown them. They're just, like, doctors.

Cardiology and family medicine, Isabel added helpfully.

Two doctors, I thought. Making doctor paychecks in America. Living in the suburbs of Milwaukee while their son, miles away, dreamed of the Maoist uprising.

My white friends with their white faces and their white lives. Their eyes watching mine. Assigning me a place on their political grid.

I could not be in Allium a second longer, have this conversation a second longer, or I would break a plate of petite German sausages over someone's head.

I have to call someone, one sec. Here's cash in case they come with the check, I said, counting out the bills. My voice dead and matter-of-fact. Fingers trembling with anger.

I stepped out, phone pressed to my ear. Isabel was already laughing about something, head leaning on her boyfriend's shoulder. Thom followed me with his eyes until I rounded the corner. This was true, maybe still, that we were, deep down, alike, that we understood the dark contours of each other.

I set forth, my boots slipping on the poorly salted sidewalk. I texted him something perfunctory.

It was a certain kind of test: Would he realize how upset I was? If he did, would he call me, come looking for his friend?

We would see, we would see.

If I walked west long enough, it would take me to my apartment on Vine. A straight shot, I said to myself. Trying to manufacture calm. I could go home. I could be alone.

What I remembered from that class about China under Mao had, like most of my education, grown hazy without disappearing. There'd been attempts to create an incremental equality through taxation and redistribution, but Mao believed that peasants who participated directly in taking power for themselves would have a far deeper emotional tie to the revolution. Schoolteachers, property owners, intellectuals: they were shot, dismembered, buried alive. The former landowners decomposing underfoot, fertilizing the soil. Land reform did create more equality. Dramatically so. Then within decades, it created mass starvation. I did not remember the cause and effect of that.

What I recalled most clearly from that class was my own reaction, the fear and discomfort that revealed to me where my loyalties lay, how I believed change should happen: civilized, inspiring, with speeches, without blood. With perhaps a modicum of fairness for people who had not made the cruel machine that was now being bludgeoned but tried to look out for themselves and live, run the train cars of their lives on the tracks laid out before them.

It was so cold, the night air. I looked at my phone. Nothing from Thom.

I called Amit. It rang to voicemail, but he texted almost immediately, Are you okay?

S
im fine

> **Amit**
> You sure about that?

S
youre busy then yeah

> **Amit**
> At work, will be until 9ish. We're
> interviewing engineer candidates
> and playing Foozball with them

S
oh by all means let me not
keep you from ~foozball~

> **Amit**
> Whats wrong. Did something
> happen with your parents?

S
im just bloody tired of people
who have grand abstract
political theories

> **Amit**
> O shit well don't ever come to san
> francisco then. What were the grand
> theories? Immigration stuff? People
> in wisco can be ignorant

S
more like . . . the politics
of renting. it really does
not matter Amit, sorry to
bother you

> **Amit**
> You're not bothering me, S.
> You never do. Maybe we can
> talk more about this in person.
> I'll be in MKE dec 21. Would love to
> see you.

S

okay sounds good

Amit

Going to take a shot in the dark here.
If you don't tell people about your
family, you can't blame them totally
if they fuck up and hurt your feelings

It felt as though one of the Lush bath bombs had lodged fast in my throat. I slid my phone back into my pocket, put my hood up. My breath suspended, white in the dark, wafting around me as I stepped.

The air ate at me. I held my body very stiff and told myself, One foot, then another, then another. Still nothing from Thom. I looked up how much a taxi would cost on my phone. I had seen the Yellow Cab dispatch headquarters from the bus, on the way back from work.

But then I would have the wait time, and if I stopped moving, I was confident I would turn into an icicle. One foot, then another.

Thirty minutes into walking on deserted streets, I got a call from Tig.

Hello 'ello! What are you up to?

Her small clear voice, all bright and good mood.

I, uh, I am walking, I said thickly.

Oh! Anywhere in particular? Got done with a silly date on the East Side, wanted to know if you wanted to hang.

I was just on the East Side. This place called Allium. I, uh, am close to home.

Allium, whaaat. I was just two blocks down from you.

Oh my god.

Yeah! Isn't that crazy—hey, what's going on? Hey. Hey. Babe. Are you all right? Why you crying?

Eventually, I blew my nose into my scarf and said some version of this: I'm okay. I'm truly fine, Tig. I wish I'd known you were that close. I would have liked to meet.

Hold on, girl, Tig said. Drop your location. I'm coming to you.

———

Blurred by the wine she brought, by my own laughter, the laughter of the recently cheered-up, I told Tig she could stay the night. I tucked her in on my tufted couch, brushed my teeth, went to bed.

I was woken up by Tig climbing into the covers behind me. Her legs were unshaven, the hair on them curled fuzz.

Just want to sleep, she said. Your living room is freezing.

Oh, I'm sorry. Of course. Do you have room.

Yeah, we good.

She put an arm around me. It felt very nice. The weight of it, I mean. Tig's skin so terribly soft.

In the dark room, the sound of two people breathing. Occasional creaks from the apartment below. In the moonlight, tree silhouettes tapped a ghost's Morse code on the wall.

Tig, I said, suddenly more awake than not. Tig.

Mmmm.

Are you too sleepy to talk?

Mmm. Nyes. No. Mm. No, I can talk, she said. Her breath sweet like old fruit.

We were whispering this, I don't know why. I chose a deep exhale and came out with it.

I just want to say, I'm sorry I didn't tell you something important about me when you asked. I want to know what you wanted to tell me.

Okay?

Between us there was a quiet equal parts comforting and combative. I readied myself to speak. Found myself unable to. To talk about my uncle and what he had done to me, about my family coming here and having to leave, it felt like too much, it was being asked to cough up one's own organs upon demand, lay them bloodied, strung with mucus, upon a tabletop.

But Tig was waiting, and, I knew, comfortable with long silence.

I could tell her part of it. The story of my family.

I came with my parents to the U.S. when I was fourteen, I said to the wall and into the dark, voice flat as paper. We moved to Aurora and kept mostly to ourselves. Barely anybody paid me much attention at school other than some teachers, but I was always like, it's fine, you American teenagers are weirdos, like my whole world was my family then. My father, he had a visa, to work for an electronics company. The company was shitty to him, like paid him poorly, tried to bully him. They did not treat most of their immigrant employees well. They don't have to, when they control your papers. My father didn't want to put up with it, I said. He's not like many people. He's not a . . . easily cowed person.

I paused for breath. Tig rubbed my back very gently. I stared off into the low dark, thinking about how to shape a life's great turbulence into a story. Considering what I was willing to say out loud.

My father had walked away from his old employer. Had started his own business with a friend and successfully applied for an updated visa. That had seemed a total miracle to me. Papa the entrepreneur, like the people starting companies in *Time* magazine. We moved from a small flat to a two-bedroom house with taupe carpets. We went to an outlet mall in Illinois and I bought a polo T-shirt that said Abercrombie & Fitch from a dark, vanilla-smelling store.

Papa's friend brought in two associates of his own, small-time investors who turned into three additional partners. My father had seemed increasingly perturbed by the arrangement. Too many cooks, he said often to Mummy, and ignored me if I asked what he meant. It was only later that I understood so much of what had happened.

Initially the company had only sold electronics for schools and universities, but the new partners had bigger plans. Now they wanted to diversify into human resources, which meant, to them, the visa game. The official line was that they were connecting immigrants who wanted to come here with jobs. My father was cordoned away from this side of the business, my mother said to me, again and again, was told to keep his focus on lecture clickers and calculators.

I could not bear to tell Tig the whole of it—the arrests, the charges, the shell companies that had filed the paperwork for H-1B after H-1B, taking the money of eager men from Haryana and UP and Punjab. My father's partners claiming he knew all along that the visas were cooked, he handled the finances, he started the company, this was his plan. I was well into my first semester at Madison. My parents were determined to protect me. Their greatest investment. I was told so little. I visited him only two times in prison. A coach bus ride, a long car drive. That was all my mother allowed. Focus on school, mol, she said. That is why we brought you here.

The words from the court case, *visa fraud, pay to play*, the names of the men they'd given the fraudulent papers to, all this brought in me a shame so total it could block out the sun. I remember holding a lecture clicker in college and feeling like I was falling to the molten center of the earth. What's wrong, Amit had said then, and I shook my head. It had been many months before I could bring myself to tell him.

So I simply said to Tig, There was trouble with the partners. Like not everything they did was legal. My dad got blamed for some of it. And after a while, he decided he was tired of fighting it, paying the lawyer fees. They broke him down eventually. He pled guilty, even though he wasn't, did what he could to get a shorter sentence, he served one and a half years, and then he got deported. Or self-deported. Basically he probably would have been deported, but maybe not if he had fought it, found a better lawyer. But he didn't fight it.

He had not, my parents had not, fought for me. Stayed for me, or tried to bring me with them. I did not say that out loud.

How old were you, Tig asked. Her voice for the first time uncertain, wavering.

Seventeen, I said.

It felt like a respectable age to have something like that happen. I had been old enough to continue living, to go to classes, to put certain parts of myself in a box and set it high up on a shelf.

Tig put her arms around me, moved me closer to her body.

My babe. I'm so sorry. I'm so sorry.

Oh, it's all right, I said, stupidly.

I'm sorry I set an ultimatum in our friendship, Tig said. I shouldn't have forced you to tell me, like, some quid pro quo thing.

I wanted to tell you, I said. I didn't know if that was true, but I said it. And I suddenly longed very much to sleep.

What I wanted to tell you the night you asked if I was in graduate school, which I felt was like, why are you still in undergrad, was . . .

I held her hand as she trailed off.

I don't know if you've noticed I never talk about my father, she began again.

I found listening to what she said next really quite painful, and I am ashamed to say I began to grow distracted, tried to pay only enough attention to get through the conversation and away.

It was difficult to sleep that night. I felt both exposed and burdened by information. Close to 4 a.m., I got out of bed. Climbing carefully around Tig, who was slumbering with her arms thrown up around her head like a great sweet baby. I was hungover from the dark cheap wine. From nowhere a memory appeared, of a recurrent nightmare I had as a small child. In the dream, the earth was disintegrating. The planet broke apart, fissured into asteroids. The very world ending. In the dream I ran, sandals thumping the ground in terror, looking everywhere for my parents. Just as I found them, I would vault off into space, drift away alone, the ones I loved lost to me.

I made myself tea, turned on a lamp, and tried to read. My pretty little apartment gathered round me like a hug. Gilt-edged mirror. Tufted sofa. A jute rug with long tassels. On my end table the green glint of a bottle of Tanqueray, a vase of dried-out flowers. Out of canvas drop cloths from the hardware store I'd fashioned pale curtains. It was possible to believe, looking at all this in dull lamplight, that the past did not matter, that it lay inert in my wake.

A counterargument to this: Tig's voice in my head, drowning out the sentences inked in front of me.

So I was the person who found my dad after he killed himself, it had said. A sentence like a gun. It deafened me.

He had stuff all over his face, and I wiped it off. I'm okay, babe, you know, please don't worry. I was a kid, and kids are very resilient. When I was in Florida I got into a program and saw a therapist for four months, this Black Taino woman, it changed everything. I have a great life, full of adventures, and friends like you. Don't trip—I'm good, I'm okay, my life's so very good.

My dad was the kindest man, she had said. He and my mom weren't right for each other, but they were always respectful, and he loved me. Rion wanted me to go to college and become a doctor or a scientist or a scholar. I went to such shit schools when I was young, and then when he died and I got to Rufus King it was too late. They weren't talking then about learning disabilities the way they are now.

What had she meant? I had been too pained by the first image, an eleven-year-old walking into a room and finding her father. Wiping his dead face. What was the substance all over it? Liquid or solid? What happened to a body when it snuffed its own life out?

Everything that came after this confession lived for me in dense fog, even as I, on autopilot, had tried to say the right things. Had said the right things.

Tig continued: I had always felt wrong, just in different ways: liking girls, not being able to do things in school. They didn't get learning disabilities the way they do now, she had said again, and began to babble, with a manic edge to her voice, about working at Disney, going to community college, getting all the books she could on CDs or MP3, but it wasn't enough.

It wasn't enough, what did that mean?

She kept trying, kept trying to go to college, trying to honor the father who had believed in her intelligence, who had said, As a Black girl you'll have to seem twice as smart, work twice as hard, who had pictured her doing more even than getting a regular bachelor's degree. He had dreamed big dreams for her. In a way that Tig's mother, a pale soft-spoken woman who rotated between a series of religions and treated her children with a serene and mute passivity, had not.

Things are a lot better now, she had concluded. I got my remedial stuff out of the way before I started at Alverno two years back. Still, it's hard sometimes, and I definitely prefer audio to text, and it takes me time.

What took her time?

And then staring back at me, from what I held in my own hands, the answer.

It moved into place: Tig never reading menus, Tig's phone set to the largest text display, the way Tig would sound words out silently when reading parking signs. It gutted me. I knew Antigone now, in a way I had never really known Thom or Amit.

I rubbed my eyes, which were very tired, even if my mind was not. I would have to save my journal for tomorrow. For now I would finish my chapter. The book in my hands was about routine work and meaning. Topical, I had thought, when I saw it at the thrift store on Brady. Its writer hung around outside factories and offices and struck up conversations with working people.

At one point she asks a woman employed at a fish cannery if she made friends with, was close to, talked with the other women on the factory assembly line. Not really, the woman answers. The woman's boyfriend hangs around nearby, ready to pick her up.

What do you do all day, then?

I daydream.

What do you daydream about? the writer presses.

About sex.

I guess that's my fault, the boyfriend apologizes proudly.

No, it's not you, says the woman. It's the tuna fish.

I told Tig about the fish cannery woman and we laughed loud. This was days before Christmas. The two of us were sipping very hot coffee and trying my first oysters at the Milwaukee Public Market, which Tig said was modeled on the apparently famous Pike Place Market in Seattle. At MPM, you walked about the warehouse perimeter, where many little shops and markets huddled, you got your tacos or cheese knife or lobster roll and carried it upstairs, where there was seating. One stall sold a canvas bag of pink crystalline salt with grandiose writing about the Himalayas for twenty-five dollars. Only in America, I thought.

St. Paul's, which we were patronizing, had a little bar where they served food. The oysters on crushed ice. A bowl of lemon wedges, doll-size bottles of Tabasco.

These are revolting, I said.

Remind me of pussy a lil, honestly, Tig said, tipping her head back.

Don't have them with coffee, Jesus Christ, the oyster guy said. Please. Take these— He pushed toward us two glasses of white. On the house, he said. Only because I can't stand it.

Tig laughed even louder, took five dollars out of my wallet, and dropped them in the tip jar.

Outrageous, I thought, but I was in a good mood. Over the oyster guy's shoulder I watched dark mottled lobsters, their claws rubber-banded, climb sluggishly over each other in a cloudy tank.

We got some soft bun things from the Public Market's bakery and took them and the wine upstairs, promising safe return of the glasses. Settled in a little nook of marble tables and spiky plants. I read a novel Amit had given me almost a year ago. Tig was taking notes on something she was listening to for school. I asked her what it was about and she said, Collectivism.

Like communism? I asked. She shook her head and began to scribble in an expensive-looking notebook.

The novel was one of these frightfully intelligent prizewinners, was all about a doctor-shoctor type walking around New York City. It seemed plotless and a little strange to me. I had never been to Manhattan, found it hard to imagine a life so contained and self-reliant, no rides needed from a friend, little fear of what might befall you when walking out alone. Something in the way the main character spoke reminded me of my mother, who thinks out loud, but carefully and methodically.

The coffee hit me. I went to find a restroom. On the pot I texted with Amit, whom I was supposed to see later that afternoon. It was our typical comfortable banter. Combative and gently vulgar. For no reason I called his female friends from growing up "the hoes." Years later I would look at my journal and read a sentence like *Saw Amit, in from San Fran. He was running late, ministrations to about six of his hoes, stacked back to back.*

When I returned from my own ministrations, Tig was not at our table. She was standing by the head of the stairs, and appeared to be shouting after two women, one blond, one with long black hair streaming down her back. They were speed-walking out of the market.

What's going on, I said, running up to her, touching her elbow. Tig's face was blotchy, her eyes wet.

The women had been arguing, quiet and then loud enough to turn heads, and then the one with long hair, who Tig said was Asian, had reached across the table and slapped the blonde.

Tig had taken her headphones out, marched over. Asked the blonde if she was okay. Things had grown heated. The Asian woman had said, Stay out of our business, called her a fat Black bitch.

Are you serious, I said, and ran to the window. Watched the two of them cross the iced street, walk toward a boxy car—and then in a moment of clean shock, saw that the blond woman was Marina.

Her hair up in a ponytail, her collar buttoned snug around her neck. She was yelling. Something I could not make out. Her girlfriend, lover, whoever, was tall and muscled, in expensive-seeming sweats. As she tossed her head scornfully I could make out a lip ring's glint.

Tig said that in the moment the blond woman hissed something like, You're so disgusting, Jenny. That was just gross. Gross.

She'd apologized to Tig for her partner without ever meeting Tig's eye. They'd peaced.

It was so weird, babe, Tig said for the fourth time. The blond cat was like, in this bored cool little voice, I'm fine, she's on her way to the airport, she's leaving me, I'm fine, I'm deeply sorry she said that foul shit to you.

I blinked. My heart was sprinting.

You're really very inappropriately silent about this, Tig said, setting her jaw.

I can't believe she called you that; I'm so sorry, I literally want to fight her. What a piece of cow dung. I just . . . I kind of know her? I'm still processing.

The fuck? The Asian one?

No. The other woman. Name's Marina. I guess *know* is the wrong word. We've only met once. Sort of. But I had a cr— I liked her for a while. But nothing happened. It doesn't matter.

I got a text from Thom as we walked out into the icy street, fake holly wreaths adorning the parking meters.

yo yo yo roomies and I having a party at the house tomorrow, see you at 8, bring wine and beer. quantity not quality pls

Y'all meet online? Tig asked once we were back in her car.

I nodded. Nothing happened, I repeated stupidly. We never even went out. I guess I hope she's okay, I said.

Tig wrinkled her nose. Didn't think you'd be that into someone like that, she said.

Like what, I wanted to say, someone beautiful?

Instead I laughed and said, Please elaborate.

She seemed pretty basic to me!

I found this small vaporous flare of jealousy more sweet than anything. I cradled Tig's jaw with my hand as she sped us down Water Street. She would drop me off at LuLu, where Amit was waiting.

All of us, I said with tenderness, are basic next to you.

Amit is warm, friendly as a dog, better than he looks at sports, a little ugly. His hair curls in glossy ringlets that invite touch. I couldn't consider the thought of sex with him anymore. Our past intimacies had been marked by fumbling affection and sharp pain. Still, from my time in college there was no one with whom I felt more comfort.

Whenever Amit was in a relationship with some girl, we were very stiff and proper with each other. When he was single we would hold hands, walk arm in arm, circle each other like two affectionate spayed dogs. We put in our orders at LuLu. With cool authority I said, The shishito peppers and the gnocchi here are excellent.

Amit smiled wide and amused and interlaced my fingers with his. So that's where things were.

How's work? I asked. You still wiping your bum with hundreds each day?

Vulgar. Low six figures makes you lower middle class in San Francisco, man. I can't afford a decent one-bedroom.

No way.

Yahweh. Look, I'm not kanjoose or anything. My appan is always telling me, Money is *for* spending, moné, just save a bit for the rainy times. And I agree, like money is for using, investing, saving, spending, whatevski. I *do* mind pissing two thousand a month down the sink of renting one *single* room in the Haight. There are other things—here Amit's eyes turned briefly wary and conspiratorial—that that money could go towards. So yeah. I'm thinking about moving. Living somewhere unconventional.

Cardboard box?

You joke. But I've seen dog kennels advertised as cheap rooms on SF Craigslist.

I went on some dates, I said, couple months ago, with someone who went to college in SF. She lived on a houseboat. Way more affordable than renting an apartment, and she could sell the boat once she left.

This was a story Pulp Fiction had shared, about an ex really, but I gave it to her. Pulp Fiction would never in actuality do something as interesting as buy a houseboat to live on.

Amit's eyes widened, brightened. He smiled but said nothing. I had chosen to be matter-of-fact, slip the pronoun in like a receipt in a shopping bag. No need to make a production. He'd known something, even back in college, about the way I was.

Our food arrived. Amit had decided to try being omnivorous, though he grew queasy still at the idea of beef. I clicked a picture of him with peppers bulging from his mouth, posted it online. He told me about how he was considering renting a walk-in closet under the stairs of a group house in the Mission. Four hundred dollars a month. I groaned loudly.

My good dude, your parents did not send their moothe moné to college so you could be the Harry Potter of Silicon Valley. Living in a cupboard ass.

Ha. I might not end up doing it. There's a girl who lives in the house who I like a bit, but she's too cool for me. Sorry, not girl, Emily uses they pronouns.

They pronouns? What in the world. Is this person a hermaphrodite?

You know, like a trans person. Well, nonbinary gender. Which is a subset, I think, of being transgender. Or maybe a superset. I'm not sure.

Oh come on.

What?

I get, I really get like, if you want to transition to living your truth as a woman or a man if you were born the wrong thing. I support that completely. Anything beyond that is elitist leftist American nonsense, honestly. Is she pretty?

I'll show you, Amit said, and began scrolling. He continued, I mean, when they and I have talked about it, they have said they just never felt comfortable as a woman, but also didn't identify as a man. That's how they realized they weren't cis. And then they decided to opt out of gender.

Oh please, I said, suddenly hissing like a goose, surprised at my own anger. Can someone tell me what it means to be *cis*?

Um, I'm not—

This shit is hard for everyone! Do people think so-called *cis* people don't, or haven't, struggled with this shit? Felt fucking weird in their bodies? Have you never felt weird about being *a man*?

Yeah, you could say I have—

I spent *all* my teens wishing I could *slice* my breasts off, have a flat and smooth body. I cut up my bras with nail scissors. Got thrashed for it. Does that entitle me to a *they*? Can I *opt out of gender* now?

Amit looked uncomfortable, chewed a mouthful of chicken sandwich, and said with a shruggy sort of smile, Don't ever move to San Francisco. This is them, he added, and showed me a picture.

Emily. Ethnically indeterminate skin, full lips, vaguely East Asian eyes heavily lined with kohl. Head half shaved. Dark, straight swords of eyebrows.

She's really hot, I said truthfully.

Do we have the same type, then? Amit joked, clearly trying to lighten the mood. How are things with your houseboat-dweller date?

Nonexistent. She's hot for some married man. Very boring.

It's distressing, how many people elect to be boring when they have the option not to be. Anyone else?

There's no one serious, yaar. I'm just having fun. The pool of females in Milwaukee isn't . . . scintillating, though. An SF four is like a Milwau-kee eight, I'm pretty sure.

Damn, we have ourselves a *hater*.

Amit. Do you feel okay about it—about, you know, me?

The silence opened up between us. My heart a bluish lobster crawling through a cloudy tank, awaiting execution.

He squeezed my hand, this sweetest of men. I don't want to make it weird, he said, but I am proud of you.

bro wtf is amit in town?? Thom texted immediately after liking my pic-ture of the boy masticating shishito peppers. bring him tomorrow. invite whoever. also no need for wine anymore bring mixers and something hard. my dude this went from genteel soiree to earnest rager.

He sent me a link to the Facebook party invite titled THE KWANZAA KEGGER.

Is a single person who lives there Black? Amit asked, smiling wryly, thumbing through racks of shirts.

Obviously not, I said.

We'd gone to the Goodwill in the Third Ward. I had nothing to wear to the party unless I showed up in a Banana Republic blazer.

I don't know that much about fashion, Amit said as I exited the dress-ing room in a wine-dark oxford shirt, rhinestone cuff links, a stringy tie with a brooch in its center. But that seems like the look for you.

The shirt moved slim down my body. I would wear it tucked into high-waisted jeans. When I dressed stylish I felt American. In the best way. I held out a shirt with flamingos on it for Amit.

Come to the party, I said.

No.

Come to the party. I will be so happy if you come.

Maybe. I have to see KJ.

KJ was Amit's one friend I'd never met. She thus held more mystery for me than the rest of the hoes. Their bond a relic from middle school, where he'd shown up a smelly dork with braces and jeans you could lose a body in, and she had deigned to be his friend. I'd seen her in pictures over the years: a terra-cotta-skinned girl who did her hair in two fat braids and always wore a watch. She called him Mitty. KJ worked in a daycare and was at some point getting a variety of social work degree. She'd had the same girlfriend since eighth grade.

I thought about telling Amit to bring her to Thom's party, thought about inviting Tig too—Tig, who had asked me once with a quizzical eyebrow lift if I had any Black friends other than her. Then I remembered it was called a goddamned Kwanzaa Kegger.

See her for dinner, yaar, then come to the party.

I won't have my dad's car tomorrow. KJ was gonna pick me up.

Fine! Don't come! Damn!

He called me the next day.

KJ can drop me off, he said, on her way back home. Meet you there?

You want to hang out the three of us? I asked, mashing salmon with a fork to make croquettes. I can cook us dinner. We'll just have to be very very very quiet. My property manager lives below me and she is a rabid dog.

Um. No, no, that's okay. We have plans.

Do you like not want KJ to meet me? Does she have some like terrible dirt on middle school you?

I do want her to meet you. And she wants to too. She's said that. We're discussing some kinda private stuff today, don't mind it.

Wow such secretiveness.

Did you think you had a patent on it? Bye.

So. Does Amit know? Thom asked close to midnight.

We were in the backyard sharing his cigarette. From the house behind us, its shingles glowing white in the dark, bass had smoked out into the cold night for hours. At the party we'd hit shots. They went down loud and burning. We chased with beer. Festooned ourselves with tinsel. We drank Isabel's mulled wine, made in the same Crockpot where Thom cooked down roasted bones with vinegar and water, lemongrass and anise. This was before the latest diet, where Isabel had decided to go gluten-free and Thom said he wanted to be pescatarian, which as far as I understood meant to eat an inhuman amount of frozen salmon and the occasional sliver of bacon. My lipstick had rubbed off to nothing. My tongue, the pucker of my mouth, all purple. We had talked in a circle around the bonfire Thom's roommate Allan had built, the multiple shots of dark rum fermenting inside me until I became loud and bold and laughing, making lewd jokes, all of a sudden asking Isabel in a falthoo conspiratorial way if Thom's dick wasn't actually—I held up forefinger and thumb an inch from each other. Isabel smiled, serene as a Madonna, wrapped herself close to her man.

I'm very satisfied, she said. No acid in her voice, just the sort of gentle adoration that was unmistakable, impossible to counterfeit. Her response filled me with a deep desire to drop my skin to the floor in a baggy puddle, then keep walking. Amit shook his head at me, disappeared somewhere.

Thom had not seemed to mind this aggression, my clownery. An hour or so later, as Allan was telling us in his droney way about Milwaukee's socialist mayors, and I tried to suppress my shivering, Thom put his arm around my shoulder. It was the most platonic thing in the world. The nonverbal equivalent of his calling me bro, that's what it felt like, but to my own astonishment I turned slick and wet. This flustered me, and so I talked some more shit, it escapes my memory, and Thom grabbed my face with both hands and began licking it. Like I was a kitten from his own personal litter. Cool slow licks, intended to subjugate. I was squealing, flapping my arms, laughing in shock. A boy with a tall mop of red hair put a video of this on Vine, where it would play in a demonic loop for years.

I went looking for Amit but could not find him. Danced next to some white girls. The slickness again, the small hands within my chest reaching, clawing with want.

Working through another cup of beer warm as the night was cold, I talked to Isabel about her teaching volunteer job. She'd turned cool and polite, still nice—Isabel was incapable of being anything but nice. Then Thom appeared, offered us a cigarette. Only one person said yes. And here we were.

I told Thom I didn't want to get on his girl's bad side. Perhaps publicly tonguing another woman's face in front of thirty-odd people was impolitic, had he considered that?

It's fine, homie. She knows you're a raging dyke.

Raging.

Does Amit know?

Know what, bro?

That you've gone and diversified your portfolio.

Pivoted my table.

Turned pescatarian.

We broke up laughing. Yes, I said, a little haughtily. I'm not hiding anything.

So you and this Tig woman boning? he asked. Is that why I haven't hung out with her properly?

Tig is like water. Impossible to pin down. She also has like three jobs right now, counting getting a degree. And no. We are not.

How come?

What kind of question is that?

Your eyes light up every time you talk about her. Which is often. Four times minimum a day, Tig, my friend Tig, my new pal Tig.

My face turned hot in the frigid air.

I really like Tig, I said, in much the same way as I really like you. Desire does not feature prominently.

At this Thom pressed his lips together very slightly. He nodded, flicked ash onto an iced-out flower bed.

I was very drunk. My head felt as though it were filled with oil in the cold night. With everything else blurred, I could feel more clearly the shape of the thing circling the dark drain of who I was.

I'm afraid, I said slowly, the words stilted and ungainly as they left my throat, that I'm not very well constructed to . . . be with anyone. For me there was only Amit and that was a disaster. Friendship I can navigate, though there are still things there that feel like too much. I can like, pull, you know, get someone home. Sometimes after I sleep with someone all I feel is contempt; sometimes I feel that contempt while things are happening, like I hate the person, like I'm thinking like sexist things, like the words *dumb bitch* will be flashing in my mind while I'm doing shit to someone. I feel like being a little cruel makes me better at sex with women, something about wanting to bring a person to their knees. But then it's over and I can't bear the sight of them. I'm afraid maybe of being with someone I also really like, because then what if I'm ugly to that someone, like—I don't know. I've never been in love. I don't have it in me to, I think sometimes. That's what I feel when I see you and Isabel: this is what I won't have.

The whole time I spoke I looked steadily at the streetlight's orange funnel: a dog cone for the night.

Thom's face. I can still see it. It was as though I had pulled down my pants and shown him a Kotex pad bulging with blood. Shame flooded and overflowed me like a bath. I looked back upward, my eyes smarting.

Forget I said anything, I said. I should eat.

Why you so intense for? Then he laughed. Come with me, he said. His smile had turned on. A flipped switch: the room now full of light.

Where?

Car.

Okay, like where?

Y-Not. You're taking the wheel.

What? I can't—

It's a four-minute drive, pussy bitch. We're gonna get fries. You're gonna have to learn sometime, quit with this I'm-an-immigrant excuse shit. Okay, this is a handbrake. Release it.

01

We were leaving Y-Not II when the thing happened. Thom was laughing about something, midchew, the car smelling of hot oily potato.

I craned my neck to the rear window, put my hand on the back of the passenger headrest like I'd seen Tig do when reversing, and stepped my foot down. Smashed swift and hard into the pole in front of us.

I screamed. So did Thom, a loud screech, high-pitched, and it seemed to me it was the fact that I'd witnessed this girlish cry that most enraged him. We ran out of the car. The front bumper scratched, well dented. Left headlight: cracked.

He was losing his mind, dragging hands through his hair, yelling into the night. Some of the Y-Not II regulars looked out the window and laughed.

I was trembling. From time past I knew something about calming an angry drunk down. You make yourself nothing. You appease and you flatter. And then you calmly assert reality and present a way forward. In their own indistinctness they may latch on to gentleness, clarity. If this does not work, you run.

Thom, I said, after what felt like many minutes, this will be okay. We will get the car fixed. I am sorry this happened. I don't know how to drive, and you insisted—

So this is fucking my fault in your book, is it, my—

No, I did not say that. Thomas, friend. Listen to me. Take a breath with me.

I reached for his hand and he snatched it away. He appeared near tears.

Thom, I said again, we will get the car fixed. I will pay for it all. Here, I'll transfer money to your bank account right now.

A look of shock on Thom's face when I pulled up my bank app, logged in. I had a little under twelve thousand dollars in my checking account—Great, I thought, more than enough to get this sorted out.

Would one thousand be okay? I asked. I can send it to you right now. I'm sorry again.

You know absolutely *nothing* about cars.

Dread bit into me. Two thousand? I quavered.

Thom laughed: a bitter bark. Then let out a loud, whitely visible exhale. With his new mustache and thick-knit brows, he suddenly looked to me like a soft-bodied dragon, nostrils smoking. He unfolded his arms, laughed again. Thom rarely holds true anger for long.

It'll probably cost four hundo, he said, still sharply. You can fucking calm down, my dude. I did make you drive the car. I will take it to a body shop and get shit sorted, and let you know about the bill.

Back at the party, Thom made a beeline for Isabel, proceeded to ignore me entirely. The Kwanzaa Kegger appeared to still be going strong. I texted Tig to ask how her night was, moroseness catching me in the ribs. She wrote back: she had taken her mother to Chicago for her birthday. were at MacArthur's, she wrote, will bring you here sometime. banana pudding is straight fire.

I went looking for Amit.

Six men and some rotating, indistinct assortment of their girlfriends lived in Thom's house. During their parties, space was apportioned thusly: cups and booze in the kitchen, bong hits in the dining room, dancing in the cleared-out living room, which gave way to sleeping bodies at the party's end, each bedroom on the second floor a small den for disparate groups of friends to chill in, each bedroom on the third floor a place for retreat or sleep or fucking, a fearsome attic that I had never been to where harder drugs apparently were on offer, but it was not much patronized—these were good boys. It was a house full of nooks, crammed with things to trip on.

I turned the corner of the stairs between the third and second floors and ran smack into Amit, who appeared pink and sozzled.

Where were you? I exclaimed. I've been texting you. I freaking crashed Thom's car.

What? Why were you driving? You okay?

Yes, I'm okay—

Don't dwell on the past. You do that too much. He hiccupped loudly. I want you, he said, to meet someone here.

I don't know if now is the best—

You'll like her. She also moved to Milwaukee this year. She's a lesbian too. I know you'll like her.

Jesus Christ, Amit. *No.*

Come! I told her I was coming to find you.

I was exasperated, embarrassed. The complete joke of this all—Amit trying to set me up with someone to prove something to himself, feel great about himself.

Why were you both hanging out *up there*?

Oh, what? I was peeing. Only unclogged toilet in this house. She's smoking down in the room with the fancy naked-lady prints. I think you'll like her. She's the only lesbian I've met—*hic*—at this godforsaken party. You must meet her, I told her I was coming to find you—

When wasted, Amit says the same thing in widening, concentric circles until the listener is tempted to break his skull. I gave in.

Who the hell asked you to try to come here and find me somebody, you absolute nosy aunty, I began to say, and as we moved through the dining room's swinging doors I saw a bird-boned woman in a leather bomber sitting very upright in the smoky haze. A lean Black man sitting next to her. He offered her a joint, she shook her head, looked up, and smiled at the sight of Amit, the troubled bored look in her face dissipating. He plummeted in for a hug, which is exactly what Amit would still do to this day. Over his shoulder she saw me. Her face froze in recognition. Somewhere between startle and spark.

My mouth turned dry as carpet.

Hey, so this is my new friend Marina, Amit said, smiling like an idiot. She's new to Milwaukee too! I thought you should meet.

And then he whisked away.

Yeah so I'd wondered, Marina said, what the *S* stood for.

A smile first vague and then in focus, wide sea-glass eyes locking onto mine, our lenses telescoping into precision, forming a clearer image. Here is the person, in the real. Here you are.

We'd perched on the stairs, watching the stragglers wiggle and grind on dirty carpet. It was the first moment that either of us had acknowledged anything—that we had interacted before. Her voice at once girlish and raspy, as though a fifteen-year-old had taken up chain-smoking. Fine pale hair fell into her face, feathered over her shoulders. I didn't want to use my name online, I said. I thanked her for the drink at Bar Louie. A flash of tombstone teeth, ordered and polished. As she smiled down at me, blood seemed to move in my veins with a new irregularity.

Marina spoke faster than I did. She was all energy, kinetic. Darting eyes, a tapping foot in cherry-red Doc Martens. She was from New Jersey, ran away to L.A. at sixteen to dance, had lived there on and off for eleven years. She came to Milwaukee in March. Nine months ago, three months before me. Yeah so tell me about you, world traveler, she said, teasing. My face turned hot with pleasure: she remembered.

She'd lived for a year in Japan, on contract with a ballet company. She loved their convenience stores, the bullet trains. She said she didn't know anyone at the Kwanzaa Kegger, but in fairness she hadn't been going out in a minute.

My friend and business partner—Shaka—he's the tall dude with tattoos, yeah, the one smoking up next to me, she said, he knows Kenny, who I guess lives here, though I don't know how, but the fact is that Shaka knows everybody, even in a city he's new in, yeah, it's fascinating, should be studied by science or something.

Marina drank white wine. She didn't like to dance at parties, didn't like pop music. Her jacket, which I complimented, was from Zara, its leather butter-soft. Her mascara, I noticed, was clumping, flaking off in tiny little pieces and dusting her cheekbones. At no point did she touch me, lean in close, or praise my looks. This worried me. She had never gone to college, and in my great stupidity I tried to square this mentally with the fact that she liked to read. She didn't know what a change management consultant did. She said it sounded hard and important. She hated cooking. She asked me how the city had been treating me so far.

I tried to put it in a few sentences, and everything that came out felt like a lie.

Why did you come to Milwaukee? I asked. In a loop in my mind the footage played: the unmentionable episode from the Public Market, the woman with the long hair and lip ring.

She had a job offer that nearly doubled her Los Angeles salary: teaching rich children in Brookfield ballet and contemporary. Shaka, her old colleague, had followed her and her better pay there from Chicago, but he'd recently quit to start a dance intensive company, where teachers and choreographers toured different cities and offered workshops and classes in a conference setting. She was helping him.

It's a lot on my plate but I'm an ambitious person, she said. I want to make my mark on the dance world.

I like that, I said, and we looked at each other. It occurred to me that for all her confidence, her ramrod posture, she might be nervous too.

Did you move out here by yourself? I asked, playing innocent.

She shrugged, her face taking on a defensive cast.

My ex came out with me, she said, but it only lasted a couple of months after that. She's back in L.A. now.

I longed to say, But I saw you together *yesterday*.

Thom and Isabel passed us to go up the stairs. Neither of them said hello. Isabel gave me a quick nod. Thom nothing. In my heart a throb of pain. White Americans could be so cold, just like that, out of the blue. Perhaps the important thing was to not let them in deep. Even Marina was starting out lying to me.

She asked me where I was from, looked startled at the answer.

Your English is so—you don't have an accent.

Funny, because you do, I said, squaring my chin.

She laughed loudly. Teeth white in her sunbed face. It's true, she said. You can hear the Jerz in me from ten yards away.

I'm going to leave soon, she added. Maybe I'll see you around?

This seemed deeply tiresome. All we had been doing was seeing each other around, appearing like small voles around each other and vanishing into the earth. If this was all she wanted, fine!

That's what I said: Fine!

Surprise in her face. Yeah so, she said, I was going to ask. Would you like to exchange numbers?

Hey, Amit said, appearing at my elbow like a genie. Sorry to interrupt.

Where have you been, I asked, not amiably, this whole night?

He looked wan and miserable.

Had to call KJ, he said. Hey, I'm tired. Can we call Yellow Cab? It'll be past two in the morning when it gets here. And I do not want to sleep on that musty carpet.

Yeah so I'm leaving now, Marina said. I can drop you both off, no it's no problem, no really, all Wisconsinites are so very stressed about accepting favors, oh Brewers Hill, that's not even far, when did it get so late?

Did you have a fun night, Amit asked me as we waved goodbye to Marina's Kia Soul and then walked up the side path to the door.

I ignored him. Between actually speaking to the woman who had been a ghostly presence in my online romantic world for months and crashing Thom's car, I did not know how to categorize the past six hours. I looked in my bag. Amit exaggerated impatience.

Hurry up, I am fully turning into a Popsicle, man.

One minute, I said, rooting through my handbag. Where was my key?

Not in the bag, it appeared.

It was two in the morning, 19 degrees, we were carless, and I had lost my house key.

Uh-oh, Amit said, in Cartoon Network cadence.

We shoved ungloved hands into coat pockets and looked at each other with some modicum of alarm.

Knocking on Amy's door, which Amit suggested, was out of the question. Her flat was dark; she and the Fiancé were asleep. Over the course of various attempts to pick the lock—with a credit card, a bobby pin, a mail key—I filled Amit in, in whispers, on what my run-ins with the terror who lived below me had been like. He looked aghast.

We can talk about this later, because I believe in only one crisis at a time, he said, but you need to move your ass out of here.

I'll think about it, I said. I don't make *that* much money, and over here my rent is free.

Huh. Is that like, a company policy?

I don't think so, why? Here, hold my bag—

It's just a bit weird, isn't it? No offense, I'm sure you're doing great work, but why add an enormous perk, like, free rent on top of a salary for a new employee right off the farm? Like you're straight from college, and pretty green minus a few internships, right?

You're being bloody rude, I told him. We have the same amount of *experience*, bucko; you just make four times what I do because you studied a topic that is highly valuated right now by markets and investors, okay? Calm down. Can we stay at your parents' place tonight?

I mean, it's not my ideal scenario, but better that than freezing.

Why is it so unideal?

Come on, S.

What.

Don't make me spell it out.

Pretend I have forgotten to read. An hour in this cold it'll be true.

My mother remembers you as the girl that broke up with her son even though I was serious enough about us to bring you home. I mean, as a worst-case scenario we can go to my house. It just won't be the most pleasant for any of us. And either way, it's not walkable. We'd have to call a cab.

So call a cab. Or call KJ. Isn't she mad nocturnal?

I do not want to call KJ. What about your friend Tig?

Out of town.

Speaking of calling people, hey, would it not make the most sense that you left your keys in gay Kate Moss's car?

Absolutely no. I'm not calling her. She'll be asleep! And I don't think I left the keys in her car, truly. If anything, it's possible I left them at Thom's house, in the stairwell; I remember playing with them when I was talking to her—

Pretty girls make nervous fools of us all, Amit said with his falthoo store-bought sageness.

Less buddy comedy. More action, I pleaded.

Amit called Yellow Cab, which informed him that a driver would get to us in fifty minutes. I'll be dead by then, Amit muttered, but gave my address anyway. Again and again he checked an app on his phone, tutting in frustration. Back in SF, he explained, there were tech companies that made it easy to hire a driver off the street, a cab coming to your door with the press of a button, sometimes in five minutes or less.

Uber hasn't expanded into Wisconsin yet, he explained. I rolled my eyes and asked again why just calling KJ was not an option.

Things are complicated between KJ and me right now, okay?

You having an affair with that fivehead? I could see it. You could hold her plaits while you gave it to her, what do they call that? Riding the motorcycle.

Why is your defense mechanism being disgusting? Ask yourself that.

Defense what, what're you talking about? I'm just making jokes to distract myself from my eyelashes freezing.

You don't have to be jealous of KJ.

I *assure* you I am nothing of the sort—

KJ and I left things on a bad note. We'll figure it out. But I can't call her.

What's going on? Can you really not tell me? I don't like when we have secrets from each other.

Amit glowered. You have secrets with everyone, he mumbled.

Not with you. Not really.

KJ has—a problem. With addiction. Drugs.

Oh shit, I said, thinking of the needle in the bathroom stall I'd kicked away not so long ago. Something from another world.

What is it, I asked, can you not say?

Amit sniffed heartily. Two tears sped down his face.

I don't want you to judge her, he said. I love KJ. She is my oldest friend. She's a good, kind person. She wants to have a family and a good job and kids with her gf. I just want you to know that if I tell you, and

I'm honestly not sure I should tell anyone. She's not had an easy go of things.

I'm not going to judge—

Shut up and listen to me for a second. You have to face this about yourself: You're a judgmental person. You act like everyone's life is within their control to change, like everyone makes their own success or failure, even though your own family shows the opposite—

Amit. Don't be fucking mean to me. I am not the same person from our freshman year of college. You have changed and so have I, and we all deserve a little grace, okay? If you want to tell me about KJ, I will listen and try to be helpful. If you don't, that's okay too. But we have fifty minutes to kill, and it seems like this is bothering you, whatever it is.

Promise you won't tell anyone.

I *promise*. Who would I tell who'd care?

It doesn't matter if they care. Milwaukee is a small town. I can't have people knowing her business.

Okay, okay. Jeez. No one.

KJ had taken pills for the first time early in high school, he told me. A couple of times, egged on by a friend or goading boys at house parties on the South Side. She liked how they felt. The anxiety and dread vacuumed out of her, replaced by a pooling, liquid warmth. For the most part, though, she stayed away from the pills and from the parties, kept busy with school and the emotional hamster wheel that was dating Cathy, her first and only girlfriend. Then spring of last year, KJ had been on her way to work when someone smashed into the back of her car and sped off.

The accident left her with a blistering, sinewy gristle of inflamed nerve connecting her shoulder and neck, while working a job where one was expected to constantly pick up chubby wriggling children. KJ was uninsured, went to the free clinic. The doctor did fuck-all, asked her to come back in six weeks if she was still in pain. Out of desperation in the face of KJ's agony, outraged that the doctor hadn't so much as prescribed her girl extra-strength Tylenol, Cathy bought a Ziploc of hydrocodone off a former classmate who dealt in those things. Friends and family discount, he'd said.

I had been prescribed hydrocodone after the dentist in India took my teeth out. To me it had felt quite beautiful. You know the foamy white soap that machines into your palms at public bathrooms, without you having to touch a thing? Hydrocodone was like that: an airy emulsified happiness frothing through the body, lightening you from the inside. My mother threw away the tablets six days after the surgery. Not good to take all this strong-strong medicine, she said.

KJ took one a day, went to work high as a hummingbird, and soon Cathy wanted to see what it was all about.

Hydrocodone is expensive. Off-market, a full baggie can set you back three hundred dollars. KJ's dealer waited for the two women to overextend themselves, and then offered much cheaper avenues to chase the same high: powder and black tar heroin.

KJ said no. She went to work for four days, shoulder a wildfire of pain, breaking out in cold sweats. Sick as a dog by the end of each shift.

She texted him, how much you need?

Amit and I had been walking widening circles around my block. I was listening, shocked to hear this, but also wondering where my friend fit in. Why he seemed so personally implicated.

When KJ and Cathy lost their apartment nine months ago, he continued, they moved in with Cathy's mom and racist stepdad, who summarily kicked them out after five weeks. KJ's mother and sister were willing to give them some cash here and there, but Cathy had stolen things from KJ's mom more than once, and the sister forbade the couple from staying. Sleeping in KJ's car was workable while the weather was mild, but ten days into that, a homeless man on the North Side had tried to wrest his way in, had exposed himself to the two women. At 6 a.m. San Francisco time, KJ had called Amit, hysterical. Could he, she begged, spare money for a motel room for the night for the two of them?

From that point on, the pleas for money had arrived, first every week. It was good timing. Amit had been promoted, was growing weary of going to mincing restaurants with forty-dollar entrees, of splitting an edible subscription service with his friends and going to art and psychedelic parties on the days when he didn't work until ten at night. Was this all there was to living well?

He was happy enough to help his oldest friend, for his handsome salary to be put to better use than it had been.

Then the requests began to ping in every couple of days. KJ calling from a gas station saying Mitty, please, I'm begging you, with no money for pads, saying I'm bleeding through my sweatpants. KJ texting from a motel about Cathy's rattling bronchitis, saying they absolutely had to stay through the week while it healed. It's very expensive, poverty. Amit was dropping everything multiple times a week and running over to Western Union. It was the disruption and anxiety of this pattern, more than realizing he had transferred over an amount in the low five digits to his friend over the months, that led Amit to decide that something needed to change.

So he'd offered to send a fixed amount going forward: Seven hundred dollars a week. No more, no less. KJ and her girlfriend could put it toward rent, the car, paying the fees at the Suboxone clinic.

It worked for a while, until she asked him for more, when they had seen each other before the party. He had said no, she'd cussed him out at Leon's as they both ate frozen custard, then burst into tears. At the party, he'd noticed that his wallet, which had held two hundred in cash before, had been emptied. He called KJ, who denied taking any of it, who said she'd never stolen in her life anyway, that was Cathy's thing.

She told Amit he had made her feel so low and terrible she had no choice but to use, after months of being clean.

So no, Amit finished, KJ, despite technically owing him the favor, would not be an ideal candidate to call up to give us a ride tonight.

No . . . way, I said.

As if on autopilot, he sniffled and replied, Yahweh.

This to me was a horror story. Amit's face was pale and drawn, his nose red from cold. We had circled the block around the locked apartment for the ninth time. I stared at him, heart aching with worry. A dog barked low and muffled from the inside of a house. And then a pert red car pulled up to us, rolled its window down.

A barely familiar voice called out my name.

Are you okay? it asked.

At the wheel: Pulp Fiction. Her doll's face, her swollen mouth. In the passenger seat was a disinterested-looking man in his forties, his hair a wispy nest.

The married doctor.

Are y'all okay? Pulp Fiction asked again. A smile cracking her face like an egg: a sweetness concealed in it. We're just headed home from the airport, she said. Do y'all need a ride somewhere?

What I found difficult to explain in the years after was how much the people I knew in Milwaukee would ride for each other, for strangers even. A true neighborliness, this in a city with so much ugly, people getting flung out of their apartments by landlords, a city so segregated that I could walk four blocks from my apartment where older blond people nodded like their begonias and told me to have a nice day, and at the end of those blocks would find myself in a neighborhood five times as poor, not a white face to be seen. Pulp Fiction and her man drove us to Thom's house to look for my keys at two thirty in the morning, said they'd wait for us so we could have a ride back.

The Kwanzaa Kegger was still going, though more blearily than before, many of the housemates having retreated to their beds.

Thom had not been answering his texts. I checked each stair for the keys like a bloodhound, walked by his door, which was nearly closed, but not entirely. I stopped. Looked.

I saw a man's rear end. Driving into a woman's. Her cool white back and dark tumbles of hair were laid out on the patterned comforter. Like portions of a meal. Thom's breaths audible in the room, hissing through his nose. Quickly, quietly, I darted away.

This is what my parents wanted for me, what everybody wanted. To be a dish laid out before a man's hunger. To be taken, to be quiet. Disappear into hair and parts. Disappear, in time, into marriage and motherhood.

As I stood in the dim stairwell I remembered the very first time Amit had mentioned KJ. We were babies, walking around our college town, the trees trembling with sunlight. KJ had told her mother in middle school that she was dating Cathy. It had been disastrous. But eventually all parties had come to some kind of reconciliation, some understanding. I remembered thinking how unnecessary it seemed, how American, to feel the need to burden your parents with that kind of information. Years later, after we had come together and broken up, Amit asked me gently if my parents would want me to have an arranged marriage. His mother and father, doting, liberal, Americanized in their way, did not wish that for him.

I'd stared off into the distance, a pale blank sensation descending upon me. It seemed like the wrong question to consider. What felt more important to me, and impossible to say, was how likely it was I would finally capitulate if they proved immovable in their desire for me to be taken care of. Which for them meant the chosen marriage, the decent paid-for man. Anything else, let alone what I wanted, bringing shame on the family.

I did not know how to explain this stubborn love for my parents that I staggered under, iridescent and gigantic and veined with a terrible grief, grief for the ways their lives had been compost for my own.

Slowly I descended the stairs. My face arranging itself into normalcy.

In the living room Amit was speaking to a tightly muscled boy with a strawberry-blond mop of hair.

I recognized him; he had filmed Thom licking my face. A hundred years ago, it seemed, not the events of the same night.

Amit, to my real astonishment, was grinning. This is Danny, he said to me, gesturing at this knotty slender boy. Danny is a gymnast. We have a plan.

Past three in the morning and we were camped outside my apartment, taking in the shape of things. We: myself, Amit, Pulp Fiction, her doctor, and Danny the gymnast. Somewhere in there I had reconciled myself to the idiocy of this whole enterprise, shivering and exhausted and nerve-riddled as I was. There was no way it would work. There was, however, strange fun in the company. Perhaps we could amuse ourselves this way until dawn, when Amy would wake up and we could prevail upon her to let us in. Then Danny began his climb, and my stomach turned to a pit of fear.

He would fall, he would break his skull. Amy would come out of the house. The jig would be up in every sense.

To my dying day I'll remember the total perfect triumph that was, after two failed attempts, Danny the gymnast coiling his body up the north gutter pipe and climbing sinuously onto the roof of Amy's back porch. Reaching up, like it was nothing, and pushing my living room window open.

Pulp Fiction screamed out loud. We erupted in whoops. Amit proposed marriage to Danny the gymnast. We heard him unlock my door, run down my stairs. Amit and I, Pulp Fiction and her doctor, we were all hugging each other, beaming. As we were enfolding Danny into our group embrace, the blinds of the window by the side door flicked open.

Amy materialized, wearing pinstriped pajamas and a look of naked hate.

We stared at each other through the glass, she and I. The blinds twitched closed.

For once I did not care. I closed my eyes and smiled to the cold sky, holding my friends and these kind strangers in my arms.

Before I slept, I felt new bravery. Sliding out my phone under the covers, I texted Marina, asking if she would like to go on a date with me.

Q1

I never did find my keys, and had to ask the Fiancé for a spare set. When I walked into work that Monday, Peter beckoned me over.

Have you been enjoying the apartment? he asked.

I nodded, eyes widening in fear.

He showed me an email exchange on his phone. Amy had written a long letter of complaint about me to my landlord. Stacy had forwarded it to Peter with two words: pls advise.

The email made it sound as though Keith Richards and Hugh Hefner had assumed tenancy. It made references to 3 a.m. parties where people climbed out on the roof. A vision of a future where I had an expired EAD, no sponsor, no option but to leave, to return dragging my suitcases up the red laterite of my family's yard—this was what flashed before my eyes.

I began to explain, as calmly as I could, why Amy's telling was a misrepresentation, but the second I uttered the words *found a gymnast*, Peter held up his palm.

I *really* do not care, he said with a great weariness, but it is important to me that Stacy and I don't have any tension about this living arrangement. I am not at all obligated to continue paying your rent and salary; our agreement can be terminated and renegotiated at will. Just fix this. Apologize to this lady who has a problem with you. She may be wrong, she may be right. I don't care. Fix it.

Burning with fear and anger, I wrote Amy and the Fiancé a contrite little note. Heartily I apologized for disturbing them as they slept. I wrote to Stacy too, an email I thought artful in its subtle redirection of blame. Her diplomatic, reasonable reply filled me with sadness.

> Thank you for this explanation. God knows we've all done our share of crazy things (oh, to be young again!). Please find a way to make it work with Amy and Tim. I'm confident in time that you'll see things from their point of view—they want a quiet, peaceful residence, as do your surrounding neighbors. We are so lucky to have quiet, responsible, responsive, and caring folks in charge of the property.

I looked for a recipe and walked to a store. In the ancient oven I baked scones with raspberries and buttermilk, dotted them with ghee. Laid the cling-filmed plate on Amy's doorstep with the note, rang the doorbell. Walked a safe distance away.

The plate and note disappeared.

I expected to never get a response, but two days later, a text pinged in from the Fiancé.

Thank u for the apology. We r nice people (+ dog) This should not b so difficult. Have a nice day.

At work the air turned sour. Thom barely spoke to me. Grunted in my direction in the break room, microwaved his Tupperware of grains and shrimp and ate it at his desk. Even after he fixed the car, I was afraid to ask him to pick me up. Anxiously I waited for him to offer up our old routine. I suffered during the fifteen-minute wait between my bus transfers, eyes welling up from the air's sting.

Two weeks after the Kwanzaa Kegger I saw him drive into the garage as I walked toward the client's campus and swallowed the rising lump in my throat. Perhaps I had no right to feel betrayal, but I did. My commute was so long, so miserable and cold. I had paid for his car's accident. He had, in fairness, made me drive it. Why was he being *mean*?

Some people find it harder to forgive you for not actually being wrong, Tig had said in her Tig way over bowls of bisque served with ragged pieces of country loaf, and we left it at that. We were at Trocadero, barside. She had started seeing someone, a soft-faced divorcée who drew blood at a clinic; the woman had a little boy and the same mole placement and straggly hair as Amy Winehouse. Even a week into this, Tig was texting less, calling infrequently. Perhaps this was the way of the world. Your best friend serving as placeholder for the real thing: the person who would audition to be your husband or wife.

On Friday I walked over to Thom's desk and asked him to get lunch. An olive branch. He grunted assent.

The client's cafeteria was almost identical to the one in college, just with more salads and calorie guidance. While I piled chicken and broccoli stir-fry on my plate, I noticed for the first time that the only Black people I saw at the client's campus were in hairnets, serving us behind the glass.

What did these women think of us? Did they, like me, hate their jobs? Before befriending Tig I would not have thought to ask myself this. Surrounded by white people as I had been ever since arriving in Aurora, I had chosen a kind of colorblindness, particularly to myself, had over time absorbed a white person's way of looking at the world. A saturated sponge, waiting for the squeeze. I bumped into the division head standing in line beside me, sending glossy chicken and mushy florets onto his dress shoes.

When Thom asked me what my ambitions were, my guard went right up. This was not, I felt sure, what he actually wanted. As I spoke, and he pressed me, I grew more certain: I was, for some reason, being lawyered.

What were my ambitions, what did I want to do after this job? I didn't know. I said so.

He bristled at this. There's no way you haven't thought about what's next for you. People who work like you do, try to win points like you, you're trying to get ahead. I'm trying to figure out what you're trying to get ahead to.

What are *you* trying to get ahead to?

I'm asking the questions right now, don't deflect.

I stabbed at wet broccoli. *Ambition* was a shiny layered geode of a word. Cut it through and you would see its variegation. To want to be a CEO, to want to be safe, to want to make your mark on the dance world, to want to buy a nice flat someday, to want to be on CNN, to want to sell enough books about philosophy that you might live in the Pink House in some hazy future—those all fell within the company division of ambition, but I knew that this stupid boy was not actually trying to get philosophical. Listen, I said, I want to make enough money to take care of myself and my parents. I want to own a house someday and not be an old lady renting, being terrorized by some Amy type.

So you want to move up this corporate ladder. You want to be a boss.

Bro, I—don't want to keep working for Peter forever? My father told me that you need to stay in your first job at least three years. I don't think I'll ever start my own thing. I will always be a wage worker. I hate—I dropped my voice—having these shit bosses, so I suppose part of me is fine with the idea that I move up, in some field, so that I become a boss, if only for the money and the idea that I may someday have fewer bosses of my own, the higher I go up. But I don't really care what industry it is—like I don't want to work for some place that is big and scary and evil, but most places seem bad. *Why are you asking me all this?*

He glowered, stuck his lip out in an exaggerated pout, and we both realized he was about to cry.

I took his arm. Walk out with me, I said, and we stepped out of the caf and into a small meeting room that was, unusually for the client, not entirely made of glass.

What is this actually about? I asked. It cannot be your stupid car.

How much is Peter paying you? Thom asked, staring at his fingers.

My stomach swooped. I saw it anew, the moment when I'd pulled out my phone to reassure him that I could pay for the car's repairs.

Twenty-three an hour, I said. Something excised *and my rent* from the sentence.

Holy shit, Thom said, shaking his head very slowly. Holy shit.

He'd been getting paid fifteen. That's what Peter had offered him. Still not the worst, he said, in Milwaukee, but damn.

I tried to think of an explanation. We'd graduated at the same time. We'd had identical majors—we met in a modernist lit class, where Thom had thought I was dumb. We were both honors students, part of the same large group of friends that originated in a sophomore-year dorm. I had done one more internship than him, in alumni affairs, where I'd gotten to go to dinners with people like Peter, learn how to say the things they wanted to hear. We had the same title: consultant. The same actuality: contractor.

And then the horrible likelihood: I had negotiated more for myself, and Peter had needed and wanted me in that moment on the project. Paying Thom as much as he paid me would have cut into his profits.

Please don't tell him I told you my salary, I begged. I don't want to get in trouble. I don't know if it's legal. My work authorization expires in two years, I'll need Peter to sponsor me.

Thom told me in no uncertain language that I had no solidarity. Corporate shill with a bourgeois mentality, that's what I was, fundamentally, and he was sorry and unsurprised to see it.

Also, don't let thousands of dollars sit in a *checking account*, assface. Invest it.

Who told you that? I hissed. Was it your two doctor parents?

Don't be intellectually dishonest. This is whataboutism, plain and simple, it has nothing to do with—

My hands were shaking so hard I had to form them into fists under the boardroom table.

I am not the reason why you are not happy, I said, modulating my voice slow and icy. Talk to Peter. Negotiate your pay, just like I did. Be a man.

He stormed out.

At the workday's end, as I walked past the mural of batteries birthing from grassy knolls, Thom waved me down.

Hey, he said, a vague and grudging softness entering his face. I can give you a ride, bro. It's wild cold.

Thank you, I said stiffly, zipping up. Earlier that afternoon I had looked up *bourgeois*, the insult he lobbed at me, which I had known only in the context of history, some French Revolution shit. I longed to say, It's been cold every day for how long now?

Sitting in my computer chair as the IT guy complained with his Swanson beef breath about a change in scoring regulations for his bowling league, I'd realized that it was the great desire of my heart to have the trappings of a bourgeois life, soft and warm as a cashmere sweater. I wanted this, and I wanted this because it had been relentlessly sold to me with the aggressiveness of a Bangalore street hawker. Had been marketed to me since I was fourteen and looking at the advertisements over the airport phone booths while we waited in line for O'Hare Customs and Immigration. To shame me for wanting what I had been taught to want seemed like a callous cheat, a wanton shifting of goalposts.

I'm good today, I said. Someone is picking me up. Let's talk soon.

I walked out through the garage and to the lime Kia Soul.

Marina had braided her hair down one shoulder. She wore a backward baseball cap and a puffy jacket yellow as Tweety Bird. As I walked up, she stepped out of the car. Small and neatly formed. She hugged me, and I felt somewhere in the lower reaches of my body a peculiar thing, a mixture of danger and yearning; it was as if my hip bones were being pushed to fold open and warm sticky blood had rushed in; I felt, even before anything had happened, unmoored; perhaps it was that for the first time I had wanted someone specific, and not only as accessory to my own want. I got in her car. With the exact right amount of force I closed the door.

I thought we could go to the Wicked Hop, she said as we sailed down the freeway. This cute little place in the Third Ward. Do you like shrimp and grits?

I'm easy, I said. This was something Peter told me to say to clients when we were trying to decide on business lunches. Shrimp to me had always seemed rather like the cockroaches of the ocean.

When I got out of the car, I saw the Wicked Hop was right by the Milwaukee Public Market. The memory of what had happened there set me on edge, and the date hadn't even begun.

Have you been to MPM? They have great oysters, I said, stupidly.

Marina laughed. I don't know why, she said, but I feel like I wouldn't want to mess with oysters here. Where they gonna come from? Lake Michigan? Not cute.

They'll come from the same place as your shrimp, probably. An aeroplane.

Oh, she got jokes! I guess I'm on a date with a funny lady!

In the end we stayed away from seafood. We ordered bulbous glasses of jammy-then-bitter red wine, fried tomatoes, a salad topped with perfect little dominoes of beefsteak, a risotto full of corn and leeks—new to me, green and oniony. We spoke about work, mostly hers. I gave her the old What Is Change Management rundown. But mostly I talked about Thom and Tig. My friends. Incandescent, funny, perpetually broke. Stretching each paycheck out like chewing gum until the snap.

I asked her how she liked Milwaukee.

Yeah so—I've hated a lot of my time here, she said. My breakup was not pleasant, I haven't made many friends, I have Shaka, but he's not always a reliable or stress-free presence, but it's been great to make a good amount of money, live in a very nice apartment. My time in Milwaukee has been mostly work, and then wines and reading and TV, like maybe trying to not kill my new plants—struggle city.

What are you reading?

This book called *Never Let Me Go*. At first I was going to give up on it, but all of a sudden there was one part that almost made me cry, and I love to cry, I sometimes think I should be a professional crier, and anyway, I've kept with it. It's by a Japanese author. I only lived in Tokyo for a year but ever since then I've always noticed Japanese books in bookstores, and you could say I'm maybe drawn to them—

I think Ishiguro is British, I said, more snobbish than I meant to sound. Like I think he spent his whole life in the UK.

She looked a little discomfited, shrugged. I watched the delicate muscles in her neck work as she chewed her steak. Her eyelashes were so long I questioned how she saw clearly.

I wondered, with a pulse of jealousy but also the naked desire to know what is not polite to ask, if she had met her slap-happy Asian girlfriend in Japan.

To occupy the lull I said, I've never met anyone who loved crying.

Oh, I think it's the best. We feel so much, most of us, and different layering things, like you can't feel only one thing ever, you know? Can you think of a time when you've felt only one thing at one time? I think crying allows us to midwife our more intense, more complicated emotions, get them outside of our bodies, and then our body feels light and free again. Dance allows me to do that too, but you can't dance about everything. My boss was a huge bitch to me last week—hard to dance about that.

I don't cry often, I said, but when I do, I make myself stop very quickly.

I don't know if I've had the experience of getting it out of my system the way that you're describing.

You need to just sit with it, get it all out. Maybe you need a surrogate crier.

Maybe! Are you offering?

I'll be so good. I'll sit and just cry my heart out for you. I'll even give you a special discount, you're an important consultant lady, it'll be good for my business.

She paid the check. Was insistent about it. During our date she had not touched me once. Had not complimented my looks or what I wore. I tried not to let in a rush of grievance at this. On the way out we stopped in the vestibule of the Wicked Hop, uncertain. Our shoulders brushed: puffy jacket against felted wool. Outside the world was fogged with cold, was dark and wet and indistinct.

Yeah so I liked talking to you, she said, and just like that my mood improved threefold.

Want to continue? We could go some other place. Only if you want.

I don't have any clients to cry for tomorrow, so yes, that could work, maybe, lead the way.

At Swig, the wine bar down the street, we set up. I sat on a bar stool. She wedged her knees in between mine. I was past tipsy. I began to hear my heartbeat, its insistent assent, in my skull.

To calm my nerves I began to drink faster, talk in short compressed bursts between swigs.

We talked about places in Milwaukee we'd been to and liked. Shared reminiscences about the Pint, the lesbian bar I had been to. She recommended LaCage, a small gay dance club. She was more forthcoming than I was, talked at a cheerful clip, drank more wine while seeming unaffected by it. We—or she—went on about how much she liked Indian food. About *White Oleander*, the book we both had in common on our profiles.

It's probably because I have mommy issues, she said with a smile.

What is your mother like? I asked, surprising myself.

Marina looked taken aback for an instant. She took a long swill of her glass of white.

My mom, she said, pensive. She has a potty mouth and a good heart. She loves tanning, the amount she goes is skin cancer waiting to happen. I guess I inherited that, though I believe in moderation. Sometimes she's very Polish and the rest of the time she's very Italian.

What does she do? For work.

When I was a very little kid she was stripping to make rent, and from some hazy memories I suspect she did a lotta blow—wow, your face right now, I want to take a picture of it.

I'm sorry, I said, trying to modulate said face into a receptive and appropriate blankness. Go on.

Where was I? Yeah so like frankly not always mom of the year. Those years she sucked, probably. Here's a funny. From my dumb child point of view, my mommy was always disappearing to dance. So I kept telling her, telling everybody, I want to dance, I want to dance like my mommy. Very awkward! So yeah she got one of her clients to pay for the classes, sent my butt over to ballet, and the rest—

No way.

Oh yes. Anyway, I was excellent. Teacher called her and told her every week. She's a proud mama. She runs a daycare in the Jerz. She cleaned up her game, got engaged to a police officer, and actually, here's a good story, it was at her goddamn bridal shower that someone outed me, just like, told her I was gay.

Air caught in my throat. I said nothing at all.

Marina continued, So she came looking for me and asked me flat out. I was so scared, but I was like, Yes, it's true.

My god. Marina. What did she do?

Girl, she walked up to the table where everyone was lining up to take a plate and just yelled. Hey everyone, my mom goes. Everyone! Listen up! My daughter is a faggot! And I am nineteen, like, just dead with embarrassment, but my mom keeps going. At six hundred decibels. She's like, Okay, and I love her! I love her! If any of you have a problem with my kid being a fuckin' faggot, come talk to me and we'll take it outside! Okay? Now keep drinking!

Marina laughed, a closed-mouthed, crinkle-eyed chuckle at this memory. My eyes were burning. I blinked hard, turned my face away, pretending to get something from my bag, until it seemed safe.

What about your parents? Marina asked.

They're no longer with me, I said, feeling the pain inside bear down upon my lungs, thinking of the mudded orange footpath, tiny ferns slipping out into the air between sharp gray stones. Of what it would mean if my parents had ever done what Marina's mother had—shouted out, Hey, my kid is a faggot, and I love her, and not cared who heard. I took a great gulp of wine. Felt its sourness in my teeth.

She looked so sorry, so tender. A small hand on my back. I realized on the way to the bathroom what had happened. What a shocking lie I'd told.

It made things simple, though. As lies can.

My parents were no longer with me. My parents were no longer with me. My parents were no longer with me. There were all the ways in which it was true. In which it freed.

As I washed my hands in the small two-stall, lit dimly by a single yellow filament in a dusty bulb, and tried to slow my heart's sprinting, Marina came in.

When I walked away from the sink, my body pressed against hers.

She peered up at me. Blade nose, deer eyes. A sharp, painful prettiness. She was smaller than me. All bone and tendon. I could feel her hot breath on my face.

Your skin is so beautiful, she said, very softly. All night I can't stop looking at it.

Her mouth smelled of wine. No one had ever told me anything like this.

I leaned down, I kissed her. Soft, first, and then furious, hoisting her body up, pushing it against the metal stall door, which only banged slightly, her arms around my neck, the cleft of her sex hot against mine even through black denim, and we ground into each other like glass, her tongue in my mouth, mine in hers, silent other than breaths warm and ragged, and I felt dizzied by all of it, by how in my hands her hips felt like the time I found an animal's skull in the underbrush of my family's home when I was a child and lifted it into the air: this hard, breakable, animal thing.

A knock on the door.

We pulled apart laughing softly, disheveled.

Let's get outta here, she said, and took my hand.

The heat went out in my apartment the way a fuse blows, with a crackling noise and an onrush of danger. This was late January. Marina had made me a card with a little drawing: it said, THINKING OF U CUTIE. The card had tiny rhinestones stuck all over it. I stepped on it while I crossed my bedroom, comforter wrapped around me. Yelped from crystals driving into my toe pad.

The thermostat was immune to my fiddling. Inert, useless. Soon my breath was fogging in the air of my own living room.

I gathered every blanket I could. I began to write out a polite and subservient text to Amy explaining about the heat, asking when it could be fixed.

But our message thread, full of her abuse, made me nauseated even to glance at for too long. I closed it. I could deal with this later.

In the wee hours of the morning my teeth's chattering woke me up. Sleepless hours later I ordered a space heater online and managed to pass out. Thom called me three times before giving up and driving to work alone.

I woke up with no chance of making it into the office before an unthinkable eleven, and feeling desperate, called in sick. Peter wrote back something short and mean: The right time for you to send this message was last night. Feel better.

The last two words an order.

Blearily I put on two sweaters underneath my coat and stepped outside, which in the sunlight seemed warmer than my house. Walked to a bourgeois restaurant with heat and a kind, attentive bartender. Ordered a cream-laden winter soup, the cheapest thing on their menu. Charmed my way into a side of crusty bread and olive oil that looked pale green on the white plate.

I spooned soup into my mouth.

Again, the slow dissolve of loneliness. I wanted to tell Marina about the heat. But it seemed too much too early, only weeks in, to lean on her. Thom and I were in the same weird place. I had been hearing less from Tig, though she'd call me now and then to tell me about something she was studying that she was excited about.

She worked at both Starbucks and Lush now, plus picking up occasional shifts at CVS. Was trying to pay off her credit card debt. Her dates with the Amy Winehouse mommy had been going well. Tig liked her kid, a shy and happy little boy with an Afro the hue of weak tea. It all seemed like too much to me, I turned sulky sometimes upon thinking of it. Oh what, you'd prefer to be with an eight-year-old? I wanted to say sometimes. She was listening to some man called Kropotkin on audiobook and got her first A+ ever. For an essay on, I think it was, Adam Smith. She told me her sister had gone off the rails, seemed to be using drugs again.

I don't know how she's even *paying* for all this, she'd barked into the phone before running into her classroom.

The insides of my legs felt very cold still, like a chill had penetrated their bone. This despite the soup, the restaurant's functional heat. I texted Marina.

Hello. I am bunking work today. Do you want to hang out?

Bunking?? she wrote back. Have not heard that one before. Of course I want to hang out with a sexy beautiful lady. Where are you at?

When we walked through the door of Marina's apartment I, still bone-cold and clammy and feeling slightly odorous, asked to take a shower. Of course, babe, she said, hunting for a towel. She straightened up, arched her back slightly.

Yeah so, would you like some company? she offered. Her eyes glittering.

Uh, ah, I want to just go ahead, if that's okay.

She shrugged. The muscles in her neck pulled taut. Her hair seemed paler than usual.

I said, Your hair looks nice. Did you do something to it?

She looked amused. You're like a dude sometimes. Yes. It's called hair dye. You know I'm not naturally this color, right?

I felt stupid. How would I know that? I said.

Have you never colored your hair ever? It's so pretty. Or I guess Indian women do henna? Right? Do you use it on your hair or just hands?

Never used henna. You'll have to ask some other *Indian women*, I said through the bathroom door.

Perhaps I was a man all along, and this was the heart of my problem, my inability to be soft like a fruit, open like a flower. Words rushed through me indistinct: invulnerable, hermaphrodite, henna, bunking, patent, cuticle. I turned the shower on to near scalding, climbed in. I splayed naked on the tub's white floor.

On the door's other side: the woman I wanted, the woman I could not say things to expressly because of that want. The hot water drilled down in mercy. I closed my eyes. Like a child I imagined the world gone dark, everyone vanished, and myself safe.

Hey, beauty, hey, Marina said when I emerged from the bathroom, looking up from her laptop with a faint smile. Headphones covering her ears: two swollen mushroom caps.

Yeah so . . . your boobs look utterly fantastic right now, she said. I like want to give them a standing ovation.

I smiled. I was wearing a very soft T-shirt of hers. Pale pink, slightly damp from my skin. The room was cool edging on chilly. It was unintentional, but probably made for a fetching sight.

When are you going to work? I asked.

Likely will head out around four? I'll be back nineish. You have me for the next three hours. Are you hungry?

I shook my head no, and got under her covers, my wet hair lacquering her pillow. Marina put her laptop away and lay down next to me. Her eyes looked browner in this light, wide and a little concerned.

You okay?

I nodded, imagining a door shutting in my chest, locking for safety.

I used some of your moisturizing cream, I said, because it seemed important to be truthful about something. What were you up to?

Use anything of mine you like. Mmm, smells nice on you, beauty. I was working on a mix for a new choreo, but you know, it can wait.

Wait for what?

That's up to you, I think.

I gave her a small, tight smile.

Then I reached for her hips, pulled them to mine. She was wearing little red nylon shorts, lean browned legs spilling over cream sheets. One of my hands at the small of her back, one hand in her hair. Her hair felt crunchy and dry, was the shade of old jasmine in temple garlands.

I hooked my hand into the fine pale mass and pulled sharply.

Her eyes flickered, shocked, then shut. Her mouth parted with want. In that moment she looked like a baby bird, with that long nose, those big closed eyes with their heavy lids. In that moment I thought I would go insane.

I peeled her clothes off, my breath tearing through my nostrils as I ripped down the flimsy shorts, the ankle socks. The loose wrap top she wore. No bra underneath. Her breasts tiny. Here she was: naked and smooth, smelling of soap and wine, eyes buttoned tight and fearful, face drawn with longing.

Kiss me, I said, yanking my handful of hair harder. Her mouth was so soft it was like lowering your lips to a bowl of honey.

Her tongue was furred, tart as vinegar, its taste unpleasant. I reached my hand down between her legs.

I'm sorry, she said, in her quiet small rasp, I got so wet.

This was the second time she had apologized this way when we had gone to bed. It was true, she was slick, juicy.

I said nothing. Turned her on her side. Spooned her from behind, drew her to me.

I spread her legs and rubbed her very gently. Measured and even as breathing.

She was quiet at first, then not. With my other hand I pinched her nipple. She let out a strangled cry. For a long time in near perfect silence I did not stop rubbing her clit, which had swollen like a raisin in payasam. Her hips began to buck and quake against mine. With Marina, everything felt like instinct. Even then, at the beginning. I knew what to do. In a way I never have. I sank my teeth into the skin of her neck. What I wanted in that moment was to devour her. To call her stupid bitch and slap her face, to spit on her tiny tits as she gasped, to hook three fingers into her as she got on all fours, to have my way with her, bypassing all mercy. I longed to lay her out on the bed's edge and fuck her with some hard and elongated object. To hold her legs up in a wide V as I railed her, sucking her soft toes right as she was about to come.

But that was too much. I knew that. And I was holding her like a lover, holding her in my arms carefully while my hands worked her. It would be too much.

She moaned: the most delicious sound. I wished I had some hard throbbing thing to shove into her mouth. By now my own wetness was streaming down my thighs.

I want to ruin you, I whispered into her ear, mad with lust, and right then she shrieked in a way where I thought the glass of her windows might shatter. Her hips shuddered with a real violence; under my fingertip I felt her clit quake like it had come off running a race. She cried out again, this time my name. Again and again, my name, the two syllables of which made me feel helpless and embarrassed. I clapped my hand over her mouth and pressed down.

She opened her eyes. They looked wet, as if glazed with tears, and dazed, and very happy.

That was beautiful, Marina whispered. She peppered my neck and face with tiny soft-mouthed kisses. Oh my god, I was so loud, right? That was beautiful and perfect, you're so good, you're so good and sexy, give me like five minutes to recover, and then I want to do you, I want to make you feel good.

The next ten days we spent together. Me staying each night at her apartment. I bunked off Taco Tuesdays, rescheduled my beer date with Thom. I cooked for Marina, went on meandering drives with her at the wheel. It was strange, how living long periods of time with a person could reveal them. Like holding a check to the light.

Marina ordered like a rich woman at restaurants but ate terribly at home. A cucumber and half a pint of ice cream for lunch. Bell peppers and Kikkoman-drenched rice and glasses of white wine for dinner. She said she missed Los Angeles, its beauty, its sunshine, its gay scene, its waving palms and sand. Its food. She ordered sushi and complained about it, drove us to get crinkled noodles in a porky cloudy broth, asked me to find a good Indian restaurant for us to try in Milwaukee. She hung out a reasonable amount with the Strive Dance teachers, or the dancers from Shamar, but did not seem very attached to them, and I turned down her invites to join them at their interminable happy hours. She seemed more attached to her friends Alice and India, back in L.A., would tell me how cool and nice and fun they were, how mystified they were by her leaving for Wisconsin of all places, how she missed them. Marina said she was not religious, though in her way she seemed as much so as anyone from my home. She believed in good energy, in karmic balance, positivity. She collected crystals and small pieces of pale sweet-scented wood she said were holy. I found these sorts of things a cross between goofy and charming. *Women!* I sometimes thought upon watching her burn palo santo, wafting its white smoke through the air.

She felt rich in Milwaukee, she said. Money went far in our new city. Her salary from the dance studio was fifty thousand dollars. I was astonished at this frankness, her tossing the number to me like a ball. I'm able to have a freaking savings account for the first time ever, she said. The apartment complex she lived in was all luxury rentals, their interiors white drywall, open kitchen with granite countertop, ceiling-high windows edged with brushed steel. I was learning something new—the lower your ceiling, the narrower your station in life. High ceilings, flooded with light, are for the moneyed, the upwardly mobile.

But she did have credit card debt. And the dance studio didn't give her health insurance. She told me this when I made fun of her elaborate twenty-minute dental routine. She flossed with string, and a device that shot pulses of water into her gums through a tiny nozzle. She brushed her teeth with a timer, scraped her tongue.

I can't afford for anything to go wrong with these chompers, she said. Would wipe me out.

Oh, I'm a contractor, I don't have insurance either, I said with a shrug, leaning against the bathroom doorframe. Honestly I have never in my life been to a dentist. No one even flosses back home. And everything is fine. American doctors just love to make money.

Yeah, but you should be careful, she said, Glide floss dangling by her canine, you could get hit with a tax penalty for not having insurance. It's a new thing. Fine print from Obamacare. Thanks, Obama!

The government is already taking so much money from me, I said. Life of a contractor.

Marina frowned. I didn't know, she said, that you were self-employed. You work such long hours. I guess I just assumed . . .

I changed the names of my parents' contacts in my phone from Mummy and Papa to the birth names I had never, would never, call them by. She drove me to work in the mornings. I would borrow her shirts, swipe her lip stain and mascara to comply with Peter's rules for his women. Thom must have noticed me coming in looking newly put together again, and without the demoralized air that had accompanied my mornings spent waiting for the bus. But he seemed unwilling to ask for details. Or speak to me at all.

I accumulated sufficient courage to ask Marina, innocently enough, about the ex she had moved to Milwaukee with. Her reply was short and unsettling to me.

She had met Jenny Shin, a postproduction editor who'd played college basketball for Nevada, through mutual friends in L.A. They dated for three years. Marina was Jenny Shin's second girlfriend ever. Jenny impulsively came out to her parents during the first time Marina had met them; her parents had told her she was no daughter of theirs. From that time on Jenny rarely left Marina's side.

She had insisted on coming to Milwaukee when Marina got her dance studio job.

I never asked her to, Marina said, more than once. She quit her job, she moved here, she broke her ankle, she got more and more depressed, and after a few months, we were done. She's back in L.A. now.

I didn't look at her for minutes after she finished. I said nothing, asked no follow-up question.

One evening she and I went out to buy plants. Down Brady Street we walked in the cold and looked at stores that sold mandala tapestries and prayer flags, browsed through vintage shops. I made fun of both.

Only Americans, I said, tracing my fingers over a metal fan, its sharp blades edged with rust, offered at fifty-seven dollars. I did not live near a single real grocery or department store but I knew that a Target would sell a fan for twelve dollars. Only in this country, I said, will people pay *more* money for something that is old and beat up.

Marina seemed put off by my scorn. It reminds people, she said with a shrug, of simpler times.

Simpler for who, I did not ask. She zipped her jacket up. She'd bought a coppery kettle, a framed poster of a 1950s woman in an apron with hair much yellower than hers, grinning over a china cup. Stroky letters announced: The Secret to Happiness Is Vodka in Your Coffee.

All these days, dark thoughts whirred batlike outside the shingled walls of my mind, successfully kept out, circling for entry. Thom at work, icy and formal. The apartment still without heat; nowhere to return to should something go wrong. How I'd texted Amy with a painful politeness and received no response. My heart began to speed every time I considered trying again with her. Susan and Peter asking me to provide daily summaries of what I had accomplished on the project, which was hard not to see as being danced closer to the edge of a cliff I would soon be pushed over.

And too large, too overwhelming to properly conceive of, what my mother and father would think if they could see me and Marina, holding hands, kissing in supermarket aisles, sitting on the couch nestled into each other.

My casual escapades with anyone of any gender were legible to me, left me more or less unbothered. They existed in darkness; they addressed a basic need of the body. No one had to be involved any more than with the question of going number two. I would sooner dip both hands in molten tar than speak to the two people I came from about the private matter of sex.

This was just normal, I knew. All decent families lived in that silence. In the past I'd blushed hotly when American teenagers on the TV screen spoke openly, petulantly, brattily to their parents about the birth control pill and intimacy and breakups. Shameless and embarrassing. It did not matter that my parents were working long hours and so not in the room with me to be scandalized. My shame lived on independently from them. An inherited trait, like straight eyelashes or fat lips. To be gay, to do what Marina and I were doing, was beyond the pale, unsayable.

I would think these things and stare darkly past the new houseplants in their knitted cream holders.

You okay, baby? Marina would ask from time to time, and I would turn the key inside my chest, smile at her, and say, Yes, of course.

On the eleventh day she asked me her question.

So—what would you say this is?

What do you mean?

Are we, like, girlfriends?

Oh. I don't know.

Yeah so I don't know either, so I am asking you.

I haven't thought about it. Not a lot, I said finally.

I've thought about it *some*. And I'm asking you to think about it now, even if you haven't before.

I just figured, I said, that we were having fun. Getting to know each other. We met in person like one month ago.

Marina turned pale with fury. Having fun, she repeated, as if trying to better comprehend.

We were in bed. It was eleven o'clock, the weather dismal. She had not yet drawn the blinds, and you could see the city displayed in all its dark sluggishness, an occasional firefly car glinting down Water Street. She had worked through most of a bottle of Barefoot. We'd watched one episode of a forgettable TV serial.

I sat upright, debating whether to put on pants, have this conversation with some semblance of dignity. My insides felt pungent. Against my mind's best will I kept returning to my mother holding me tight—bright stiff sari, jeera and sandalwood.

It seemed important to not hurt Marina's feelings, to not have a fight.

The idea of her upset frightened me. But I was beyond irritated also at this pretty woman who would not let something just *be*, who wanted to Define the Relationship, as Thom called it, one month in, when less than six weeks ago she was with her tall scary girlfriend. Something she had not, to this day, been honest with me about.

I was afraid to say all this. So instead I told her that I was a slow burner, that I did like her, that I wanted to keep taking things slow, what was the rush? These were phrases I had heard from my friends, mostly the boys, in years past, ways of keeping clinging women at bay.

She began to cry, her thin back to me, visibly shaking. A terrible pressure began to assert itself upon my rib cage. I tried to put my arms around her, and she shrugged angrily out of my embrace, walked to the bathroom, slammed the door.

Marina, I called to her. Don't be like this.

Something crashed against the shut door and broke.

A compact new fury taxied in me. Vaulted airborne.

Dumb drunk bitch, I said under my breath. I shrugged on my clothes and strode to the balcony, slammed its French door shut behind me. This weak crying woman. Asking for more and more, throwing tantrums for attention, that's what she was doing.

I could walk away. Could say, Keep an eye on the wine and cigarettes, my dear, you're cute now, but not cute enough to keep pulling this. Could say, in the cruel cowboy-descended repartee of some American TV show: Enjoy cleaning up after yourself, sweets.

Marina slid the French door open.

Her nose was very pink, her mouth puffy with hurt. Every eyelash separated by tears, long and straight as those of an ostrich. The sight of her face sliced open my pretending.

This was, this had become, a person I cared for.

Marina leaned against the balcony's railing, cradled a cigarette in the clipped cold air. I was wearing a coat. She was not. I reached out my hand in an attempt at conciliation. It lay limp on her bare shoulder as she stared grimly over our temporary city, and after an awkward moment I put it away.

It seems to me you want a lot and really fast, I said, the words coming out in a rush. I am still getting to know you. It matters to me that I get to know someone, I don't want to get into a relationship with somebody with whom I'm not suited and then break up—that's happened before to me and it really hurts. It matters to me to really know someone. I have liked this time with you. You are fun and beautiful. But there's so much I don't know about you still. I saw you at MPM with your ex—with Jenny, like the day before we met at the party. My friend Tig said she saw her hit you, which is awful if that's true. You were with her so recently, dude. Like days before we met. You've never been up front about that.

She finally spoke, her smoky voice now barely a croak, her speech tired but even. Her eyes were alive and angry.

I don't want anything from you that you're not prepared to give freely, she retorted. But some advice from a woman a smidge older than you: the process of really getting to know anyone is a process of years, and for most people there is just a switch that flips and they decide, Okay, this could be my person, I'm making the choice to commit to them. I'm very happy to tell you about the backstory with Jenny, which is not what you think. You can't really fault me for not getting into the gory details when the only times I mentioned her you glared off into the distance and got quiet! Shit. There's so much I don't know about you either; I don't even know how your parents passed away, or if you want to stay in Milwaukee, or what you like me to do to you in bed. You bear some responsibility for our failures to communicate, you know!

Air forced its way into my lungs; I had forgotten to breathe ever since I'd heard the phrase *parents passed away*. Marina continued.

Yeah so I will be honest and say I'm not used to this, I'm a Gemini sun, Pisces moon, have my pride and my sensitivity, and maybe more to the point I'm just not used to someone I am dating not wanting it, I mean not wanting more? I'm not some indiscriminate U-Hauler. I have standards. I'm a picky bitch. I like you, I thought that was very mutual. You've spent eleven consecutive days with me. We have eaten every meal together and spent every night in my bed. You wear my clothes to your work. You use my makeup, all my products. I had to buy a new Stila lip stain! It's like you've moved in unasked but I'm not good enough to be your girlfriend. I'm sorry, but that is some messed-up shit. I thought you were better than that. It's hurtful.

My ears rang like church bells.

I'll pay you back for the products, I said, a choking sensation at the back of my throat. I didn't know you cared about the clothes. I'm sorry. I won't wear your things again.

It's not about that at all, you're missing my whole point, she spluttered, but already I was running back into the apartment, scrambling into shoes, struggling with the laces.

Marina stood astonished by the French door, one foot in, one out. Come on, she said, the thin gray wisp from her cigarette pirouetting around her.

I had a single goal: to leave before I cried, and I was very nearly not successful. Marina blocked my way out.

You don't want me here, I said, and in that moment my old accent came back, like some dam had been breached and the warm and hot and round and jagged tongue I had been raised with gushed in, laden with consonant and debris.

Yoo doan't vont me hyur, I heard myself say in a burst of hurt, so I will getoutofthe waye.

Come on, man. That is not—

Pointlessly I tried to tame the demon in my throat. I said, trying to get past her: Excuse me. I will pay you back for the things we talked about. I'm sorry I hurt your feelings, I'm sorry I took advantage of your kindness.

What are you saying? Marina asked. I can't figure you out. I can't figure out what you want.

Shit, me too, I said stupidly. I took hold of her shoulders, very gently.

Moved her out of the way like you might a table with a breakable glass top that did not belong to you.

Thinking it was my only option, I left. Through Marina's great white museum of an apartment lobby and into the street. I heaved into my hands. It was a forty-five-minute walk in the snow to an icy apartment perched above my personal Hades. I needed help, and I had to become better about asking.

Tig picked up on the second ring.

She would come get me. I could stay in her room and she would stay with the Amy Winehouse mommy, who, when I met her in the passenger seat of Tig's Honda Fit twenty minutes later, was a very kind woman named Diana and told me multiple times it would all be okay. Marina texted me, you really hurt my feelings. think I need some time and space.

But first, Tig said into the silence, we have to take care of something together.

When we pulled up to my place I walked toward the side door; Antigone did not.

Around the corner she whipped. I staggered behind in snow.

She was rapping smartly on Amy's front door. Even though it was midnight, even though Amy was a wolf in an asymmetrical maroon haircut. Even though I was terrified, what came to me in that moment was laughter—a dry dizzy chuckle cracking through the ice air. The apparition of Amy's face, shocked and pinched and angry. Fixed on Tig's broad solid form in disbelief. How very funny.

Good evening! was what Tig said, with a smile of steel. I know it's late. You the property manager for the apartment upstairs, right? It hasn't had working heat for the last ten days, so very obviously it's dangerous to live in. She's contacted you and heard nothing. What're we gonna do to make this right by your tenant?!

In a cloud of malevolence Amy fixed the gas—it was the pilot light—two days later. My apartment became habitable again, at least on the temperature front. When I'd walked in I almost gagged. Quickly shut the abandoned fridge, full of liquefying vegetables, stews studded with pale coins of mold. Tig said her interaction with Amy told her all she needed to know about why she'd been a dog to me.

That woman is Ray Cyst. That's at least part of why she has been this way to you, Tig told me. She also probably just doesn't want someone young and cute with friends living above her, making her feel bad about her ugly self. In her ideal world it's nobody living above her, but she's not in charge of that, since she's not the landlord—yet—but ideally you'd be a lil old helpless woman with snowy curls who is scared of her.

I thought about moving. But every time I did, it felt as though a temple elephant had made to sit down on my chest. To have the savings I did, to have the security to take care of my parents, pick up the tab sometimes for my friends—that seemed important. I looked into why Peter had offered to pay my rent and made two discoveries. One was that Stacy, my actual landlord, whom I'd only heard mentioned by first name, was the wife of a local multimillionaire, a man mentioned in an online magazine as one of Milwaukee's Movers and Shakers. Stacy and the husband were friends Peter appeared to be cultivating—on his social media I found pictures of their families skiing at Vail, with Peter commenting, You must come with us to Chile next year!

The other was that I looked up his company, and noted that I was claimed as an employee, not a contractor, and that the business he ran was registered in Wisconsin, not the state Peter lived in, and most notably that it was registered at my address in Milwaukee.

It's not totally nefarious, I guess, Amit said, when I called to tell him. More annoying than anything? He probably wants to curry favor with Stacy and her husband, get more connections to possible clients in Wisconsin. He also gets to pay lower taxes if the business is registered there. Businessmen gonna be businessmen, I guess. Sorry, I got to go. Back-to-back meetings.

For hours I cleaned the apartment. I had a plan. I had spent too much time agonizing about this tension with Thom—the back-and-forth of it, convincing myself that I was in the wrong then in the right like some anxious metronome. What felt plain in that moment was: I was a fool for not seeing, from the beginning, that we should be on each other's side. That we had common interests. Nothing else felt particularly worth litigating.

Hey, he said when I opened the door, two necks of Schlitz in his right hand.

Put those in the fridge, I said, playing winning hostess. I'm gonna make us real drinks.

We discussed Tig, Isabel, the prospect of his eventual marriage, how he liked the idea of old-school communal living, a big family house. We made predictions regarding the possibility of gay marriage. Thom gave it ten years. I scoffed. That kind of wild upending, people deciding a whole ancient institution can just be different, that would take, I said, no less than half a century. After our second round—I'd flooded a double of gin with lime juice, shaken the lot with cream of coconut and walnut bitters—I decided it was safe to bring up work. We popped the caps off the Schlitzes.

Let me start at the beginning, I said, and told him all of it. From my first offer from Peter onward.

You should negotiate for more with him, I said. The rent here is five hundred, so yeah, you could factor that in.

I'm sorry, I added, about earlier. I didn't know like, what was legal and what wasn't. But please be careful when you talk about it. It's really fucking stressful working as an immigrant without residency, you know? It feels like at any moment the floor might give way under you . . .

Yeah dude, he finally said, after much silence. I really do get that. I'm not always the best, I'll admit. At like, imagining what it's like in your head.

When I am very drunk I am most likely to forget to maintain the partitions between what I tell and what I won't, most likely to forget to lie. Toward the bottom of a small bottle of Jim Beam, even though I had no intention to from the outset, I told him about my father. What happened in college. The bus ride from Madison. The lecture clickers.

He listened quietly. Really listened. At the end of my soliloquy, he got up off my tufted couch and walked over to me.

He raised his arm, whiskey on his breath. I flinched.

He pulled me toward him, held me close. I'm so sorry, my dude, he said. I wish I'd known. That is insane.

Within me I felt the hot flush that signaled tears, but my eyes stayed dry.

In my leaner mirror with its gilt edge I saw us both. Two friends in chubby sweaters and boots crusted with salt. Two friends locking into each other, choosing what seemed so rare to me: to trust and to forgive.

Again Tig and I grew closer to inseparable. We walked by the river with its Frappuccino ice, cheeks growing pink and chapped, laughing about the things we laughed about. Tig was running low on rent again, after giving her sister money for car repairs. She took me to buy gifts for my trip to see my family. Kleenex and lotion, they'd asked for, Hellmann's mayonnaise and Johnnie Walker. Godiva chocolates, rubber sheets.

Three years ago, when I was going back home and having my dental surgery, my uncle had cheerily requested cologne. Passing the JCPenney cosmetics counter I remembered my stone-faced refusal, felt an asthmatic tightening in my lungs. In my peripheral vision Tig sprayed an aerosol halo from a dark glass bottle. Walked through the cloud of scent like an emperor. I laughed at her, my nostrils filling with wood and musk. The fist in my chest slackening.

Taco Tuesdays had resumed, now with Diana in attendance. Diana taught me how to blow a chewing gum bubble while we waited to get seated at BelAir. She said the strangest things with the straightest face. My whole family would sleep naked in the same bed, all six of us, she told me in soft dreamy tones. That's my favorite memory from childhood, she added.

From little hints they dropped and I ignored, I think Tig and Diana might have been interested in sleeping naked in the same bed, with me included. A bristly feeling inside at the idea. I did not know how to reconcile my love for Tig, the shimmering regard and gratitude I held for her, with the frank slime of want. I feared these two women could unearth something ugly in me. As their friend I was my better self: dry and laughing, spiky but kind, trying to peel the world like an orange, eat it by the segment. I wanted to keep it that way.

So instead I waved goodbye to them after home-cooked dinners and painting nights at Diana's house, and went and met girls from the apps. Pulp Fiction texted me saying her car was stuck in the snow. I walked thirty minutes, helped her shovel it out, and then took her to bed. Pressed her face down into the Target-pattern pillow, let her struggle just long enough. Every time I remembered Marina, I pushed it back into the dark pulped ice of my most buried thought.

Sometimes she texted me. Passing by Wicked Hop, thought of you, one said, and added with a pained formality: Hope you are doing well!

Another time: bored @ wine night with the dance girls. meet me in the bathroom?

I responded to these with a carefully calibrated flirtation. Semaphoring affection. Promising nothing.

Do you think you blew shit up with Marina on purpose? Thom asked me in the break room while we watched food turning slowly in the microwave. Because you don't want to come out to your parents?

I glared at him. I was not in the market for this two-paisa psycho-analysis. At work we were now on two different projects, him staying with Susan and inbox change management, while I had been transferred over to creating a series of training modules and workflows, occasionally getting pulled back in on project inbox transition. This meant we saw each other far less. Still, he usually waited for me in the garage when I worked late and drove us both home. He'd negotiated a five-dollar raise with Peter, never mentioning me. He wanted to save up enough for a down payment in three years, which was, he said, around when he wanted to marry Isabel.

My stomach hurt at the thought. I imagined it: my friends peeling off one by one to fall in actual love, buying three-bedroom houses in far-off suburbs, growing too busy to call. While I, either alone or in some airless marriage with a paid-for man, would crawl from bed to bed in the dark like a cockroach.

It's not that deep, was all I said to Thom, chucking him under the chin like Tig might have, walking away.

From the first time I brought them together—something I had avoided out of a vague anticipatory jealousy—Thom and Tig took to each other like Parle-G and chaiya. It was mostly beautiful to see. Though wildly different on paper, the two of them thought alike, listened to similar podcasts, used the word *proletariat* with the same frequency. They were two funny, easygoing, radiantly decent people with the same area code but none of the baggage about who was mean to who in middle school. Days before my flight to India, the three of us drank beers at Y-Not II and talked about Peter and Kim Kardashian and Marx and Tig getting fired from Lush.

She'd been scatterbrained about restocking the bath jellies, gone off-script when soaping customers' hands, been insubordinate when denied her bathroom break on a five-hour shift.

I said to this dizzy bitch, I think the hell not, you want me to pee in the demo sink? and walked off, Tig said indignantly. I was back on the floor in *one* minute, but she was not having it.

Things were precarious, had been so even before this. Until now she had been able to keep up with rent, was just sending it late every time she got a pay-or-vacate. Her landlord had been trying to get her and her roommate out. Most likely to sell or flip the place, raise rent higher than the lawful margin for lease-renewing tenants. A slew of new gastropubs and cocktail bars had popped up in Bay View, Antigone noted, by way of explanation. I'm so sick of this shit, she said. I've been evicted before. It fucking sucks.

She gulped the last of the pale ocher brew and said, I don't want another one on my record. I'll highkey never find a place again.

What's it like? Thom asked, topping up her stein with Rhinelander.

Tig closed her eyes.

You don't have to explain it to him, I said, bristling in her defense. Google is free.

She shook her head. How will we learn about the world if not from each other? she intoned, eyes widening.

I couldn't help but smile. What a wildly Tig thing to say.

She told us. The rumble of moving trucks, the fist thumping at the door at six in the morning, marshals with their tow-colored mustaches and badges, your things lining the curb. Right before she'd left Milwaukee for Disney, her mom had gotten an informal eviction. Tig's mama had been late on rent. Her sister had made the grievous mistake of calling to complain about black mold in the kitchen setting off her asthma, had mentioned the tenant bill of rights. The landlord had had enough. Served them a notice to vacate, no court papers, and simply took the door off its hinges.

Rent is the bane of my existence, Tig said.

Well actually, landlords are, Thom corrected. Tig gave him her most magisterial smile, went, Say that!

My desire to partake in a second round of this conversation was not particularly strong. I went to the bathroom, then meandered to the door, raised my phone to my ear in pantomime, and stepped out in the cold air. Above me in the display window loomed Y-Not II's electric chair, arcane and huge.

I owed Amit texts back.

He'd written a long worried screed about KJ. She was spending a fortune on motel rooms while she got clean. She was gaining weight from the Suboxone. Couldn't fit in any of her old clothes. She sent Amit a four-hundred-dollar bill from Kohl's and he'd wired her a reimbursement from Western Union. Later he noticed the date on the receipt—August of last year. He asked KJ why she'd lied to him. She flew into a paroxysm of fear, begged him not to stop supporting her.

Jesus Christ, I wrote. How much money have you given her so far?

I watched the ellipsis that signaled he was typing. It appeared, then disappeared for long minutes. My hands were so cold.

Stepping back inside, I looked to make sure the bartender was distracted, and sat in the electric chair.

Like a throne, it felt. Wood and leather. Restraints on the arms. My wrists slid into them smoothly, slid just as easily out. I looked at my phone. Amit had stopped typing.

S

in later news i think i messed
it up with Marina

> **Amit**
> Oh. Sorry to hear that. It seemed like
> you were both vibing pretty well.
> What went down with that

S

idk it all happened fast. i
didn't want a relationship yet,
she did. lesbians u kno? she
blew up at me. she's very
emotional. i don't know if we
would have worked long term
anyway. Whatever long term
is hahah

> **Amit**
> Hmmm. You don't come across as
> *not* emotional, not to me anyway

> **Amit**
> But if you weren't compatible you
> weren't compatible I guess

S

think we started off on a
weird foot. not the most
honest.

Amit
What do you mean?

S

she didn't tell me that her
ex-girlfriend was with her in
milwaukee literally until the
day before I met her at
Thom's party. Tig and I saw
them at the public market.
and the gf hit M and cussed
Tig out. I wasn't there, it's
what Tig said and I realized it
was Marina later. seems like
some really messy shit. i don't
know if I want to deal with any
of that. and honestly its easier
to sleep with women than to
date them

Amit
Sounds horrible.

Amit
For what it's worth I don't
think having and leaving an
abusive ex is really any kind of
wrongdoing?

Amit
She may have wanted to tell you but
been ashamed, like worried about
how you'd take it

S

i should be frank. it was
also me. i messed up in a
way i couldn't really recover
from

Amit
You want to talk about it? I can call you.

S
i actually don't think
I can say it out loud. also
am at Y-Not II with Tig
and Thom

Amit
Okay lol don't let me
keep you

S
basically I let M believe my
mother and father have
passed away

Amit
What the fuck

S
it was a misunderstanding
and the misunderstanding
made things so much easier. i
guess i feel like for a few
weeks i got to pretend i was a
white girl

Amit
Most white people have
parents lol

S
wp get to own their lives.
they get to feel like their
lives belong to only them

S
for about a month i got to feel
that way. not like all my
choices are mortgaged to the
people who have made my
life possible

Amit
Listen S I know you feel like you
have a choice between being a good
daughter and finding real love

S
that is an unecessarily
dramatique way to put it

Amit
Okay. How would you put it

S
Do you remember Intro to
Physics

Amit
Barely, but yes

The specifics of the theory I recalled only vaguely. Quantum units in a box. Sometimes they were waves and sometimes particles. In fact they were both, but any one observer could only perceive them as one at a given moment in time. They collapsed into a steady state when observed.

Something is either green or blue. That is true in most places. A young woman is a decent daughter, chaste and godly, educated but not too much, successful but not too much, on her path to marry a decent paid-for man. Seen another way: a girl migrates to a new place but is too scared to grow up, still a Mummy and Papa's girl, traditional to a fault, clinging to the old ways, choosing obedience over happiness out of childish fear.

A young woman, corrupted by the new place, turns into a pervert, wrong in the head, crawling from bed to bed, kissing another woman's neck like a deviant. Seen another way: a girl comes to the new country and finds freedom, finds herself, finally lives in the truth of her desire and ambition, lives like her life is her very own, lives like an American.

These were the frames I could choose between, the choices I had. Green or blue. Blue or green. A or B.

Sometimes green and blue collapse. Indistinct. Smudge into sameness.

We know this. You could look at each of them and think, These are the same, only different based on who is looking. The way I had trained myself to think, I hovered between each of these quadrants, unstable. Had built careful firewalls partitioning the two halves of my life: the one that belonged to my parents and the place that I came from, the one that belonged only to me, shaped by this brash selfish country. I typed for many minutes to Amit, sending nothing. The many beers in me were collapsing my thoughts.

Babe, Tig's voice said, and her hand was on my shoulder. My friend's lovely face. Big-cheeked, honey-skinned, creased in concern. She'd walked into the display window. Was staring down at me.

Are you okay? she asked. I was about to answer with assent when Marina appeared across the street.

She was with Shaka. Both of them so lithe and beautiful. Marina in her yellow puffer. Pale hair piled upon her head in two small knots. They had walked toward Shaka's car, which was parked across the street. My heart began to ricochet against its restraints. As Marina opened the passenger door she looked up straight at me.

I imagined the scene from her eyes. The girl who'd jilted her sitting in this old-school electric chair in a display window. As though I were a mannequin for this trashy dive bar. My hand, of its own volition, jumped to my chest. Pressed down.

You can go to your girl, you know, Tig said drily. Taking in the scene at a glance.

I can't, I whispered. I've ruined everything.

Go, Tig repeated. She's what you want.

Marina, still looking at us over the top of the car.

I stood up and walked unsteadily to the door. But by the time I was outside, she'd gotten in the car. Zoomed away.

Tig put an arm around me, pulled me close.

It's never too late, she said in my ear. That's what Rion told my mother. I was a kid, listening at the door. I never forgot it. He said this. While two people are still alive to try, he said, it's never too late, and it's never the end.

I slid my hand into hers.

I love you, you know, I said.

It was the first time I had said this to another person. It was what I felt. A painful swell of tenderness and regard and gratitude. My best friend. No one better.

I love you too, babe, she said, with her easy smile.

When I put down my card for our beers, I got a text saying I had a low balance alert. This seemed strange. After Thom's jibe about investing I'd moved money out of my checking account into a high-yield savings account and a one-year CD, but still should have had plenty left over with my incoming paychecks. I logged into my bank app on my phone.

This was how I discovered that I had not, in fact, been paid. Not in January or the first week of February. It was careless of me to not have checked for so long. I would have to ask Peter about this.

Tig, I said in a low voice while Thom chatted to the bartender, I was thinking about you. I'm going to be in India for two weeks. If you need to stay at my place, you should. Here, here's an extra key.

She pocketed it, asked, What about old girl downstairs?

I'll take care of her, I said, if you need me to.

I wish things were different, Tig said sadly, looking into Y-Not II's pink neon signs. Talking to y'all has got me thinking, for real. I have bigger dreams than running from place to place, trying to survive. It's what animals do. Spend their lives desperately looking for food and shelter. Black and brown people in this city, we are just animals. Hunted down.

I know, I said, though I did not. I added, I'm so sorry.

There has to be a better way, Tig said. I'm going to think on it. I'm a philosopher. It's my job.

Later that night Amit texted me.

So I did the math, he said. $47,140.

I stared at the white number in its lime-colored cell. It beggared description. In Milwaukee, that was a down payment for a midsize house. That was more money than I made in a year. Rich people were so stupid, so unaware of the actual cost of anything.

She was using him. There was no way his dear sweet middle school friend was not rampantly doing drugs with his cash infusions. Nothing else could cost so much. This fool was likely keeping an entire coterie of her friends awash in heroin.

This was too much. I would have to reply later.

I got ready for bed. Lazily began to touch myself. But my body remained tense. I rolled over in bed and reached for my phone.

S
hey. how are you doing?

Marina
I am okay. How are you?

S
i don't know. kind of flat. i
think i always kind of feel
that way. except when i was
with you.

Marina
Yeah?

S
i felt very happy when we
were spending time together.
maybe the happiest i'd been
in so long. i've never properly
had anything close to a
girlfriend you know. for me it
felt distinct from hooking up
with women, desiring women.
i think it's like, partly because
i thought in order to properly
like be a lesbian, have a
girlfriend, i would have to
become different, renounce
parts of myself, shave my
head, dress terribly. but when
i was with you i was just
myself. nothing actually
needed to change.

Marina
Lesbians are not some alien species
lol. Lots of different ways to be one.
Butches at the Pint. Hollywood
producers and Bollywood actresses
and car mechanics. I can be a Stila
lipstain lesbian. If you want so
can you

Marina
Yeah well I also felt very happy
when we were together. I didn't
know you felt that way too. You are
not easy to read. At all lol. I felt like I
didn't know how to make you happy,
to be what you want

S
can I just ask. what happened
with you and jenny shin? i

should have just asked and
not let it fester.

Marina
Ugh. I'd prefer to have this
conversation in person.

Marina
But here's the short version. Jenny
came out with me to Milwaukee. I
didn't particularly want her to, but
we'd been together for a minute,
you know? Anyway, she's here,
she loses her job, she's totally
miserable, hates it here but won't
leave. I try to break up with her. She
won't accept it.

Marina
When I'm traveling for work she
falls down the stairs leaving our
roof and breaks her foot. Now she's
on my couch, won't leave. I'm
going absolutely insane. I tell her
fine she can stay while she heals but
we're not together. I go online, try to
date other people. But in practice
it's not going to work because my
crazy ex is on my couch and is
calling everything I'm doing
cheating. Finally she gives up.
After months of this. I've been
losing my mind, just burying myself
in work, I slept at the studio some
nights.

Marina
I delete the apps, I'm not even
trying to date anymore. Her foot's
better. I tell her if she doesn't move
out I will, and that I'm prepared to
pay the insane fee my building
charges to break the lease. She
buys a ticket the next day. I can

understand why it was upsetting for you if you saw her and me the literal day before you and I met at the party. But you have to understand. J and I hadn't been romantic for months. It had been over for a long time. She wasn't my brand-new ex. She was my squatter.

Marina
Okay maybe not so short after all.

S
good grief

Marina
Yeah man

S
thank you for telling me.

S
i think the story made such an impression on me partly because it felt so shocking, the idea of this woman slapping you. in public. made me feel crazy

Marina
Look she didn't like beat me up on the reg or something. I've seen that happen with some gay women. Just like awful violent shit. There were like two times with Jenny in our literal years together. One I gave back as good as I got. The second I was so glad I was getting rid of her I was like ok got your suitcase? cool. I was not like, abused lol. I'm a tough Jersey bitch

S
yeah. you are.

s
when i saw you today i felt
overwhelmed

s
i think you are what i want.
and that feels very scary

Marina
Do you want to try again? I'm
trying to understand what you
would like.

s
i really do like you. i would like
to try again, and take it slow

Marina
I can try to do that. What are you
doing next Saturday?

s
i'll be in india for two weeks.
won't have much internet
there or anything, and no cell
reception. but if you're free
for a late dinner after work
wednesday, i would love that.
or after i am back.

Marina
Weds is good. It's on my calendar.
Sweet dreams, baby

s
sleep well.

The room felt warm, an expanse I could dissolve in. The glowing rectangle I held illuminated its dark, but only barely. Under dusty sheets I kept looking at her last text, clutching my phone tight in my hand as I fell asleep.

Peter called me into a boardroom. He had sent a cal invite at 7 a.m. for an 8 a.m. meeting. A tremor ran through my hands when I saw it. The training modules were again badly behind schedule. Susan was on the warpath. The master spreadsheet for stakeholder engagement had been deduped with errors, so you had AVPs getting the newsletter blasts intended for mere engineers and battery specialists. Peter had not responded to my timorous email about my paychecks. The client retreat was days away, my India trip in twelve hours. The very air appeared wetly saturated with tension, ready to circuit into storm.

Both Thom and I had worked on the spreadsheet recently. In the depths of my abdomen a pooling suspicion: I had mis-selected a range when sorting, causing the cells to lose relationship with each other, garbling the data for senior leadership. I could not know for sure. Thom, Peter, Susan, and I had sent the spreadsheet back and forth to each other about a hundred times.

You will be okay, I told myself again and again. You have savings now. You will find something else. You will survive this.

The night before, I had checked Marina out of the emergency room at St. Luke's. When I'd gone to pick her up for our date—we'd been planning on legit tacos, at Guadalajara—she'd opened the door, sweaty in joggers, hair ponytailed, face terrifically puffy.

Sorry, pretty, I'm running late—

This was when I knew for certain something was wrong. It was as though there were a small hot potato in her mouth. Every word muffled.

What is going on? I asked, following her into the bathroom, where she was doggedly styling her hair. The strands hissed and steamed as she pincered them with her straightener's ceramic beak.

I don't know, she said, in the same garble, flickering her eyelashes over a goopy mascara wand. Yeah so I had a sore throat last week and like it was bad, but it doesn't hurt right now. I don't have a fever or anything. I think I'm fine, honestly, other than losing my voice today. Had to yell teaching.

Yeah I don't think you're fine, I said, wincing at the sound of her voice. Let's stay in. Watch a movie, order takeout? Okay?

Okay, quavered the hot potato, in tones of defeat.

Come here, sillybilly, I said. In my arms she was avian, pneumatic. As though her very bones were filled with air. A dark fluid rushed up in me. A warmth that left my head tingling. I did not dare say anything. To attempt putting words to this—a bridge too far. I divested myself of my blazer and skinny tie. Slid off Marina's shoes. I said, Blankets and soup for you, old lady.

In the middle of the night I woke and heard her mother on the phone.

In the stories I'd heard about Marina's mom, of beating up a thieving fellow stripper, of hollering Listen Everybody My Daughter Is a Faggot to a yardful of revelers, I'd pictured a loud, brassy woman, and the volume of her speech even through the bathroom door did not give lie to my imaginings.

I don't care if she's your girlfriend or what! Don't be a little *chooch*! You make that girl take you to the damn hospital!

From her daughter I heard nothing. Fearfully I knocked on the bathroom door.

Marina looked the palest I'd ever seen her. She did not attempt to talk. Her eyes pleading, she scribbled on a turquoise Post-it.

CAN'T REALLY BREATHE

In the St. Luke's waiting room I forced myself to quit looking at WebMD, which was doing its level best to convince me that she had either sepsis or cancer.

Marina wrote me that they were about to do a CT scan. She would leave her phone behind.

Pacing around the waiting room's vending machine and plastic palms, without the distraction of texting her, the reality of my trip home surfaced. I missed my parents and longed to see them. But there was also the question of my uncle. His death, stowed neatly away in the other half of my life, had never grown more real to me. In my mind he walked around still, mundu folded securely, hands clasped behind his back. His face kindly, blankly circumspect as it was when he reached into my seamy tops and underwear and hunted for whatever he was after—something I suspected he barely knew himself, and which I as a child was in no place to identify. Could only provide a facsimile of.

Finally I was allowed to see Marina. They asked my relationship to her. Uh, we're, um, my friend, I stammered. The woman in scrubs looked at me like I was a child lying about having peed my pants.

The infection in the wisdom tooth had likely begun years ago, the pain dying as the nerve did. But the rot remained. Had spread from the tooth through her maxillofacial planes, wormed into her throat. Swollen her tongue and encroached on her breathing. Marina was on a drip. Her mother was flying in tomorrow. She would need an extraction, and a hefty course of antibiotics. She was already trying to plan for the hospital bill.

But she was fine. She was alive. I held her neat hand with its fine bones and we laughed. I thought of how light she had been to hold, and a dark scaled feeling folded around my heart like an eel.

I know you're leaving tomorrow. It'll be okay, Shaka's coming and then my mom will be here in the evening. But listen, you better write me when you're in India, she said, a little fiercely.

And I said, I will, I will.

———

For the first time in history, Peter brought in two mugs of coffee, which solidified my confidence that I was about to get axed. He offered one to me with a thin smile.

I drank it like Socrates upon receipt of the hemlock. The wildness of the past twelve hours felt like counterweight. This was only one more terrible happening in a white room flooded with clinical light. Deep breaths. Try to take this with grace.

I wanted to check in, he said, and ask how you were. How is your capacity?

Quite good, pretty open, I said, calculating whether a desperate apology would make any difference to him.

Peter told me some changes had been made. I would need to take on more responsibility when I returned. Particularly on Susan's project. There had been some resource streamlining, he said.

Okay, I said, not understanding, willing my lungs not to explode with relief. I would not be getting the sack. That was all I knew. All that mattered.

As I got up to go, Peter said, Safe travels, and oh, by the way.

Yes, boss? I asked.

Like an afterthought he mentioned my paychecks. They're delayed, for all of us, including me, he said, because the client only pays upon project completion, and Susan has extended the timeline again and again. My company is not doing particularly well at the moment. I simply can't afford to keep assuming the cost of your wages. You'll be paid eventually, of course. Just when the client remunerates me.

Okay, I said, in a ghostly whisper, trying to make sense of what he'd said.

It's the hardest thing, being a business owner, Peter said, shaking his head. Just one headache of responsibility after the other.

I'm sure it is, I said, voice deferential. Full of sympathy. Have a good day, I added. I'll update you on deliverable status before I leave EOD.

My heart having puffed up a size with relief, I attacked my projects—complex spreadsheets, audio cleanup on a training module—with such concentration that I barely saw Thom in my peripheral vision. Then I looked again, turned from my monitor.

He was walking down the hallway, face blank as chalk. He carried a cardboard box with a cardboard lid.

Oh my god, I said, and ran toward him.

Get away, Thom said, barely audible. I'm not supposed to speak to any of you.

I stepped backward like I had been burned. I watched his back as he receded down the hallway, stepped into the elevators by the battery mural, disappeared.

Across the baggage claim aisles my mother called my name. There they were. Mummy and Papa. I was groggy from the long flight and smelled bad. My skin was dry. I should, I thought, have brushed my teeth before coming through customs.

My father with his silver goatee and rimless specs. My mother in an organza sari of pale pink, her hair oiled into a bun with such precision it was as though her scalp was painted. At the edge of her waving hand a neat steel wristwatch.

I saw it in her face: she wanted to run to me, but I was the child, and the parent does not run to the child. There is a way things are done.

I walked fast. Fought the emotion that climbed in me like well water in rainfall. When I was about a meter away, my mother darted forward and clutched me to her body. She said my name, again and again, and I felt sick. I told her, Stop it.

My mother cradled my face. Sneha. My Sneha, she said. We have waited so long. You've come home.

I shrugged out of her arms.

There is no need whatsoever, I said, voice like the winter I had left behind, to conjjellify like this. You came in an auto? Poaam, come on, let's go.

They

Oru madameh vannu ippum!

Bincy Varughese hooted at me from her chicken coop, from where she had been scattering feed into the red dirt. She threw her head back and laughed like an old parrot. Oil-haired, gold-toothed.

Her daughter washed the front steps of their tiny cement house, smaller than ours. She avoided my eye. As children we had played together. One afternoon we gathered every millipede we could source upon an elephant-ear leaf. While they wormed over each other, the two of us, dizzy from our giggles, chanted, Doing *sex*! Doing *sex*! at them with the ardor of ancient priestesses. Two thin bucktoothed children, delighted by our millipede orgy.

Bincy was mocking me for having come back a foreigner. Not merely a foreigner, but a madama. Full of hot airs and mincing graces. I stood dully by the Varughese gate, my mind pickled by jet lag. When my parents were succeeding, she had been exceedingly solicitous to them, calling them over Reliance for every birthday and holiday, sending food over to my grandparents. Like many people I had been fond of when I left our town at fourteen but now felt venom toward, Bincy had taken Papa's deportation and newly straitened circumstances as a personal affront. The equivalent of buying what you were told were blue-chip stocks and seeing them turn out penny. Now she had only scorn for us.

The entirety of my first and second day back home I'd stayed horizontal under thin cotton sheets, alternating sleep and staring up at the fan whirring patiently above me. A bone-deep exhaustion had settled into my every limb. I left the room to eat curd rice and pickle, to say evening prayers by my grandparents' bedside. They gazed off into the ceiling, their gums bared in slack smiles.

On the first day my mother had sat next to me, stroked my hair, cooed how tired I must be. On the third day she roused me with some sharpness at six in the morning. Required me to take a well-water bath, to bring my grandparents chaiya from their folding bed trays. By the way my mother moved I could tell she was ashamed of me. By my short unplaited hair, my late rising, my mannerisms alternating between mannish and slatternly.

The last time I visited, I had been a student mid-university. Had brought two suitcases, one for schoolbooks and my clothes, the other crammed to its weight limit with necessaries for my family. A leather briefcase, orthotic shoes. My father had not then given up searching for job after job, pushing hard against the taint of scandal that had followed him across two oceans. When I was here last, my postextraction cheeks swollen in a reprisal of childhood chub, I had not been asked to lift a finger. My only job was to study, I was told. To do well. Graduate with distinction, secure a decent-paying job. Success at these had been met with no celebration, only a transfer of expectation to the next desired milestone: marriage and readiness for it.

Come be in the kitchen with me, my mother snapped, watching my freshly bathed head drift toward the ancient family computer like a moth drawn to flame.

For once, she said, angrily lighting the wood stove, *learn* something. This is your home, keto? Not a hotel.

I went to fetch the coconut grater before I dared to retort from the safety of the next room, This is a hotel. And I, like you, am a servant in it.

The kitchen was, despite Mummy's daily cleaning, eternally covered in a thin layer of wood soot. Gingerly I stepped around in it, surveying what my parents might need in the future. The pressure cooker was ancient, likely hazardous. For next Christmas I could buy them new Corningware casseroles or perhaps a better-working mixy than the one they owned, a present from marriage that had journeyed overseas and sullenly returned. One day, when they were older, perhaps even a dishwasher. A quarter of my mother's day was spent hunched over the sink, plying steel wool. I felt colossally indignant about this whenever I considered it from my vantage point in the States. Still, I could not say I felt great desire to share in this work now that I was here.

Upon beginning to prepare breakfast we discovered that the storage cupboard was out of both sugar and black kadala. I—the visiting-from-America mol, the consultant mol, the mol demonstrating that this family was not yet ruined by ill fortune—had been dispatched down the street to Bincy's to rescue our morning meal.

How is Amayrica, mmm? she jeered. You are doing very well there?

In the distance I could see the rubber fields. Tree trunks thin and massed like hairbrush bristles. The place I come from is a beautiful one. Its pained immodest loveliness outstrips anything in the new land.

Doing well, I replied, my voice dripping with dislike. Doing very well.

What I might have said, arrived at much later, once I'd replayed our interaction in my mind about a hundred times: Madam, I am not a madama, I was taken to a country when young, and I was taken there because Amayrica is the sun, and we are moved, most of us, by light and heat and power, and I am happy I am there, to the extent I am ever happy about things, because the sun orders all happening around it, and you, stupid woman, you live on a dusty asteroid that nobody thinks about. Because I am crazy I sometimes miss the asteroid, long for my family who were taken away from me, yearn to be back with my people. But when I am back, I remember how the people treated us, what my own kin did to me, become reacquainted with how much I wish every single one of you would fall down dead. And to escape my hatred, to stop it from burning me up, I jump back where I am stuck, between these worlds, in thick, dusty space.

Sardines deep-fried in a coating of earth-red masala, fresh hot rice with butter-colored moru, glistening achinga sautéed with onions cooked down until they turned the same hue as our skin. When we were not cooking or eating what we cooked, if there was not work to be done—felling a tree, pressing a mundu, fixing a cane chair, darning a mosquito net—we sat on the veranda and received a mighty stream of guests who talked a great deal and said very little. My grandparents we fed kanji and pire. Their teeth had given out. Every night my mother soaked two sets of dentures in solution. Out of my grandmother I cajoled the proper recipes for saaru and idli, no box mixes needed. I asked how to make olan. My favorite. If you can't get cowpeas in your Milwaagee use the white beans with a dark mouth, my grandmother said to me in a burst of lucidity before fading into reverie.

I daydreamed myself months from now, stewing pumpkin chunks and black-eyed peas and coconut paal with cumin seed and curry leaf, serving it to Marina and her friends. Oh, this? I would reply in the face of their compliments. It's so simple. A family recipe. The friends would leave, won over, and I would take Marina to bed, hold her through the night.

In the afternoons when everybody slept, or in the late reaches of the night, I sidled to the computer. My time with Marina felt a world away, and for this reason I found it hard to know what to say to her. Still, I took seriously my promise to write to her often. Hope you are healing OK, I typed, feeling stiff as an ironing board. Please let me know when you feel back to normal, also I hope the extraction bill wasn't too taxing. To Thom I wrote two different emails, long and pained, cursing out Peter, suggesting avenues for redress, aching for him. Days passed and I received no reply.

Tig wrote, hey, am in your apartment.

> Hope that is okay. My pig land lord made good on getting me + Turk out. Bet he is gonna flip the house no way is he actually living there. Turk is moving back home for a husband setup. My mom place is a whole mess and my half sister is crashing there and if I see her pull her usual junkie bullshit I will go upside her head. Thank you for the key and planning ahead for me (lol things I need to work on). I am being very very extremely quiet but also can you tell your scary neighbor to not like shoot me or call the popo.
>
> Love you be well now headed to class. We are reading Amartya Sen and Sojourner Truth. Just finished Vindication of Rights of Women. lowkey decided I wanna write a manifesto someday

Sublets are not allowed under lease terms, the reply from Amy zinged back almost instantly when I wrote her a note about Tig's short stay. We will need to bring this up with Stacy, it added.

To lower my heart rate I took an achchappam and crunched it while pacing up and down the red dirt of the yard. Everywhere the trees and the steps and the stones of the compound wall were gathering moss.

Dear Stacy, I wrote in my next email.

> Hello from South India, where I am visiting family. I hope this email finds you well. This is simply an FYI that while I am gone someone will be house sitting the apartment, watering my plants and collecting mail. This is not a sublet, formal or informal. I am cc'ing Amy so we are all on the same page. Have a nice day, both!

Sounds good! Have a wonderful trip! Stacy replied.

Amy remained silent.

U out-whiteladied the raining champion of the whiteladies!!! Tig wrote, when I forwarded the exchange. Absolute king shit!!! one more favor to ask. Found a place I can move into in two weeks. Landlord wants two months rent and I'm $200 short. can you Venmo me a lil cash, like $150, and I can pay you back soon??

Papa had felled two of the teak trees on the property and I offered to help him split them into slabs to sell. We worked in the bright sun, our necks wet, the air too damp to absorb our sweat. I liked this kind of work, found it calming in its way, enjoyed how it obviated the need for speech.

Two hours in, my father mopped his forehead, stood back and surveyed our progress.

Good, he said simply, the corners of his eyes puckering in warmth.

At sunset we went, at my mother's suggestion, to the river.

Not good to stay huddle-shuddled in the house full-time, she said, although this was, most any day of the week, all they did.

Past neglected fields of paddy, past the kallukadas and vegetable stalls, past the State Bank of Travancore outlet we walked.

Impossible to find people to work in the rice paddy anymore. This Shreyadarshini was telling me her difficulties, my mother said. Sad it is, this is what makes this place beautiful. People these days are getting too big for their boots.

They want more pay than the old poverty-stricken rates, my father said shortly.

Aiyay, how much can you pay to harvest rice? If you pay so handsomely, if you give a pension and salary and all, then the rice only will cost more. Then how will the common man eat?

The Meenachil curved ahead, bluegreen, greenblue. Since I had come home last, concrete steps had been set into the riverbank's descent. Above us, pepper vines coiled around the limbs of trees beginning to swell with armored green fruit. My mother held my hand as we walked down the stairs. She was so much more demonstrative now than she had been when I was a child. It made me uneasy.

The river of my childhood smells now of fertilizer and the bubblegum-and-rot tang of jackfruit. In the summers it grows sluggish and dry, the water millions depend on barely knee-level in parts. But in February the Meenachil is beautiful still. It had been a long time since I had come to this exact spot, years before we immigrated. I squeezed my mother's hand.

You know *Americans* sell chakka now? I said. In fancy supermarkets and all? They put barbecue sauce on it, use it as meat. Selling it for eight, nine dollars in the market! My nose wrinkled.

You always had this big dislike for chakka, my mother said. You didn't like the smell. One day you came into the kitchen, you were a small pengkutty only, and took my big cleaver outside, and Monchayan found you, you said to him you were going to cut down every chakka tree. You said, Every single one.

I laughed while feeling a cold pale vine creep around my ribs. I don't have a memory of that, I said in our language.

Sneha, my father called from higher up on the riverbank, look here. Sneha! Ividey va.

He was brandishing something in his hand, pointing to a copse of young trees, shorter than him. As I moved closer I realized what he held—the dry brown bean pods, their contents rattling. Widely I smiled, in uncomplicated and childish delight, and reached out my hand.

The deep crimson seeds knocked into my palm.

We called them manjadi kuru or gulgangi mar, depending on which side of the family was talking. Children love the look of them, the red and beautiful beads scattered across the ground. I used to collect them in an Amul jam jar.

Very nice, I said, fingering the small crimson spheres. Lovely.

My father appeared to search my face for something more. Some kind of recognition. You don't remember? he asked, gesturing toward the copse of manjadi trees.

Remember what, Papa?

I myself had forgotten, he said, until seeing you and Mummy down there, holding hands. You and some friend and Mummy came here, you were maybe six. You girls both said you were going to plant this manjadi kuru you had been collecting. We told you spread out the seeds, don't put them so close. And you said okay, and still you planted them this way. Stubborn. Look—he gestured upward to the thicket of pod-laden trees—what you planted, so many years ago.

I reached out, squeezed a greenwood branch. The trees were spreading, riotous with oval leaves, rustling in the wind. Truthfully I had no recollection of the story he'd related. Most often when I considered my childhood, a miasma of confused sensation and blurred events rose in me. I looked at the trees, some of them my height, and thought, You are here because I was here, because I made a choice that I barely considered.

How strange, was all I could think to say.

I dropped to my haunches, began to pick the seeds that peppered the uneven ground. My mother took a few sprigs of leaves to make a decoction for my grandmother's digestive problems.

On the long walk back home, she and I periodically flung a bright red manjadi kuru along the roadside, or into a decaying field of rice, leaving it to chance and nature, the question of what would grow.

Midway through my trip, after a morning sunshower, I found my father in a red cotton lungi on the veranda, watching Bincy's form retreating to our gate.

Upon waking I'd oiled my hair and begun to organize the pile of my warped and dusty college books, until I saw that this was leaving greased Parachute fingerprints on every cover. Papa offered me a plantain fritter from a steel tin that once held Danish butter cookies.

Want chaiya also? he asked. When I nodded, he tossed his head and said, Then go in the kitchen.

My father and I are alike: tall and reedy, loyal to those we love, broken by the hint of failure, alternating soft and ornery.

Eee Bincy aunty, I said, sitting down in a plastic folding chair.

Mmm.

Why she's coming here?

Papa shook his head. Her son is wanting to rent the empty flat, he said with a shrug. At least that is what she said. Might have been a serious inquiry, might have been one big purana so she can peer at you. At us. Who knows with these people. She was asking where you were. Mummy didn't want to say sleeping.

I wasn't sleeping, keto. And she's already peered at me. Right when I came only she called me a madama.

My father snorted. If the mundu fits, he said, not unkindly.

You also think I am? A madama? My question crouched somewhere between curiosity and hurt.

Don't ask me such things. Bincy is of course little jealous. Wants to send her mol to Gulf or USA. Mol is just now studying computer science. It may work out. Or it may not. I told this lady, No guarantees, over there. Wheel of fortune, some people are on top and that pulls other people below. You cannot count where on the wheel you will be.

A tremor of pain flickered over his face, quick and quiet as a thottavaadi's wilt. This was the closest we had ever come to speaking near the knock on the door, the prison cell, the signing away the right to live in the same country as his daughter. The fact that I, in the eyes of the world, was the successful one, not him. Was his single investment that had not foundered. This was the closest we could go. My family is a geode of silences. You would need a hammer to smash it open.

He hitched up a smile. How's work? Engené onde? Generally happy with you they are?

He had asked this question before, on my first day back. This much I knew: he would ask it of me reflexively throughout my stay.

I nodded tightly. Walling my mind off against what had happened to Thom, about Peter possibly only paying me many weeks from now. They're giving me more responsibilities, I said. Project deliverables.

Adhe sheri. Very good. Very good. Make us proud, keto?

We'll see.

This Peter, he's said anything yet about sponsoring you?

No, Papa. You will be the first person I call if he does.

Good, okay. Godwilling it will work out well. You just keep doing a good job for him. I'll say a prayer. Thankfully you have the authorization for now.

You are okay for money, mollé?

It was my mother who asked this. She had come out to the veranda bearing two steel cups of tea. Soon she would leave for work at the local clinic. Part-time. Paid peanuts.

Yesofcourse, I said, sitting straighter. How about here?

Things are little tough, Papa said, looking off into the sopping green leaves of the rhododendrons, picking up his chipped cup from where it was being mobbed by ants. But godwilling we are okay. Don't send anything. Enjoy a little. I think you must be working overtime. Remember the other important things in life.

My mother nodded, watching us.

Don't end up like me, he added with an attempt at an ironic smile, his large eyes narrowed and unable to meet mine, and in that moment I thought my heart would fissure, shatter outward like a dropped clock.

D2

As they went to sleep, I went to the computer. Read my unanswered missives to Thom once more, my chest filling with heat and pain. Enough, I said under my breath, but I said it in my first language, even though nobody was around to hear or care. Madi. Enough with this sniveling. Just as romantic love faded or fractured, so too could friendship end.

But nobody consoles you after a rupture with a beloved friend. There are few movies ideal for watching while your tears salt pints of ice cream, no articles in women's magazines that you can skim at the hairdresser's. You have only the ache. No script to accompany it. No ritual to give it shape.

As we'd chopped onions for dinner, my mother had asked me with a great abruptness if I was unhappy because of a friend. By which she meant a boy.

I shrugged, then jerked my head into a fraction of a nod. It was not untrue.

Don't get involved in any silly business, keto, my mother said.

In the dark quiet of the sleeping house I looked at Marina's social media. For the first time it saddened me that there were so few pictures of us that announced who we were to each other. I found myself longing for the opposite of what I usually desired—to be legible, visible together to the world.

I would send her a really nice email, I decided, beginning to type. It would be long and winning and poetic, not my usual staccato questioning. I would reminisce about our happy moments together, our *silly business*, check on how she was healing from her extraction. Ask after the hospital bill. I would tell her about this land I came from. How the air felt, warm and velvet wet. How I spent my hours—necessarily sidestepping in my writing the existence of the two people who shaped them. I would tell her the lessons of this place. To bring water up from a well, you pull the rope hand over hand, as though you and the well are dancing a coy dance of seduction. To chop many red onions fast you need a very sharp cleaver and to slice down the onion half as though you are marking five-degree intervals on a protractor. To feel powerful, touch a thottavaadi, watch it shrivel and collapse at your finger's brush. To know the limits of power, walk by it again in twenty minutes, when it is revived, standing as tall as if you were never born.

Once I could barely hold my eyes open, I switched off the CPU. Made my way down the dark passage.

A guest bedroom, they called it, though there was shared understanding that this was not a construction for the present, but an investment in how my future husband's family would see them. Three-BHKs are the known domain of the middle class. They signal you have arrived, that you have enough to consider trivialities like where visitors lay their behinds to sleep. I came back wishing to be thought of as a guest, and commandeered the bedroom afforded me. No one offered it up. This was taken by all as proof of my Americanness, this imperial grab for space, and was, like most everything else visibly wrong about me, tolerated in mute sorrow.

To aunties' and great-uncles' houses we went, borrowing one uncle's car, bumping down hours of potholed road. We sat on veranda after veranda, drinking tea, refusing appams, eating the appams that were foisted upon us regardless. I was asked about my fancy job and teased about marriage and my hair, which had in the humidity turned into a coarse halo of fuzz. My mother combed it with force and rancor each time we exited the car.

It sounds sweeter than you're making it seem, Tig wrote back to me. Hospitality and investment in each other, going to people's homes, not just restaurants. That's the shit that builds community, you know.

Well, I replied, I am not all that idealistic about community.

After a day of drive-by stops followed by a visitation from an old school friend of Papa's, I lost all aptitude for interaction. My mother found me hiding in the guest bedroom, examining the damp heap of books from my early college years. *The Norton Anthology of American Literature. Gardner's Art through the Ages. Interpreter of Maladies.*

Avan poi, my mother said with a hint of reproach. He asked to pass on a goodbye wish to you, keto.

I grunted at this, stuck my nose in an old Goethe novel to get rid of her.

What is it you are reading? my mother asked, moving closer to me.

I flipped it closed. A glossy white cover, curlicuing red font. A remnant of one of the few classes Thom and I had not been in together: The Bildungsroman through the Ages.

Wilhelm Meister's Apprenticeship, I said out loud.

Good?

You want to study it now? I asked sardonically.

Her eyes flashed. I did not mean to put her down. What I wished for was to be left alone.

Still, in this moment, our eyes locking, I was reminded of our respective places in the world, the world she had brought me into—could, as she had reminded me during my adolescent rages, take me smoothly out of. This was my mother. My mother who loved me.

Switching into contrite obedience, I told her: Yes. Strange and long but good. The novel tells the story of Wilhelm Meister, a boy who wants to be an actor and an artist. His parents want him to be a sensible businessman, marry a woman appropriate to his station. But he doesn't want all that. He leaves to find his place in the world and joins a traveling theater crew.

My mother appeared to be listening more carefully than usual. It occurred to me that this conversation might be driven less by her desire to discuss Goethe—my mother tended toward Dan Brown and Chetan Bhagat; her most-read volume was a Christian devotional for nurses—than by her need to wear a spot of the geode thin enough to break through, say what she wanted to say. Something in me wished to put off her speaking for as long as possible, and I kept on.

There are some parts where it feels like it is just blabbing on forever, I continued, but this book created the idea—I suppose the Western idea—of youth. Before this, you were a child just until, fata-fat, you were grown up. Wilhelm Meister has a period of freedom in between. He gets to have this time. Time to become himself. Learn what it is he wants.

In a moment of what felt like boldness, a new kind of sharing of my actual thoughts, I added, This cycle, you know, of pressures, then rebellion, then freedom, and then choosing the traditional path of one's own choice, that is how we all understand, now, what it means to be young.

My mother dusted the top of the sewing machine, appearing to digest all this.

Tomorrow we are going to our cemetery, she informed me abruptly. It is Vellya Appachan's orma. We can stop by Monchayan's grave. You haven't seen it even.

The words darted away from me, fleeing their home in terror.

Mummy, I'm not going.

She appeared not to hear me. After that we will go back with Lalitha-mai to her house. Mol— And here her face opened into an expression I never saw, somewhere between shy and eager. She continued, I wanted to say, not now but maybe in the next two years, will be the right time to . . . find you someone. Lalitha is more well-connected than your papa and me, and also very smart and sensitive about these matches. The boy she chose for Shebin's daughter was so sweet, and they are very happy now. So I want her to have a good impression of you. Please comb your hair and wear something proper, okay?

I don't *want to go*.

Mol.

If Lalithamai wants so badly to get me married in two years she can come here and we can talk about it then, not in a graveyard slipping on moss. Madi! Why are we always running after dead people, carrying them on our heads? Let them be dead, I say.

Ente mol, she said, her voice full of danger and love. She said it again in our language: my daughter. Those two words in my mother's mouth: a branding iron.

We are going, she continued, let us have an end to this talking back, okay? Don't you make me call your father in here—

Listen, woman, someday I will come to *your* grave and do orma and all. But that is it.

Her slap popped my ear. Hand cradling my face, I bared teeth back at her. I was Susan after the conference chair had been thrown. Widely I smiled.

He was not good to me, I said, as calmly as I could manage, since some form of explanation seemed required if I was to ever be left in peace again. He was not. Monchayan, I mean.

As I said his name I remembered his smell. Yardley's talc and cigarette smoke, chickpea flour soap and vodka. His finger sliding into my underwear like a fat grub.

I don't want to go see anything of his with you, I said quietly. I don't want to say falthoo prayers for his soul. I suspect I know where his soul is. *Fat* lot of good your prayers will do there.

My mother appeared at a loss for words, searching my face for meaning. Not good to you, she repeated.

I said it the only way I knew how to in the world I come from. Voice husky with, flattened by, humiliation.

He—troubled me, I said. For years.

My mother's eyes bulged. She opened her mouth, then closed it. A dying fish.

When she spoke it was whisper-quiet, terror-scorched.

What are you saying, Sneha? *How* can you tell this, now?

It honestly doesn't matter, I said coldly. It is not some big thing I am always thinking about. I just want to tell you. Your brother was a— useless pervert, I am not going to see him in the cemetery.

How can you say this, after all this time? What am I supposed to do? How could you keep this from us?

I am not going anywhere tomorrow, was all I was capable of saying, tears finally storming their way into my eyes, plopping in wrinkly sunbursts onto the opening pages of *Wilhelm Meister*.

And to my great shock they acquiesced. Left me behind. I sat with my grandparents, walked in the small yard amid the breadfruit trees, touched the well's slippery moss, ate at the plastic-covered table alone. After they came back my mother seemed frozen, quiet. Her eyes red. She stepped around me, spoke to me gingerly, as though I were some great glass sculpture sitting in her house.

The day before my flight Papa said he was going to drop off some slabs of teak at the Mar Thoma church. Asked if I wanted to come.

During his interminable conversation with some achchan or the other, I, sweating in the borrowed car, finally unable to resist, walked out and alone into the cemetery.

Where I am from, bodies are buried above the ground, encased in concrete. The earth too wet and uncertain to allow for anything else. Alone I wended my way past the crypts of Eapens and Pillais and Mathews and Kuruvillas.

SAMUEL J. MATHAN

LOVING SON AND BROTHER

1968–2013

BLESSED ARE THE PURE IN HEART,

FOR THEY SHALL SEE GOD.

MATTHEW 5:8

What ruined me, standing before his stone, was feeling, in place of the sweet creamy hatred I hoped to savor like soft-serve, a terrifying dissolve into pity. For this small cockroach of a man, who had never found a woman he could convince to marry him, who was so alone in the world that he chose a child. From pity my heart moved, sliding in a neatly fluid mass like egg white, to a terrible, shamed love. This despite every attempt at rescuing the calmly kinked malice that had protected me so well for so many years.

And the love, the feeling of missing Monchayan, it was too much, too much to bear, it nauseated me, it left me wishing to set fire to this entire land, to vanish and teleport to the cold wide country I was trying to force to accommodate me, become my home, away from *mess*, from *blood*, from *entanglement*, from every cascading unfreedom that had marked my small stupid life.

With all my strength I spat upon Samuel J. Mathan's grave.

My saliva lay, white froth on the concrete's grain. Again I hawked. Here was one more thing I could never speak of. A thing relegated to the blue / green / A / B breach of my twinned lives.

The foam on the beige slab made me think of hydrocodone, took my mind to KJ. To go through life can be so painful. Like being born or hatched, your body extruded into the screaming world. Who could fault KJ for choosing what she chose to blunt things? Truly I understood the appeal.

Three final times I spat before turning on my heel and walking back to the car, no longer caring if I was seen: thoo! thoo! thoo!

As the cold Wisconsin air with its dandruff of ice coated me, a panic soured my mouth. It was as if I had come off the wrong flight, landed in the wrong place.

You belong elsewhere, the cells of my body appeared to chorus as my belly clenched. You come from a place that is not here, a hot place with red soil, where everything bursts with life.

Goodbye, mollé, my mother had said, hugging me painfully tight. Come home again soon. I had only nodded, not trusting myself with speech.

Despite some degree of aversion to self-pity, I had longed, walking across the blue-carpeted airport, watching hordes of cheerful-seeming people greeting loved ones with unfeigned warmth, to have been born a slightly different person. Subtract my uncle from my life. Subtract my father's deportation. Subtract the coldness and dislocation that appeared to run through my personality like electrical wiring ran through a house. All this, the very facts of who I was, could be different. I could be a person refigured: warm, charming, loving, loved.

Outside, I walked along the row of cars, shivering, squinting.

Hey, world traveler, a voice called.

Reaching for Marina's face with both hands, from the passenger seat of the Kia Soul, I kissed her with an abandon that surprised each of us.

To return to the new place makes it less new, moves it something closer to comfort, to safety.

I'll be done with work by nine, but you'll probably be exhausted after that flight. I'll drop you off at yours and maybe we can do dinner tomorrow? I've got six weeks before Shaka and I go on our intensive tour, Marina said, coolly whipping through traffic, her small fingers interlocked with mine. I'll be gone for a long time. I'd love to see you lots before then.

There was a pause, and then she said, a little timorously, I missed you.

I missed you too, I said, squeezing her hand, looking into the horizon's line.

From Tig I learned that Thom was doing poorly. He had been taking his feelings out on Isabel, and Isabel, who knew her worth in the larger scheme of the world, had tearfully demanded a relationship break and had a friend drive her home to Minnesota. In the wake of this, and at Tig's urging, he had been to see a psychiatrist. This person gave him pills to make him less desperate and sad, to still the eddies of panic that pulled him into their vortices. So far he'd scored one interview with a company that sold paper goods. They gave the gig, an entry-level position, to somebody with seven years of experience. Four hundred people had applied.

I heard all this from Tig, since Thom would not speak to me. From the moment he had walked out with his box of things from the client, he had been putting on a play. A performance where I had been subtracted from existence, where he did not know my name. This hurt me to a degree I did not realize was possible.

He'll come around, Amit wrote to me. It must be painful for him. To know he failed at something and you didn't.

It's not like that, I typed hotly back. The fact was that Thom understood that I'd always, somehow, had the upper hand between the two of us. Had been better suited to performing obeisance to our overlords, to signaling eager competence, playing the part of the underling rock star who was so grateful to be allowed in the fluorescent corporate board-room, so *honored* to get to be there. And that performance, the dance of the bought-in underling, had been more important, ultimately, than who actually made the mistakes, who actually delivered on the project parts. In Thom's view, our loyalty had not, in fact, survived capitalism. He was angry and struggling and mired in his own sense of shame, a shame he did not deserve to feel. I wrote this out. My throat sore. Then changed my mind, pressed down on the small x, disappearing my reply.

Two weeks before my twenty-third birthday, at drinks after the driving lesson she gave me, Antigone and I had our first real fight.

It's time for you to learn, was the pronouncement handed down. I want you to have this freedom, she said. To not be dependent or afraid.

This was the heart of Antigone's burgeoning religion, a set of guiding beliefs I was watching form and cohere in our time together. A newborn star. The core of what I want my life's work to be, Tig had said to me on the way over to the Miller Park parking lot for my lesson.

I want everyone to be free, she continued. Free from money. Free from gender. Free from debt.

Diana had shorn Tig's hair close to the scalp. Over this, a red woolen hat with a tiny bobble on the end. I wanted to pet it, pull it tighter over Tig's small ears.

Nobody wants anyone to have more freedom than them, I said. Maybe some very good people will settle for: as much.

We're taught that everything is finite and zero sum, Tig said. Money, food, houses, freedom. Zero sum when it ain't need to be. The whole thing is that some things multiply. Create feedback loops. Like love and honesty. Like generosity. Creates more of the thing itself.

I was silent, considering this. Some of it I agreed with in principle. But it grated slightly to hear Tig say this so soon after I had scrambled to PayPal $150 across continents. I did not regret this, don't mistake me. To help Tig, who had supported and loved me through so much, this had not generally felt like some great burden. But now I was actually worried about my cash flow. The client had not paid Peter, which meant he had not paid me, and I did not know when that would change. The finiteness of my own money was wearing on me, grinding me down like glass under highway traffic.

Tig took the on-ramp and continued: There's enough. The lie of the world is telling you there is not enough. The government can print more money, can buy fewer tanks. We could build houses and share land and not be afraid of eviction marshals showing up at six in the morn. We could organize our lives a different way.

What did you mean about like, free from gender, what you said before, I asked, a cold feeling snaking around my belly.

Tig merged lanes, dreamily said, I don't know. Only thought about it recently, talking to Diana. She's encouraged me to work through it. Fact is, I used to feel like a woman, but now I do less and less. I was drunk last weekend and we were watching a galaxy on TV and I thought, I feel more like a galaxy forming than a woman. I don't know though, I think about if I weren't a woman, if that would mean I was less in solidarity with a feminist struggle. That matters to me. It matters to me a little that I have that category in common with my comrades like you. But I think I still would anyway.

Okay, I said, a nameless sorrow settling in me. I thought things useless to say out loud. What did it mean to be a woman? What did it mean to be a dyke? If I felt more like a crow scavenging in the dustbin than a woman, what should that mean for how the world saw me?

Tig, I noticed, was looking at me nervously. I remembered, now, writing scornful emails about Emily, Amit's paramour.

What? I said.

I am going to start going by *they* in the future, not *she*, Tig explained. But I really don't mind if the people who have known me the longest, the people who get me and see me at an elemental level, especially other femmes, call me something different. You totally can still say *she*. Always can. It won't change anything for you, I promise.

I felt very slightly like crying. Listen, I said, trying for a casualness, I may not understand everything to do with this—

Tig nodded, seemed about to interrupt. I pushed on, trying to find the words.

But like, respect is free, I said. Costs me nothing to call you what you want to be called, like maybe I'll forget, but I love you. Generally our friendship is not work, whatever you may say, but an ongoing pleasure, pretty much any day. If this is what you want, if you feel like a galaxy or a rocket ship or an asteroid versus a lady, that's fine, yo. I can do a bit of work and call you what-the-hell-ever you want to be called.

Tig seemed surprised. Appeared greatly relieved, and this hurt even as it was understandable. Squeezed my knee, said, Okay, time for your lesson. Watch out, streets. She's comin': vroom vroom.

After, we went to Trocadero. At first I had demurred, but Tig insisted, wanted to celebrate me. Me driving, me coming back from India. The exhilaration of doing donuts, speeding up and down the length of the Miller Park lot. You own the car, Tig had said firmly. It doesn't own you. You a free bitch. Slam that pedal *down*.

When we were about to be seated, Tig added, Can you get me? All the cash I have left till payday is five dollars.

Sure, I said, beads of sweat beginning to gather at my hairline. I asked the server for the soup. With a luxuriant smile Tig ordered a Duvel and a chicken piccata. I glanced at the menu.

A Duvel was the most expensive beer Trocadero even carried. Nine dollars. The chicken piccata was eighteen. And no doubt Tig would tip generously. With my money.

What's wrong, Tig asked, as my face reddened.

Nothing, I said.

We ate in near silence.

You have to tell me what's up with you. You're making me anxious.

I love you, but sometimes I think you think I'm comprised of cold cash, I said.

Tig recoiled. You certainly make a lot more money than me, I just figured you were okay—

First of all that's not really true. You just hear the title consultant and think I'm flush. It doesn't matter, I feel bad for caring—

But you do. So what's changed?

Let's drop it.

No.

You *can't* make me do this, I burst out. My voice suddenly a yell, echoing around Trocadero's tile and glass. I'm so *glad* you feel so *free*; well, someone is always paying for someone else's freedom! You can't drag me here and therapize me for feeling stressed about how I spend *my own money*, and make *your expensive tastes* my problem! You can't! This is absolute rank cow shit!

Heads swiveled around to us. Tig's eyes bored into me.

In a voice like ice, they said, I see, and continued eating. The chicken was browned and oily. They speared it with a glinty fork, chewed carefully, all the while looking at me.

I want to go home, I said. I'll pay for this.

You don't have to. I'll put it on my credit card.

You're in fucking credit card debt. Come on. It's fine. I just want to go home. Have a splitting headache.

Not another word was said until we were driving toward the Hill. Tig turned down the volume on Robyn and burst out, You know all my business, don't you? And think it's entirely okay to not be sharing yours?

What the fuck do you want me to say?

What is going on with you would be a start! You want to wait until things are very wrong before you unburden yourself, want to blow off steam and feelings being entirely out of pocket, being a rude ass to me in our favorite restaurant, acting like some benefits administrator making sure I ain't buying frozen lobster with my EBT card, uh-huh, okay, be my goddamn guest, bitch! But recognize it as a choice!

Snowbanks whizzed by us.

I massaged my temples.

I'm sorry, I finally said. I am—quite—stressed about money. I haven't been paid since December.

What?

Freakin' Peter's going to get me the money I'm owed when the client pays him, which will happen at the end of the project. It's just stressful. The prospect of living off of savings for so long. I—I—I'm pretty low on cash.

Antigone's anger appeared momentarily blunted. Fuck. Wow. I am sorry he is treating you this way. Babe. You *have* to be fucking honest, Tig said, their jaw set tight. Be *honest* in your relationships. You have to be honest with me, your *best friend*. Otherwise you're just skating on ice, and one day you'll fall through.

'S not that easy, I said weakly. My skull was pulsing, my vision beginning to blur as we pulled onto my street.

Can you like apply for unemployment?

I felt a tear leak from my left eye, slip down my neck.

I'm an immigrant, no. Besides, I am technically employed? I don't know how any of this works. But if I ever get to apply for becoming a citizen, they'll ask if you ever committed crimes or if you ever took government benefits. Not great incentive to—

Shhhh. Your eyes are so damn red. You need to rest.

I feel quite bad, I said. I did.

Tig took me upstairs, put blankets over me. Everything felt dark and vaporous. They made me drink a mug of microwaved water, swallow a Tylenol. A cold damp washcloth on my head.

Tig's weight next to me. A hand smoothing the blanket on my back.

In the throes of a painful, fitful sleep, I cried out, then whispered for my mother.

She's not here, baby, Tig said, voice very soft in the dark. But I am. Shh. Go back to sleep. I'm here.

On the day of my birthday my heat went out again. The apartment was the inside of a freezer. Wrapped in blankets, I crouched by the space heater and called Yellow Cab. Went down to the basement with a box of matches and tried to see if it was the pilot light. It did not seem to be. My fingertips were burning. Snow on the ground. The cabdriver asking where I was from, meaning originally. My insides felt sour and red. At work I ducked into the copy room when I saw Susan bearing down the hallway.

My parents wished me.

You were so beautiful when you were born, my mother wrote on WhatsApp, attaching a picture of me that most resembled a large naked mole rat.

So sweet and pure, the message continued. We gave you your name because of your eyes. So wide open, full of love.

I stared at this for a long minute. Sent it to delete.

What plans do you have, birthday bitch, Tig texted me, and I responded with a picture of Kanye shrugging. Thom had not wished me. He was still ignoring my texts. He had still not found a job.

Come meet me for a toast to the next year. Von Trier, nineish.

Okay. Love you.

Love you.

As I wrapped up the day's work, Marina asked if she could call me.

What's up, pretty lady? I asked, hopping into a focus room, pressing the cool metal tile to my ear.

Marina's voice: liquid smoke and baby food. Hello, hello, happy birthday beauty, surprise, I'm in your parking lot. Here to take you out for dinner.

Oh my gosh. What! Thank you. That's so kind—

But?

Oh, um, there's no but, really.

There's something! Don't tell me you have to work late.

No, no I don't. I told Antigone I would meet her, uh, meet them, for drinks at Von Trier. At nine. I didn't know you had plans for me—

On the other end of the phone, a silence.

I see. Well, I can happily drop you off. Or I could come.

Oh?

Unless you don't want me to meet your friend—

No! I don't know why I didn't think of that, I said, tracing over the glass door's brushed steel frame nervously. That'll be nice. I'll just check with Tig. But it should be nice. It should be good. Okay! Grabbing my coat and running out to you! Ahhhh!

Marina had dyed her hair. A pale glassy green. A green shot through with blue, which is to say, maybe, with itself. It startled me. Surprise, she said, laughing. You're hot, I said. She took me to Buckley's. Many times we'd driven by it. You're ordering the agnolotti and that's final, she told me. It is *godly*.

Her eyes were starry, her energy high.

Buckley's was beautiful. Blue-gray paint, mirrors everywhere, palm fronds and white marble. Everyone there unreasonably attractive. I'd dressed for work in an inky blazer, a lilac oxford shirt underneath. Worried out loud that I looked square. Marina linked her fingers through mine. Squeezed.

Go to the bathroom, she said, and take your shirt off.

My breath came faster.

What do you mean, I asked.

Take off your button-down and put it in your bag. Listen to this L.A. girl, okay? Okay, good, you're wearing your black bra. It's so good. That and your blazer. It's all the look you need. A birthday look. Do it.

I like when you boss me about, I said. My pulse drumming. Obediently, I got up, my fingers already touching the shirt's buttons: round and pearlescent, small and hard.

We had time to kill; we chose to kill it in the car. Over in an empty parking lot by the brewery on Commerce. The passenger seat of the Kia Soul swung as far back as it could go. Marina on her knees, tonguing me. Her fingers reaching up, twitching my nipples beneath the bra's lace.

Get up here, I said, pulling her onto my lap. Her breath smelled of sweet wine. The T-shirt she was wearing under the Zara bomber was thinly soft, a heathered gray; quickly I dispensed with it. Marina purred with pleasure as I nuzzled her tight chest. Her skin felt like her leather jacket—oiled and soft and hot.

Will you do what I need? I asked, holding her hips, looking up at her.

Yes.

I touched the Kia Soul's gear stick. Get naked, I said. Then put your mouth on this.

A look of uncertainty flashed across her face. Still, she complied. Contorting her torso to stay perched on me. Her generous lower lip and its slender tremulous companion, pink shot through with brown. Her mouth, parting.

Pleasure this, I said, taking in the bemused look in her eyes, feeling the vague gathering mists of foolishness—and of course, real wild desire is braided tightly with foolishness, with all that is awkward and stilted. I had to work against this. To safeguard the moment, which still felt savable, felt swollen with blood and heat.

Pleasure it, I said, as if it were my cock.

Her eyes closed. Air whistled through her nostrils.

When she worked the way she did now, you could see the intelligence compressed taut within her body, her ability to form line, to engage muscles I barely knew existed in order to keep herself aloft. With a great gentle decisiveness I hooked my fingers into her. Two, then three. Her shoulders quivered. It was as though all the air in the car had turned to oil.

The noise of her sucking. It made me an animal. Aggressively, inexorably I began to rock my hand back and forth, motioning with my fingers as if to say, Come here, come here. Minutes upon minutes of this; both of us sweating in Milwaukee winter, her head bobbing in a perfect obedience. In that moment I wished I could slide my whole hand into her silky cunt. I did not want to hurt her. With my thumb I pressed against her small neat asshole, not entering, only vibrating it slightly, and this was what undid her. Marina came. With a long shiver and howl, a cry that rose in power and volume until I covered her mouth with my sweaty hand.

She let out a gasping laugh.

Clutched at me, shivering. Nestled into my neck. Her body shaking. It was then I felt the first punch of a nameless feeling: warm, redly dark, fluid as blood itself.

Marina kissed me closed-mouthed. She pulled away. Stared into my eyes.

I will do what you need, she said, and I felt the punch again.

It was when she was working me that I noticed the wine bottle.

Barefoot, it was, the label white and green. Half-full. Corked. Nestled by the brake. I was too occupied with her tongue, soft as Jell-O, flicking like a lizard's. Closing my eyes, I gave myself over to this. Much later the image would jam in my mind, paper fed badly through the printer, calling attention to itself.

12

Through the door of the smoke-hazy Von Trier patio we walked in. Orange-glowing heaters crowded the ceiling.

Surprise, Tig said, and a chorus of voices cried out: Happy birthday!

I looked around in pure astonishment. Thom's roommates, Danny the gymnast, Diana. Thom. *Thom.* Looking slightly fearful, face closed like a door, but still, here. At a bar-top table a plastic packet of grocery-store cupcakes. What a sweet thing. What a sweet thing.

From the car on we had held hands, but a second before I swung the door open Marina had let her fingers go slack. Her deference to my shyness about us. I felt a small bolt of sorrow at this, and a grudging respect for her sensitivity.

Instantly Tig bore down on me. I flung my arms around my best friend's neck.

Thom was next, though less demonstrative. Happy birthday, my dude, he said with his easy smile on a leash, a nod substituted for a hug. It was a prophylactic, this demeanor, against difficult conversation or emotion. His eyes widened slightly as he took in the bra-and-blazer outfit.

I watched Tig watch Marina. Tig looked at me, cocked an eyebrow like a gun. In the display window of Y-Not, my friend had told me, Go get your girl. And they had been right.

Hey, I said, smiling around at the birthday party I had not known was waiting for me, the one I'd never before had. My heart singing a big loud song.

God, I said. Y'all are amazing. Wait, I need to introduce you.

I put an arm out, pulled her gently to me. The flicker of warmed surprise, delight, relief across her small sharp face told me all I needed to know. Even as it cut me.

To my gathered friends I said in a single breath, Hey all, this is Marina, my girlfriend.

For a time I was so happy that my own life appeared unreal, calling to mind phone pictures filtered to absurd saturation and luminosity, where dour midwestern skies were transformed to electric blue and everyone's teeth blinded. So happy I was capable of setting on ice, for a period, any worries about work or cash flow or the consequences of my lies.

The night of my birthday, Marina had asked to go home. To my place. Around my friends she had been funny, loud, a lightning conversationalist. Even Tig had seemed to warm to her. We can go to mine, but the heat has stopped working, I said baldly. Then added, We can make do with blankets, though. On Marina's face surfaced an expression of pure confusion. Stay at my place until you get it fixed, she said, like it was the most obvious thing. Let's go by, she said, and you can pack up a bag.

Each morning I woke up before her and made chaiya for the two of us. I steeped inji and one peppercorn and two cardamom pods in boiling water, answering 6 a.m. emails from Susan from my phone in the meantime. Added three tea bags of black tea, tied them to the saucepan's handle. Heated milk in the microwave, winced at its loud beeping. I spooned in manuka honey from a large glass jar. By her side of the bed I'd set the cup and climb back into the covers to wake her.

She taught me how to make margaritas from scratch, with tequila she had infused with serrano peppers. I would look over the top of my book, watching her set choreo before her evening class, playing YouTube videos of Kate Jablonski or Batsheva Dance for inspiration. Some days she drove me to work, and the days she didn't, I played like I was taking the bus, but walked downstairs and hailed a yellow cab on Water Street. Once each week Tig and I would go to BelAir for tacos, spend the wait drinking Rhinelanders down the street. Once Marina and I became official, Tig stopped inviting Diana to Taco Tuesday, announcing it was reserved for Friend Time.

A little strange, isn't it, Tig said, munching on carne asada, that we both ended up with whitegirls.

I shrugged. I haven't *ended up* with anyone, I said reflexively. I'm twenty-three. Basically still an infant. It's never too late, remember, it's never the end.

Ayyyy, Tig said, clapping the air like it was a stripper derriere. Then added, smiling, I think you want to hoe more than your heart is in the hoeing.

I like you so much, Marina told me after bowls of mazemen ramen at Tochi in Shorewood, which abutted a bourgeois plant store. The March air smelled like sap and malt. I was touching the glossy leaves of a ficus tree, thinking about my apartment, which I had once taken such care of, had bought leaner mirrors and tufted sofas and World Market rugs for. I had let Amy take this from me. Hadn't been back in weeks.

It's quite mutual, I said softly. I bought her an air plant in a little glass bulb. Fishing wire to hang it in front of her window.

Air plants are great, the salesgirl said to me, appearing to size me up. Need very little care.

Marina's hair was shedding and splitting—brittle jade strands on the couch, strewing her soft pillows. Take a break from dyeing it, na, I said.

She laughed. You wouldn't recognize me, she said. Would kill my brand dead.

You're a person, I said. Not a brand.

I microwaved three spoons of coconut oil from her pantry in a little bowl, added a pinch of red chilli powder to it. Standing behind her at the sink, I massaged the oil into her scalp, let it coat her strands. Her eyes closed, her breathing softened. As I rubbed the crown of her head with my fingertips I watched the white hairs on her thin arms stand up like soldiers.

All this while the business of managing change dragged on interminably, all this while my savings dwindled. Surreptitiously I applied each week for other jobs. Monster.com. Indeed.com. On LinkedIn, but carefully, lest Peter realize something. Mostly, as Thom had found, there were simply no jobs, certainly no good ones. I applied to work weekends at Wolf Peach and LuLu, jobs that my parents would have been upset about—they had not brought me to America, lost everything, left me behind, for me to work in shops or eateries. No calls back. Amy wrote me tersely for every bill that came in—water, electric, gas, Internet. When I considered asking her again to fix the heat I broke out in a sweat. It seemed easier to wait it out, hold on until it was no longer cold.

The cab rides wore a hole in my wallet. I was unable to stop taking them.

The tenants in my family's rental had moved out months ago, and no one appeared to be on the horizon to replace them. Walking some tightrope between pride and bravado, I sent my parents $1,800 at the end of March, another $50 claimed for the wire transfer fee. This would last them a good few months. It's okay, I muttered, taking deep breaths to calm myself, looking at the amount left in my accounts. Less than two thousand dollars, all together. That was still a good amount of money. Peter would pay me. He had said he would pay me.

Marina and I went to the Pakistani market. I bought methi and sambar powder. A creeping pepper vine of anxiety brushed against me every time I moved my hand toward hers. We went down the street for dinner to Anmol. The restaurant was deserted apart from one family—brown, a son and father in identical rimless glasses, the mother in cardigan and sari. Marina ordered chicken nihari. I asked for the goat biriyani and she wrinkled her nose. The servers never looked at her, only spoke to me. It was the opposite of moving through the world outside Anmol, where she would always be noticed first, be catered to.

We were midway through the meal when the woman in the cardigan came over.

Marina had been recounting a joke that Jenny Shin told on their first date. It went, What's more dangerous than running with scissors?

The answer is, Scissoring with the runs.

I groaned loudly.

Excuse me, the woman said from behind me.

Her sari was pale chiffon with an embroidered border. Her blouse looked polyester, small sweat stains under its overtight armpits. She spoke only to me; Marina might as well not have existed.

Please give your father's number, the woman said.

Fright and confusion sawed through me, dusting everything around. Had she overheard us being vulgar? Was she calling to complain?

Had she seen the two of us walking in holding hands and determined she must tell another Indian parent—Bhai sahib, I am sorry but your daughter is a deviant, is going around with these blond-blond girls, going around lesbianing!

I am sorry, aunty, why? I replied.

The woman seemed bemused at my recalcitrance, gentle as it was. Again she said, I would like your father's number, please.

Marina appeared frozen, taking everything in.

Could you tell me why? I asked. Attempting to infuse my voice with firmness.

Because I would like to speak to him, the cardiganed lady said with great dignity and severity.

My heart began to sprint. No, I said. I can't, I am sorry.

The aunty appeared to falter.

You are unmarried, no? she asked me. I would like to talk to your father, please. She gestured back toward her table and continued, a pleading note to her voice, We think you are quite pretty. We would like to make family inquiries.

In total shock I glanced back at the table. The son, her slight bespectacled boy, was bright maroon in the face. Hanging his head down, an unwatered plant.

I'm sorry, Marina said—and I almost clapped my hand over her mouth, terrified she would say something like, she's my girlfriend, she's gay, take a hike.

I'm sorry for cutting in, Marina said, fire in her eyes. But her father is dead.

I let out a great, shuddering exhale. Marina continued, eyes boring into the sari'd aunty, who had put her hand to her heart.

Yeah, so she cannot give you his number, right? And she has already said no. Please enjoy your dinner. Thank you!

I can't believe it, Marina said, laughing as we got into the Kia Soul. So wild, the whole thing. Just like, Oh hi, I'm a total stranger, give me your father's number so I can get my loser son a wife! Like you would have no preference in the matter—

In my guts I felt a terrible churning shame, the sensation that I had backed myself into a corner, barking dogs bounding ever closer. Yes, I wanted to say, that's all very nice, but these are my people. They are *my* people. Yes, I am glad that I am here in this country, for a thousand reasons, including the latitude to hold your hand in public and kiss you on the forehead, but the people of this country are not my people, and most let me know every day. I thought perhaps unreasonably about Marina asking about henna and rhapsodizing about Indian food, and a line from the novel Amit had given me hurtled into my mental foreground.

> You are different, okay, but that difference is never seen as containing its own value. Difference as orientalist entertainment is allowed, but difference with its own intrinsic value, no.

Out loud what I said was, Yeah, it was a bit weird, but you know, that's just how things are done where I come from, please try to understand.

Yeah, but do you think it's a good thing? Are there gay people in India? What do they even do?

I *assure* you there are gay people in India. You sound bloody ignorant.

Oh, I'm so sorry that I didn't go to college like Miss Fancy Consultant! That I'm not a *world traveler*! I'm sorry that I ask questions!

This has nothing to do with credentials, which you should know I don't care about. Listen, I don't want to talk about this. Can we go h— back to your place?

I want to know, Marina asked, very seriously. Do you think you could even be with me if your parents were alive?

Staring into the Anmol awning—green and red and blue, the letters fat and friendly—I found myself unable to say a word. The pressure of Marina's small warm hand descended upon my own. I closed my eyes.

Baby, Marina said, voice so soft and gentle, will you ever be able to tell me what happened with them?

I don't know, I whispered.

I turned to look at her, my eyes wet and burning. My throat sore.

To my great surprise, Marina's eyes welled up instantaneously at the sight of mine, tears barreling down her cheeks. She let out an anemic laugh.

I told you, she said, pointing to her face. Great crying surrogate.

I reached out and wiped her cheek dry with my hand. We can schedule a weeping session soon, I said, stretching my face into a smile that felt painful.

Kiss me, Marina said, a pleading in her eyes. Obediently I leaned in.

We broke apart; she began reversing out of the parking lot. I looked up to see the family in Anmol goggling at us from the curb, growing smaller as we drove away.

She

She slept with her lips parted. Eyes buttoned and peaceful. Hand lightly coiled upon itself, resting on her linen pillow. Light crept into the room, the neon red of her alarm clock morphing closer to seven. I did not want to go in to work. I moved toward her, palming her warm skin. Tracing down her spine's curve.

Soon she would wake up, stare at me, all pleased vulnerability; soon she would croak, as she did each day, Morning. Soon there would be coffee for her, chaiya for me. I would leave, she would stay. I'd return, and she'd be gone.

The night before, we'd gone to the hardware store after she'd finished work, called in a takeout order. We bought Edison bulbs and drill bits. All for her, since I was still ignoring my own apartment with great fastidiousness, using the heat as an excuse. Only stopping by once a week or so to pick up some clothes and turn a blind eye to its growing disrepair. The plants now dead. Freckles of black mold in the fridge. Everything now collecting a thin layer of dust.

After dinner we'd stacked our bodies like spoons on the couch, watched *Chopped* on Netflix. Marina loved this dumb show with a passion. Would narrate along, pretending to be the bitchiest Jersey judge. Maybe one day we can have a *Chopped* party, she said, watching a contestant massage octopus while sweating visibly. Invite your friends and mine, all together for a change. I like throwing parties but don't like to do it all alone, you know? Everyone needs to have a partner in crime—

What'll you put in my challenge basket? I asked. Wanna be prepared.

Are you asking for an *unfair advantage*?

Yes. Exactly.

Mmm. Your basket. Chicken wings. Coca-Cola. Ummm. Cabbage. What's that stuff—sambar powder.

That is revolting. You are a sadist.

Don't make excuses! Work with what you've got, chef! That's all any of us can do in the world! Let's see it, chef Sneha!

Okay okay *okay*, I said, having watched enough episodes now to understand that composing the idea of a dish that performed well on a show like this was simply a matter of attaining fluency with a certain kind of language. Perhaps this adaptability, this ability to read a situation and accommodate its needs, was one of the only things I had a halfway solid aptitude for, I who had grown up on the other side of the world, and still squared my shoulders and walked into the dyke bar, trusting I could find my way.

Marina elbowed me in the ribs. Okay! I exclaimed. Let's see, okay, I—would—make—Singaporean noodles with braised cabbage and a sambar dipping sauce. Soy sauce– and Coca-Cola–glazed chicken wings. With star anise and cumin.

Holy shit. Her mind, ladies and gentlemen. Ten out of ten. Wait, nine. You forgot dessert.

Onscreen a *Chopped* contestant was crying, shaking with rage.

What do you mean dessert? You give me some falthoo cabbage and chicken wings in my basket and want to make me come up with a bloody *dessert*?

Excuses, chef! She nibbled my neck. You gotta work! You could make . . . a Coca-Cola cake. My mom used to when I was a little one. Don't make that face, don't yuck my yum, okay, it's *really* good. Like a Texas sheet cake. Okay, pass me my wines, please, Miss Consultant.

Thinking of a child-size Marina scarfing Coca-Cola cake, twirling in the smallest tutu, I smiled down at my sleeping girl. As if on cue, seawater-green eyes peered at me blearily.

Morning, she creaked out.

Hello. You want coffee?

Mmmyes. Cuddle me, please. Had a bad dream.

I scooped her closer to me. Her breath sour, a tang of old chardonnay and pond surface. In this person I had begun to feel a kind of safety. A trust timorous and partial, and because of my own mendacity, perhaps irredeemably compromised. But I felt good with her. Felt some facsimile of belonging. Soon she would leave, I remembered, dread veining me. Would be on the road in a matter of days, and I would be alone again. Have to fend for myself again.

What was it, baby? I asked, smoothing her hair. My heart bending like hot plastic. I said, I'm here now.

The night she departed for her tour of dance intensives, she asked me to do three things.

Water her plants for the next few days, since her subletter would only move in mid-April.

Get Amy to fix the apartment's heat. (Baby, she's required by law to do it, promise me—)

Not mind or take it personally if she only texted once or so each day. The intensives were busy, draining affairs with hundreds of students milling about.

The tour would take her to Illinois, Ohio, New Jersey, and New York over six weeks, netting her and Shaka nearly twelve thousand dollars apiece.

I'll buy health insurance when we're back maybe, she said, grimacing at the memory of the ER bill, which had wiped out the majority of her savings. This mami needs new headphones too.

Good thinking, I said, my guts feeling tight and tangled. I pulled her close. Her skin against mine made me feel in place, anchored me.

You need me, I whispered in her ear. Her eyelids fluttered closed. She nodded, reaching confidently for my mouth, tracing the outline of my lips and hooking her finger in. I sucked hard.

Yes, she said so softly, eyes now alive with desire, yes, yes.

That Saturday I returned to my long-neglected apartment, looked around at the dust and insect carcasses, thought of the next six weeks without Marina, time at work seeming to stretch forever ahead of me, and started a headache that would not end. A small god of fire was dancing upon the crown of my skull. Burning wherever he leaped. At some point hunger came for me, but I could not abide the thought of preparing anything. I looked up the closest cheapest food—a Wendy's, a thirteen-minute walk away. Ate a fried chicken sandwich in bed next to my space heater. Drank glass after glass of water.

Nothing seemed to quell the headache. I took paracetamols my parents had sent back with me. I managed to walk back to the Wendy's. Bought four chicken sandwiches this time, put them in the fridge, ate them at successive mealtimes. Ignored Marina's attempts to talk on the phone, saying I was busy and felt sick.

On the third day of pain, in desperation, I called my mother.

I felt something was not right with you, was what she said, picking up on the first ring.

My mother told me, Bite the tip of your little finger until you cannot stand it. Then breathe in several deep lungfuls of air. Take crushed inji and ground cinnamon and clove and drink it with hot water, apply it on your temples also like a compress. Take paracetamol but since the pain is very bad, you should also drink strong black tea with it.

In my state I could not go in to work or face the walk to a grocery store. In the freezer I had a knob of ginger in a Ziploc baggie. It was spongy when it thawed, its thin brown skin easily flaking off. I chopped it up. Put it in a dusty mug with two cloves and a pinch of pumpkin pie seasoning, poured boiling water on the lot.

I went in to work Tuesday and got told that I was getting pulled off the project.

There's some other deliverables I have for you, potentially, Peter said, glaring at an empty corner of the room. The pain in my head returned, turned to wildfire. I considered standing up and screaming my head off, shrieking without stopping until they carted me to a loony bin.

Peter said that his company would keep looking for new clients. Would work with Susan and accounting to make sure the firm got paid, so he could pay me. In the meantime, I would work with him on ghostwriting the book he wanted to publish.

You'll work from home, he said; you'll document the process we've spearheaded so far into a methodology others can follow, I will send you notes and voice memos, and we will check in weekly on your progress.

Changeology, I was thinking of calling it, he said dreamily, and it was in that instant I realized Peter had been fired too.

Day after day I slept in. Scheduled emails with Boomerang to auto-send at six and seven in the morning. It was relatively easy to fake productivity, a Puritan work ethic. I missed Marina awfully and texted her very little at all. I knew she was busy and did not want to impose; I felt unable to describe the plain facts of my situation, having hidden them so far and so well.

The last of winter fled, the chill receding from the air. In a burst of executive function I walked to a corner store in Harambee and bought canned food, a bag of rice. In the afternoons I wrote arrant bullshit for Peter, attempting to compile our spreadsheets and charts, his adages and formulas, into something coherent for a corporate audience. I paid my taxes with an online program. My bank balance now at six hundred dollars. Still, over the days, the pain in my head began to dissipate like mist. Some mornings it would come back down, a smooth cold fog in the brain, and burn off by the afternoon.

Maybe you were allergic to working there, girl, Tig said.

A fortnight after getting the ax, and with Tig protesting that they never saw me anymore, which felt a bit rich considering they were impossible to make a plan with these days, I'd felt well enough to make it through dinner. They paid for the beers, our burritos. We'd gone to the lovely, amiably peopled Riverwest Public House, one of the seventeen-odd places that had rejected my application for actual paying employment.

We pulled up to my curb.

I want to show you something, Tig said, an uncharacteristic shyness suddenly in their face.

What, I said.

Ugh, Tig said, blushing. Okay, I feel dumb. Don't laugh. Okay?

They fumbled in their bag. My diaphragm tensed. I saw it then—Tig would pull out a velvet box, the diamond ring. I would have to be excited, happy for the two of them. Ask prattling questions about how the ring was chosen, how they would plan to propose to Diana. The crown of my skull began to throb. My friends all would leave me behind in life, one at a time. That was one reason to choose the traditional route. Find your own person to go off into the world with, take your place in the expected order of things. Wilhelm Meister, forever dogging me.

But I was wrong. Tig pulled out a small black leather notebook.

Laughed shyly. Said, I've had this dream. I haven't been able to stop thinking about it. Yooo, I feel silly! Read it? Give it back to me next Tuesday?

Okay love, I said. I put it in my coat pocket, squeezed Tig's hand. Said, Thanks for dinner and thanks for the ride.

It was when I was unlocking the side door and beginning to zip my boots off that they ran back out of the car, flagged me down. Asked to use my bathroom. Sidestepped my panicked refusal, my realization that the apartment was still absolutely filthy from my time away, that in weeks I had not washed a dish or picked up after myself.

Do you want me to pee on your doorstep or in your apartment? Tig asked, wobbling in batik-print pants. It's one or the other, girl, one or the other.

I sat on the tufted couch, cheeks burning with shame. Around me: the reek of old trash, bowls crusted with old food, cans of tuna and chickpeas left pell-mell on every surface. My footprints visible in the floorboard dust. The stopped clock with its broken glass. Sheets and couch tufts full of crumbs.

What's going *on* with you? Tig asked, stepping around my apartment. No, bitch, don't tidy on my account, leave it, I'm asking like, are you okay? You live like this now?

Tig swiped waxed energy-bar wrappers off the couch. They fluttered to the floor. My friend perched next to me.

I'm a hot mess, I know, I mumbled.

Sneha, Tig said, and I winced slightly at this unnecessary invocation of my name, girl, I don't want to like, offend you, but you ever thought about seeing a therapist?

You think there's something *wrong* with me—

I think you're maybe depressed, on some level, and it's an investment in your mental—

Leave me alone, I spat, losing my temper entirely. Are you a whitegirl or something? Get out of my bloody business, who asked you to come here? You think that all that needs to happen here is me pay some lady with glasses on a chain to listen to MUH TRAUMA? What does it mean to be *investing* in my *mental health*? To be healthy? Show me a healthy person! Is it *you*?

I opened the notebook, feeling bruised and sulky. This after Tig told me I absolutely could not talk to them like that and left, closing my door forcefully.

The notebook was black leather, imitation crocodile, its edges gilt. Some little expensive store in the Third Ward would sell a thing like this, price it at twenty, thirty dollars. This was a total Tig move, I thought, to buy this sort of expensive frippery while living paycheck to paycheck.

On the book's first page, Tig had written down, in a looping child's hand:

> *This is my dream for myself. This is my dream for my beloveds. This is how I hope to leave a legacy. (I also hope to write books . . .)*
>
> *My name is Antigone Clay and I am a philosopher, a barista, a so-called gig-worker, a subject under racial capitalism, a student, and a genderfluid Black child of the universe.*
>
> *We create our lives saying one small yes to one small thing at a time. We create the world that way. That is how heroin users and racist suburbenites and political revolutions are made.*
>
> *We say yes to something better! We dream of a pink house with land around it where all the people we love can live safe!*
>
> *We promise ourselves we will bring this to be!*

In my bed full of crumbs and Wendy's wrappers I read the rest. A manifesto-meets-project-vision.

Tig wanted to band together with people who shared the same beliefs. People who sought security and community. People who were tired of being ground down by landlords and bosses and corporations. People who were willing to share: power and resources and money and dreams.

Together they would save up money, pool those savings, and buy the Pink House. Would learn construction and rearrange the innards of the property. Build a pizza oven and raised garden beds. Install an outdoor shower and a hot tub—*we dream*, Tig's pendulous writing said, *of a hot tub full of women, lovers and friends.* They would hold house meetings to process dispute and idea. In time they would build, on the Pink House lot's southern edge, tiny insulated homes for people who were homeless in the city. They would share money, they would protect any family member who fell upon hard times, they would never have a landlord again, they would in this manner grow old together.

Part of me was impressed. Most of me sneered. How would they get the money for this? What if someone in this idyllic-ass commune wanted or needed out, desired to leave? The 1960s called, and they wanted their ideas back. I turned the page. Tig's blueprints.

In smudgy pencil, they had sketched the house out, using the floor plan from its last selling. A wing of the house had my initials on it. On the next page was a hastily scribbled rendering of a garden, dotted by small cottages. One said *Mama and Kelli Jo*. One said *Writing Studio*.

One by the vegetable garden said, appended by a question mark, *Sneha's Parents?*

I closed the small notebook and held it to my heart; I burst into tears.

For so many years I didn't speak of what came next. Told nobody. Afraid to set down, to say out loud, what it felt like.

Rice and lentils were inexpensive but effortful, undesirably redolent of the place I came from. I ate bread and Kraft mayo for the daytime meals. Peanut butter was more nutritious, but I did not like its stickiness, how it coated the teeth and tongue.

From the road, Marina had taken to sending hearts in our texts.

I needed to eat more protein.

I would walk to the Wendy's in the brisk spring evenings, sunglasses on, bundled up, wishing not to be recognized. The chicken tasted of nothing besides crispness and salt.

Marina had said nobody ever felt only one thing at a time. Food was like that too; every real flavor a layering. A mango from back home was flowered sourness and honey, buttery heft, slivers of green bitterness in the flesh near its skin. But every part of the Wendy's sandwich had a single note. The faintly sweet bun, the crunch and salt of the patty, the mayonnaised slick of wilted lettuce.

I ate it like it was the food of the gods. This is what it is like to be hungry: you are on fire, smoke suffusing you, the heat inside impossible to ignore. What it is like to be hungry: time loses meaning, turns elastic and useless, traps you in knots. What it is like to be hungry: like no good thought can stay within you for long. Happiness itself metabolizes in minutes, your body sopping up its calories like bread with soup, reverting to the preexisting ache.

Marina on the road, us missing each other for phone dates, barely talking, since I felt unable to speak of the one thing that the rest of my life was warping around. Tig frustrated at my meanness, my unwillingness to take help, pulling away, off cavorting with Diana and her kid. Me, pretending to write, to be capable of writing, Peter's stupid bloody book. *Changeology: A Manual for Navigating Your Company's Transformation.* I copy-pasted sections from articles about OCM and organizational strategy into a Word document, kept a bibliography in Microsoft Excel using Son of Citation Machine. Which is to say, I pretended not only to Peter but also to myself that there was something of his rock star left in me.

I asked him over email when he thought I would be paid. The client still has not processed our invoices, he replied curtly. Four days later. My bank account now was at three hundred dollars. This after the most careful spending, hoarding my dollars and cents.

Three hundred dollars. This was, after one accounted for sales tax and the electricity and Internet bills, the cost of 177 of the Wendy's chicken sandwiches. Which meant that if I ate them for every meal I would have sufficient calories to stay alive for the next eight weeks. I could not decide if this was a long or short time.

how are u, I texted Tig from my bed, trying to will myself into confiding in them. Even after I apologized after our tiff in my disgusting living room, a mild chill seemed to have set in between the two of us.

A day later, they responded, hey thank you so much for asking. it's been really hard. Police killed a black man in red arrow pk. Did you see? My sis knows his brother. Shit is fucked up. I went to the march though I'm not sure what marching will do. Actually headed to another one for him right now. It's really horrible. This kid Dontre didn't hurt nobody he was mentally not well and just resting in a park. they just shot him like twelve times and he was unarmed like the fuck is wrong with you. Don't worry too much abt me babe just send good thoughts. Diana's taking good care of me. Times are just hard.

Tig and I had walked in Red Arrow Park, talking, laughing. Cold air and fledgling sunlight in our faces. For many minutes on my phone I stared at the photograph of Dontre Hamilton. He was smiling handsome, a dimple in his cheek.

im so sorry, I wrote back to Tig. Self-disgust and helplessness, sorrow and loneliness flooding me. They killed him, I thought. They killed that man. I wanted to be the kind of friend to say, drop your location, babe, I'm coming to you. Touching my fingers tenderly to the glowing screen, I wrote out what I could then: i love you so much. im really so sorry. im glad you have Diana.

There was one full day I spent in bed, staring at the gray-blue paint of the walls. My belly prickling, then expanding in bloat, feeding itself on emptiness. At night I wanted to relieve myself, and it seemed like such a great effort, like facing down the starting line of a marathon, the idea of getting out of bed and making the walk to the bathroom. So tempting, the thought of simply relaxing my muscles, letting myself go.

I thought of my mother's face, imagined the smell of old urine, a smell I knew from my grandfather's bed—sweet and acrid, choking the nose like burning plastic. After an hour I succeeded in moving my body the requisite twenty feet to piss in contemporary plumbing. Rested my head in my hands. Every pair of underwear I owned was marked with dried-out white paste. Surreal to think that I had, mere months ago, ordered lobster and oysters and coconut-gin cocktails. Taken my girlfriend out for meals that cost more than a hundred dollars. Spent over a grand on a plane ticket.

I worried that if I looked terrible and unhealthy, Marina would notice when she returned at the end of my chicken sandwich diet. Might no longer be attracted to me. Into a search engine I typed *how much sodium die of heart attack if young*.

I walked to a food pantry. Wore my floppy boots from Goodwill, ruined by salt. Once, I would have cared. The pantry was in St. Casimir Church. This for some reason struck me as being in bad taste. I wished for the ability to fill my bag in a facsimile of a supermarket. All clinical light and gusts of cold.

Standing in line, I felt people's eyes on me—younger than the other adults, not one of the children milling around in jeans and bright over-alls. The color of my skin, the set of my face, in this country, signaled software engineering, 7-Elevens, suburban homeownership. Not penury.

The paperwork was less extensive than I feared. I was asked my age, my race, my religion, my dietary profile, and whether I was currently employed. If you had a boss but were paid nothing were you currently employed or not? Blue? Green? Who could say? I took all the vegetables and protein I was allowed. Refused the offer of a shopping cart. I don't have a car, I said softly to the old lady directing me, her hair so white it was almost blue, and she said, Oh honey, this city is not meant for the walkers among us.

They served me egg casserole and baked beans and pale bulbous straw-berries. Big fluffy pieces of French toast, custard yellow with a brown tracery that called to mind henna stain. I took the paper plate to a table by myself.

Through all this I felt a terrible dislocating shame, a feeling that choked me with its fumes, that refused to let my mind turn from my parents, of how they would feel if they saw me now. I could never tell them this, the same way I could never let Marina or my friends know how skewed the image they had of me was, how deep my failure ran.

At St. Casimir, they called charity cases like me shoppers. Two shoppers trailing small children asked to sit at my big round table. Tersely I nodded, concentrating on my egg dish. It was pale and sulfurous, its curds smooth like plastic.

How are you doing, honey? one of the shoppers asked me, apparently incapable of reading social cues. She was white. Short and sandy-headed with big teeth. To my great surprise, she had a job. Taught chemistry at a local school. I just come here when we need a little help, she said, her teeth shining at me. Sometimes there's rent and there's bills and there's just one thing too far, like a doctor's bill, and then it's the start of the month and you end up here. You know? There's no shame! I hope you don't feel bad, if it's your first time!

All right, I said, eating my eggs.

The Black aunty next to her seemed put off by me and this nice nervous horse of a woman alike. Come, she said to her small granddaughter. Swept off somewhere. On her feet were violet suede kitten heels, and I thought how strange people were, to dress nicely to come to a church and beg.

I texted Amit, hey, miss you, let's catch up soon? how are things with Emily? anything new with KJ?

As I was walking out of the lot with my four straining plastic bags, the aunty with the purple shoes pulled up by me.

You need a ride, baby? she asked.

One real kindness in this moment would pop me like a balloon. And truthfully I felt the voice of suspicion, telling me that anything could happen, trust no stranger, even one in the same straits of pain as you, especially not one in those straits. The woman's eyes were large and tired, her eyebrows plucked to two surprised Cs. The child, with hair in tiny bright-bead twists, waved at me from the small junker car. My back hurt.

Oh, thank you, I said, but it's okay, it's a very short walk for me.

You have a good day now, I added, trying for a folksiness.

The woman looked at me in a searching way, and I feared she understood the calculus of my answer. Without saying a word she drove off. Alone I walked the forty minutes home.

I woke to Amit calling me. His third try.

KJ's in fucking jail, he said without preamble. Cathy blew my phone up and then stopped responding to anything, I can't get through. Maybe their phone got turned off. I called the courthouse but there's no information, I don't think they've set her bail yet—

Oh dear, I said. Typed *milwaukee courthouse* into the search bar on my phone.

She's in the county jail, by the Public Museum, he said. I know she must be scared. I don't know what happened. S, please. Will you go see her? I'll help you register in the system online. And I can send you money for a cab—

It's okay, I'll walk, I said quietly. Let me know what I need to do.

Not how I pictured us meeting, girl, KJ said to me, the ghost of a smile in her sleepy brown eyes. Will you get me a pop or some Takis? Machine is behind you.

I was at a hundred and ninety-two dollars. Still, I did not find myself able to refuse.

KJ's face is plain but her voice is quite beautiful. It was the first thing I noticed. On this particular morning it was scratchy and hoarse, but you could hear what girded it underneath: sound with all the gradient of a sunset. In the county jail, its light fluorescent, its floor scented with Lysol and danger, I thought useless senti things about roads not taken—my father's, KJ's. In a different life the voice I heard could have been that of a singer, a music teacher, a yoga studio owner. I didn't see the things I expected from Amit's stories and my ideas about addicts—I had pictured vacant eyes, needle marks down arms. In the crook of her elbow was some variety of boil, healing, purple at the edges. KJ's small hands rested on the Formica table between us: dimpled and velvety, nails bitten down nearly to disappearance, calling to mind a neighbor's lipless smile.

Don't tell me anything that could get you in trouble, I muttered quietly when I first sat in front of her. Like we were in some TV crime serial.

KJ, I would learn later, had been for once in her life very lucky.

She'd used in the morning, driven to get a frozen pizza from the Aldi. On the way back, fought the drowsiness descending upon her.

What the cops had seen: a Black woman weaving in her vehicle. They stopped her. Tested her. Searched the car.

Days from now, KJ would tell me, Before I left I'm thinking, I'm finna bring a little skag with me, just a gram, go pick Cathy up, can you imagine if I'd gotten possession instead of an OWI? I must have got an angel looking out for me.

She would be charged with drugged driving. A first-time offense. The ticket would be $850, and upon receipt of payment she could be released to a family member.

But we knew none of that in the moment. The only person KJ had been able to speak to from jail was her sister.

Her eyes grew wet when she said, Tell Mitty I'm sorry, okay? Feel like I let him down so bad. I want to get back to the program, but they make it so hard. It's like some obstacle course shit, but your whole life. And it's expensive as hell! Only reason I can do it at all is cuz Mitty pays for it.

Amit loves you, I said, not knowing what else to offer up. I added, stupidly, It'll be okay.

KJ leaned forward. In this moment she seemed so young, younger than me. In my mouth I tasted a tenderness cut with exasperation. Like a rise of bile while you drink sweet tea.

Will you come to my court? she asked softly. I don't want to be alone. Will you? And like see if Mitty can send me anything? I hope he's okay with money, like for his own rent and shit. Man, I'm so over myself for ever trying skag, one trash decision, and—mmm. It's so crazy, I have no idea what's gonna happen. I don't even know if my sis gonna come to court for me. She sick of my shit.

I'm sure your sister will come, I said with a bright emptiness, nodding my best sympathy.

It turned out I was right. I walked into the courthouse waiting room, and there—grim of face, in a straining blue button-down, hair metamorphosed into short stiff waves—stood Tig.

The fuck. What you doing here?

What're *you* doing here? Amit's middle school friend is up for drugged driving—KJ. It's been a whole thing. What about—

Bro, what the hell. That's my sis. That's Kelli Jo. Bringing drama like usual. Also girl, no offense, only love, but you need to shower. Funk is real.

My world was spinning like a washing machine. KJ is your *sister*? I asked, incredulous. Amit has been spending tens of thousands of dollars on *your sister*?

Is he Kelli Jo's sugar daddy? The fuck?

Honestly, it's gonna take too long to explain now. They're starting. Let's go in.

Your parents named one kid Antigone and the next kid Kelli Jo? I could not help but ask during the break.

We have different fathers, Tig said primly.

What still stuck out to Tig after all the administrative bullshit masticated us sufficiently, after we drove KJ to their mother's house, after the check for the OWI ticket had been written—a two-day logistical nightmare involving draining Tig's savings account and calling their mom to transfer over an additional two hundred dollars—was Amit's role in things.

Once they'd connected the friend I'd spoken of with KJ's stories about her homie Mitty, once the two of us absorbed the shock of the cumulative amount Amit had spent supporting KJ—over fifty thousand dollars—Tig would not stop speaking about this. And with a far more positive spin on the facts than my own.

It's rare, Tig mumbled into an al pastor taco at BelAir. To see someone willing to give, and that much, because he cares about somebody, not getting anything out of it—

He got to bloody feel good about himself! I pointed out.

Like, okay! But to give money, lots of it, no strings attached, to a Black woman and trust her with it, that's so very rare—

Honestly, babe, I love him but he's a fool. A well-intentioned, good-hearted fool with a need to feel as though he's the most moral person in the room. Kelli Jo could have overdosed. His whole platonic sugar daddy routine paid for her treatment stints when she was in treatment and kept her off the street in winter, okay, but it also probably kept their whole friend circle awash in heroin—

I want to get to know the brother, Tig said, setting their jaw. They mopped guac off their T-shirt, which said in cursive letters REMEMBERED IN LOVE: DONTRE HAMILTON. I feel like you don't want it to happen and Kelli Jo doesn't want it to happen, they said. He's making good money, he's a brown dude with Milwaukee roots. I keep thinking, like, he could help fund the commune.

The commune?

You know. The Pink House.

Why would *he* fund the commune? Do you want him to live there?

I don't *not* want him to live there. Right now I don't know who gonna live there. Other than me. Haven't heard from my friend Sneha yet, that's for sure.

It was time to discuss this, apparently. It seemed a relief, to consider the abstraction of communal living rather than the tangibles of my fridge or bank account. I straightened my back. Dug in my bag for the black leather notebook.

Thank you, I said flatly as I handed it over.

What did you think? Tig asked, reddening a little.

I took a nerve-filled breath. It is terrible to know that with a few fumbling words you might either wound or exalt somebody you love.

I'm really impressed, I said, voice squeaky. By the idea, by how much work you've put into this. It's, like, an incredible visioning statement and a great project brief. Thank you for sharing it with me. I'd never pictured anything like this, you know? It feels hard to imagine, but also cool. You know?

Tig stayed silent, watchful, a vague mistrust in their eyes.

I really meant this, was not just supplying them platitudes. All my life, when I imagined the future, I thought of each of us as small atoms, individuated, settling down, getting a flat somewhere, wearing out one job and then another, like successive pairs of shoes. You grew up, you were found a person to marry, you went sullenly to work, you kept a house running, you did the requisite paperwork or paid the price, and then for two hours of the day you might cultivate a pastime, like yelling at sports on the television or forcing the lawn into submission. It took a bravery to imagine something even slightly different, let alone follow that imagining through.

My parents had been in possession of a version of this courage. Comprehending this at twenty-three in a Cali-Mex taqueria, thinking of the two people I came from, on airport escalators with their reinforced plastic suitcases, my stomach began to hurt.

But still, I said out loud, after a pause, I guess I like wanted to see more of a . . . project plan? The *how* of it all seemed mad opaque to me? Not even just getting the money. How the legal side of any of it would work. How can eight, nine people own a single house? What happens if someone leaves, like needs to move, or tensions rise in a way that can't be resolved? Do people get bought out? How many years of saving up would it take?

Okay, so I went deaf, Tig said, the second you let out the words *I wanted to see more of a project plan*. A project plan . . . bitch. Gott im Himmel.

I laughed. I'm serious, though, I said. The difference between it being an actionable plan and a beautiful dream is a clear map of how to get there. Right now I don't have a map—

Tig drained the drink in their hand and said, It's interesting to me that you want *me* to provide the map, do the work, dream the dream, and research the property law of it all. What I'm actually asking is—same's I'm asking Jervai, Thom, KJ once she has her shit together—is like, are you in or are you not? These are the things we do *together*.

Their voice took on a peculiar boomy tone as they said, You wanna stay with your old dreams? Or dream something together?

I said nothing.

It should have a better name than the Pink House, though, they said, appearing to think out loud. I was thinking about calling it—Tig's eyes turned wet—after my father.

What was his name again, boo? I asked softly. Touching Tig's shoulder.

Rion. Rion Clay.

I looked into the pale clouded green of my drink, hoping my friend would offer to pay for dinner. I was at $187. The thought of this number, the fall it represented, caused my stomach to heat and churn.

Thankfully, a sliver of good news had arrived in my life: Danny the gymnast had put in a good word for me at Leon's, where he knew the manager. Even I could scoop custard. My first shift was two nights away, my first paycheck arriving in another week and a half.

What do you think? Tig asked again, staring me down.

I let out a great exhale. Tried to imagine Rion, the two-million-dollar pink mansion where our friends would never be evicted, where we could eat the food we grew ourselves, where we could sit together in our hot tub under the stars. There was something indistinctly moving to me, in a world where everyone was laser-point-focused on individual striving, to reframe anything around collective ambition. I also wished to throw my margarita across this restaurant. How was anyone expected to dream loftily about the future when the present ground them down to powder and nothingness?

I don't know, was what I said. Hey, I can't do tacos again for a while. Need to keep my expenses low. And I'll give you Amit's number. I added, You're right. You should know each other.

I see you avoiding the key question here, Tig retorted, smiling, but I'll forgive for now.

13

Marina and I were arguing. I had been missing her calls, primarily because I was sleeping through them. It feels like we're not even together, sometimes! she shrieked.

For a small person she could yell very loudly. I laid the phone faceup on my side table and ate a piece of bread with mayo. I could hear her clearly. It was as if she were on speakerphone.

She would return to Milwaukee in two weeks. Finally, out of defeat and in a bid for some emotional leniency, I told her about Peter not paying me, leaving out the trips to St. Casimir, the state of my bank account, stone before a river.

Oh my god. Are you serious? Baby. It's called wage theft, what Peter is doing to you, and it's not legal.

Peter will pay me eventually, I said. Thinking of my father. Who had chosen to stand up to his bosses, to walk away from mistreatment. How he might still be here if he had not. This is what it means, to come here as an immigrant. You are here on sufferance. You are a form of currency, not a person, and only a person has the right to desire, which is to say, to be difficult.

Peter had asked to look at the draft chapters of *Changeology*, and I had been studiously avoiding his request. I marked the email as unread, headed out to Leon's. The job was okay. Not enough to live on, certainly not on two shifts a week, but with my rent paid at least it meant a little more money for food. I had to wear a uniform. My forearm pulsed with pain after hours of scooping custard. Most of all I held a terror that Susan from the client would walk in, furry coat on, child in tow, and see me.

Amit and Tig spoke on the phone every few days, with the direct result that neither of them deigned to talk much to me anymore. I lay in bed and looked on Facebook at other people's lives, feeling a degree of disbelief that anyone in the world had energy enough to get engaged, start a dream job, move cross-country, travel.

Tig's friend Jervai said she was in for Rion / Project Pink House. Thom had asked to think about it. I felt a thrill of smug anger when I heard this. This was the thing, when your politics all started as abstract theory, as axioms at their most distilled. You had to negotiate the growing gaps between the principles you railed about in darkened bars and how you actually lived.

For myself, I did think a great deal about Rion. While I lay in bed, while I wrote corporate gobbledygook for *Changeology*, while I dragged myself to St. Casimir, sometimes after I masturbated and lay back in my sheets, my brain feeling smooth and clean like it had been run through a car wash. Tig's words took shape in my head as color and picture. I dreamed of the hot tub full of women. The outdoor shower. How it might feel to gather tomatoes and squash from our garden, to be close to my parents as they grew old. How quietly lovely, the idea that I would never have to eat a meal alone again unless I wished to.

Unrealistic as I mostly still believed it to be, the thought appeared: I could, at the very least, help them.

I duplicated the Gantt chart Peter and I had built for the Microsoft Suite transition, renamed it RionProjectPlan.xls.

Began to draw up a budget, break down how many people they'd need, how much a down payment would cost.

The apartment had grown nearly unlivable from my neglect and dirt-baggery. In some strange way I found comfort in what I saw around me—the confirmation staring back at me from the sink and couch and counters that I was in fact slovenly, worthless, no good. Still, the fridge's smells had quit being encased by the fridge, and I was having to hold my breath every time I walked by it to the bathroom. I got a garbage bag, tied a scarf around my mouth and nose, began pulling things out to throw away.

Five minutes of this and my eyes were streaming, my mouth tasting something pungent and intestinal. I walked the garbage bag to the bins outside, came back in, and lay down, sapped of all energy.

What had Tig said? *I think you're maybe depressed, on some level.*

No shit.

What I'd neglected to say that night was that I had, actually, been to a therapist before.

A professor had twisted my arm. I'd been missing classes, oversleeping. My work was complete, my exam scores good. I was one of the smarter people in the seminar. Still, she said, she might have to fail me. Participation was 40 percent of my overall grade. I had thought then of my parents, banished from this country a year before, counting on me in myriad ways from afar, and got so upset I ran out of the room and vomited.

The university therapist I was ordered to see looked like an ironing board with glasses.

Near the end of the third session—reams of surveys, rabbit-hole questioning about my parents, pontification about immigrating and classes and ambitions for the future—I was presented with her findings.

High-functioning depression and anxiety, mild compulsive patterns, and complex post-traumatic stress disorder seemed most likely, but additional diagnostic work might be needed—

I began to laugh loudly.

The ironing board looked askance.

I am not a war veteran or child bride, I said. Perhaps American students feel pride in getting handed this sort of litany, get some validation.

I sincerely doubt I have—and here I traced quotes in the air with my fingers—"complex" "PTSD."

The therapist appeared to regain her footing by a half shoe. With a gritted gracious smile plastered upon her face, she went over my "symptoms," the likely "trauma triggers" behind some of them, how I might begin to heal.

It is not uncommon, she said very gently, for someone with this diagnostic profile to have difficulty building trust with a provider. I am happy to give you a referral to another therapist, if you prefer, but I urge you to consider treatment. It is an act of courage to want to change your life. Don't you think you would like that? To have a better life?

I bit the inside of my cheek. Hard, then harder. Thus far in college I had been a quote-unquote student leader, had been responsible for budgets and decisions and administrivia. I'd had a research apprenticeship with the head of the history department, had trawled through archives to support chapters in his eventually award-winning book. On boards and committees I'd sat with professors and alumni, which was how I'd first met Peter, impressed him. I had good grades, a friend or two.

I was not some broken little bird, whatever this woman in linen trousers might need to believe.

Again I looked at the worksheet on my lap. Growing up, who treated you as a special person? Who did you feel safe with, as a child? These were questions that had made my heart speed until I felt sick.

My scores and answers indicated, among other things, she had said, a lack of excitement about the future. Sleeping a great deal or sleeping very little. An ongoing melancholy.

My laughter burbled up again, helpless, irrepressible. It was the first time I had been this disrespectful to a grown-up.

If you *cured me* of all these, I told her, I don't even know who I would be. It would be like getting lobotomized. I would not recognize myself.

Setting the clipboard down, I thanked her, still chuckling lightly. Walked out.

What the questionnaires had not asked that might have been useful to me:

Do you wake up each day for yourself or for someone else?

Do you believe your life to be your own?

I walked back to the fridge. Stared at its closed door, my nose watering. Something settled in me, clicked into place like a cog.

When I rang Tig it went to voicemail. I got another garbage bag. Its scent called to mind a clean diaper, spritzed with lavender.

I began to work through the apartment, picking up the trash, consolidating the dried food bowls by the sink. I got on a chair and took the broken clock off its shelf. Enough, I thought.

Aiming for the dustbin, I tossed it like a cornhole bag. The clock missed by an inch, shattered across the floor.

Yesu! I yelled out loud. Can *one thing* go right?

The only answer to my question was silence and a filthy apartment. With a broom I began to sweep the shards up, capturing also in the process a truly repulsive quantity of hair and lint and vegetable scraps. I tossed the yellow plastic body of the clock in the trash. A text from Amy arrived with a bing. Its contents nothing if not predictable.

be quiet!!! it said. you are so loud and rude! will be noting this to stacy. we are tired of trying to make this work.

You are truly batshit insane, I typed back, and I suggest you go live in the woods with your grunting Neanderthal away from all normal people who elect to stay in cities, which means proximity to other people, which means sometimes you hear the noise of other people LIVING. I hovered my finger over the send button.

My phone began to buzz in my hand. Tig calling.

Hey, I said, my breathing hard, trying to dial my adrenaline down.

Hi, babe! What's up? You okay?

I closed my eyes.

I wanted to tell you, I said softly, pacing around the kitchen, I wanted to say that I think I'm in. For the Pink House, I mean, for Rion, at least, I'm in to help plan it with you. I also think I should find another full-time job, move out of this place. Maybe I can stay with Marina in the interim, keep working at Leon's and save money. If she'll have me. She may be over my bullshit. Tig. I'm ready for my life to go better. I also just want to say—you know you're remarkable, right? When I think about your life, when I think about the hand you've been dealt, and the actual shit you turn to gold, I'm—it's very moving to me. It's hard for me to think about the future. But it feels more possible, things feel more possible with you, when I'm not alone in it. I'm ready to change my life.

A long pause.

I'm fucking de*light*ed, Tig said. Babe! I think Thom's in. Amit wants to advise us, give us at least a little money. And now this. Shit. You're gonna make me cry, bitch.

Ha, don't though. I started making a project timeline for Rion—don't roast me. I'll send it to you. You have Microsoft Excel on your computer?

I knew I was smart to get A Consultant on board, Tig joked, and right then I stepped on a shard of glass the length of my forefinger and let out a full-body scream.

Tig drove over right then. Walked in, sized things up, and decided they needed reinforcements.

To my shock and chagrin, it was a full car that pulled up. Thom, Diana, KJ, Diana's *child*. I was on my couch holding a dish towel to my foot. I jumped up, and nearly fell over.

No, I said, face melting from shame. I didn't— I don't want this, please—

Listen, S, you need help right now, Tig said bullishly, brandishing a plastic bag of cleaning supplies. We all need help sometime. You can't even stand on your damn foot. Diana will take a look at it. And like, we'll help get your apartment to a place where you can like, live again. At least until Marina's back in town and her subletter's out.

I'm fucking—mortified, I said, almost in tears. It was the truth.

They got to work. Each taking a corner of a room. Except the little boy, whom Diana placed on my bed with an injunction to play with his iPad. Tig blasting Swedish pop on Thom's Bluetooth speaker, dancing with the vacuum Diana brought over. Years later I can look back on that moment and see it as the act of devotion it was, to pick up somebody's disgusting mess and dispense with it. The kind of thing my parents would have done for me. That I would do for those I love most. In that moment, though, it felt like someone had lifted my head off, vomited into the urn of my body.

And this was before Amy opened my door, walked in bold as anything.

Parties are not allowed, is what I remember her saying, her maroon head shaking in anger. It's on your lease.

Get stuffed, lady, Thom said. He and Tig had moved instinctively in front of me, two human shields. Are you even allowed to walk in like this? he continued.

You all need to leave right now, Amy said, or I'm calling the police.

What do you plan to report to them? Thom sneered. This is very clearly not a party. We're helping her clean the apartment. Do you know that filing a false police report carries penalties?

Amy said, a new fragile, pleading note in her voice, It's nine o'clock at night. My fiancé and I need to sleep.

We'll be done by ten, said Tig, and added very softly, bitch.

Tig stared at Amy. Amy stared at Tig. Amy whipped around and ran down the stairs. Thom bolted the door behind her. I think Diana whooped.

Bro, you need to move out of here, Thom said to me, throwing dusty papers into a filing box.

Two days later, this would not be a matter of choice. But that night we laughed, feeling as though we had won, making the oldest, most time-honored mistake this land had seen—bringing the knife to the gunfight.

The email Peter forwarded to me had only Notice as its subject line.

Please acknowledge receipt of this email ASAP, and confirm you will be able to comply, he had written. Send me your most current version of Changeology immediately. I will be calling you at 2 p.m. today.

The email he'd forwarded on was from Stacy the landlord.

> Peter,
>
> Per the lease agreement, I am providing your company with 30 days' notice to vacate the upper unit with vacancy no later than Monday, June 30th. As you may recall, I have not required a security deposit from you, so I would ask that the unit be left in sparkling clean move-in condition, including the bathroom, stove, and fridge. The keys can be left with Amy Cable in the downstairs unit. We also need to work together to ensure the tenant pays final gas / electric / water bills since they have continued under my name. Please let me know that you are in receipt of this email and if you have any questions.
>
> Thanks,
> Stacy

I scrolled farther down in the chain. Feeling my own body to be unreal. A simulation. The email from Amy to Stacy simply said, Lease and pictures attached. It had been sent to her two days ago.

Inline were compressed cell phone pictures of the apartment. The apartment at its worst. When I had left it dirtiest. Amy had come in when I was gone, without my knowing, it appeared, as recently as last week. Taken pictures of the dishes in the sink, the couch papered in fast-food wrappers, stained clothes covering the bedroom floor. Saved them up, apparently, to deploy at my next infraction. To deal her death blow.

Again I read the bloodless polite email, and felt a surge of nausea.

The apartment is clean now, I wanted to scream out. I longed to run downstairs and smash all of Amy's windows. How dare she come into my house without notice. How dare she do this to me, after everything else. I was a child, sputtering impotently, paralyzed by the sensation of the world so much larger than me, so much more powerful. She had won. Had won from the very beginning.

At 2 p.m. Peter called me and matter-of-factly said he was letting me go.

I have not heard back from you promptly multiple times in recent weeks, he said. The situation with the apartment has impacted a business relationship. And frankly, I have little to show for your work on *Change-ology*.

What was most terrible was that I could see myself quite clearly through his eyes, through Amy's, through Stacy's. I understood why they viewed me the way they did.

I called Marina, heaving so hard I could barely speak.

Listen to me, baby, she said into the phone. I know you don't believe this, but take it from someone who has a few years on you: You will be okay. Getting fired is not the end of the world. This was a shit job. You hated it. You'll find something better.

There's nothing here, I choked out. I've been applying to other jobs for months. It'll be even worse now because I've been fired. Who will want me? I'll never be able to face my— I ruin everything I touch.

That's not true, Marina said softly. Listen. My subletter is leaving in three days. My friends are visiting from L.A. for my birthday and it'll be nice to have a moment at my place before they descend on me. I'll come home, be with you. Shaka can carry our final intensive.

No, don't do that—

Sneha. Like. I don't know how to say this, but yeah, *I* get to decide this, Sneha. Sneha, baby, let the people who love you take care of you—

I felt the punch of the hot red feeling at the word. In my head it rang like a bell, like a lie—love, love, love—

Stop saying my name again and again like that, I burst out helplessly.

Okay, like, why?

Just— I'm just under a lot of pressure, okay—

Why are you so . . . nervy about your name?

I can't do this right now, man. I have to go.

L3

The Kia Soul returned to Milwaukee. From my window I watched it swing down my street to rescue me, and I thought about the stylish novel Amit had lent me, with its solitary hero walking all day in New York City, and once more about my own life, the walks with my uncle, taking auto rickshaws with my mother, all my people with their cars that I had depended on in unwalkable cities.

Days later, Thom and I sat on his front steps while he told me that he'd finally landed a decent-paying job.

He would be a construction laborer with Rabine. Twenty-three dollars an hour, with the chance to go up to forty. How do you feel? I asked. Weird, was the reply, but damn glad to make some money. Sorry about Peter, homie. So ironic that he fucked up basic cash flow.

Who change-manages the change managers? I quipped.

Thom laughed but in an anemic way.

Summer's blessed warmth rolled in, humid and certain. I applied for jobs every day. In the city, in my college town, on LinkedIn and Monster.com and Craigslist. In Marina's high-ceilinged apartment I lay in bed for hours. Sometimes I pulled up my computer and made incremental additions to the Pink House project plan, if only to engage in the fantasy that I could still plan a project, still get the client to their definition of success. Evenings I cooked, grateful that Marina filled her fridge with groceries and never asked me to chip in. She made us smoothies, verdant green, redolent of frozen pineapple. All day she edited mixes for her choreo at her kitchen counter, sipping on white wine. Her Shamar company show with Shaka was three weeks away.

And then, two days after, I would need to leave my apartment, or contend with the eviction marshals.

When not in bed or on LinkedIn, I worked my Friday and Saturday shifts at Leon's, growing steadily sicker of the smell of custard. The ache in my arms sometimes shot down my spine. It paid $8.75 an hour. Still, it felt like honest work in a way that the gig with Peter rarely had—there was something fraudulent and invented at the core of that world, even if I was too stupid to correctly articulate it.

From time to time my parents rang. I took the calls in the hallway outside the apartment. Nothing to report, Papa, I would say. Work is keeping me busy.

I got an interview with an architecture firm that needed a receptionist. From sleuthing online I saw that Peter and his family were on vacation in Chile. There were pictures of him and his bony wife in an infinity pool overlooking lush mountains. So much for no cash flow.

Marina helped me write a polite email asking for my money. For days there was no response. I wrote to him again.

I am evaluating your invoices, he said finally in reply, as I am not sure of their accuracy without consulting against my own records. I am disappointed in how you have chosen to approach this. I began our engagement with very high expectations. Every employer has to make a calculation with a new hire—will this person make me money or lose me money? I thought you would be a great investment. Clearly I have been proven wrong.

This absolute bastard, Marina said when I showed her the emails. She smacked her granite countertop with a balled fist. This complete cocksucker. How dare he. Hey, baby, come here. This is not your fault.

That's not how I feel at all, I gasped out. It *is* my fault. I feel like I've destroyed my life.

Shhh.

I said, I'm telling you, I ruin everything I touch. I'm ruining this too, us too. I can tell.

Marina leaned her pale green head to my chest, locked her arms around me. Tears were leaking down her face. My throat felt like I had swallowed a cactus.

I won't leave you, she said. I'm here.

Marina finished her cigarette and asked, Yeah so you'll come to my show, right?

Was planning to, it's on the twenty-ninth?

She nodded, appeared to hesitate, and then asked, Do you know, like, have you thought about where you'll go after you move out of your apartment?

I was silent for a long moment, vulnerability descending upon me like dew.

I haven't thought about it, I finally said.

Oh. Okay. It's in three weeks and change, though?

I stared at her, throat raw with anger. The architecture firm had just turned me down. Clearly I was not good enough even to answer a company's phones. Here she was, not offering her home to me, knowing I couldn't bear to invite myself in, knowing I didn't have money enough for a first month's rent in a new place, let alone a security deposit. It was only later that I thought back on this moment and realized she might not, actually, have known these things I believed patently obvious simply because they were pressing on me with the force of a landslide.

I've no idea about any of it, I spat, not until I get a job or that wastrel pays me—but don't worry, I won't impose on you any longer than you're comfortable!

As night fell, Marina left the scene of our fight to drink with the Strive Dance crew. I called Amit.

What I wanted was to ask for money. I could not bring myself to. Strongly I hinted. Talked about my notice to vacate, how my job search was turning up peanuts, how Peter was not paying me.

You should get a lawyer and get it from him, that's outrageous, Amit said. Or threaten him with small claims court—

What will I pay the lawyer with, bhai sahib? My pussy?

In exasperation at his cluelessness and selective generosity, I settled for tormenting him about Kelli Jo.

Did it feel so *good*, being her savior? I asked, in a voice trembling with malevolence, equal parts ice and acid. Did it feel difficult to disentangle from her problems, from feeling so good about helping her? Do you think you were—maybe—struggling—with an *addiction*?

Amit let out a long, slow breath, said nothing.

You can say something mean back, I said. No need to be so holy. Not with *me*.

S, Amit said in a tone of exaggerated patience, what do you want me to say or do? I am very sorry you got fi— let go. I know you will be okay. You always are. You should talk to your parents, if you can. And I am happy to help, as your friend—

Then help! I burst out. I have two hundred dollars to my name, and three more weeks of having my own roof over my head! I'm alone in this bloody godforsaken country, my parents have enough problems of their own. Help me!

Another long pause.

I can send you a little money, if you really need it, though truthfully my savings are pretty depleted right now. Didn't you say you had some money in a CD? Can you break it out?

Yeah, but it's like a two-hundred-dollar penalty, Amit—

I think, he said, that you should consider if what you're asking me for is what would actually be most helpful to you.

Listening to this, I could say nothing. In the reflection of Marina's living room window I watched a woman, phone to her ear, crying in silence, face twisting against the sullen night.

Amit said, Hey, look, will you just update your résumé and send it to me? Emily's sister works at a contractor for the National Archives. Her division is looking for a program associate. They told me today.

National Archives?

Yeah, in D.C. I think you'd do project planning, maybe work on some events, get to learn a lot of history, poke about a bunch of papers. It's random. It might not pay *that* well. But I don't sense you wanna stay in the consulting game? And I think you could do the job.

But, I said, my nose full of snot, I hadn't really planned to leave Milwaukee. I don't know anyone in D.C.

You didn't know anyone there when you moved there.

Also like, my work authorization will end in less than two years. Peter said he might sponsor my green card—

Listen, my friend, Amit interrupted. It is time for you to get reacquainted with reality, because this man is not sponsoring shit.

From a scooping shift at Leon's I returned to find that Marina's friends had done up the place. White and gold balloons were leashed to corners; the Chemex now housed a gargantuan flower display.

Alice and India had hated me upon sight. From the minute they disembarked and found me waiting with Marina on the acres of commuter-blue carpet at MKE, I confirmed their worst suspicions, and they mine. India was tall and blond; she wore feather earrings and ankle-brushing cotton dresses. Deadstock, she said with a shrug when I complimented them, and I nodded, not knowing what she meant. Her voice was very, very soft. It was as though you had taught a kitten human language. In her many-ringed hand she clutched a glass carrier cup half-full of what appeared to be carrot juice.

Alice was a yoga instructor, with a sleeve of Hindu temple tattoos to prove it. Her skin was bronzed a deep, startling orange. She wore an old-time mechanic's shirt, its short sleeves rolled tight. The name *Dean* was embroidered over its breast pocket. Her hair, which she'd dyed a braying pink, was styled in a cropped bob that sliced little crescents into her cheeks.

I watched them hungrily, trying to better see my girl through these two new tinted lenses. The three of them were squealing, jumping, hugging each other. Primarily to feel like something other than airport furniture, I took phone pictures. Three heads together, smiling big and white, hair crushed together in a thicket of gold, pink, green.

Awww, I said, in earnest. Y'all look like the Powerpuff Girls.

Marina laughed softly. No one else made any reply to this, and we piled in the Kia Soul.

The Powerpuff Girls had reunited, which is to say, Alice had invited herself and India over to Milwaukee on the occasion of Marina's twenty-eighth birthday. Clearly assuming I had planned nothing for the occasion, the two of them set about contriving their idea of an appropriately grand celebration. I felt trapped and uneasy. Still, I melted before Marina's visible happiness.

We had been having a tough time of it, she and I. When I told her I got an interview for the job Amit had helped connect me to in Washington, D.C., she'd startled cold. I don't see myself in D.C., she said, the dance scene there is not what I want for myself. She added, Not that you're asking me to go there with you, clearly.

Still, she helped me prepare for the Skype interview. Did my makeup. Wished me luck. That is the problem with Marina. She believes various unfortunate things about herself, thinks herself bad, like so many of us have been taught to. But she has a clean heart, goodness pumping through its ventricles. She is nearly always generous.

I muffed the interview, I thought. I answered the questions well enough, but I did not have nearly the amount of experience they wanted for archivist work. I tried to explain the change management process to my interviewer, a tough-nugget dyke with an auburn ponytail, round glasses, a picture of her wife and her on the wall. Again and again I attempted to summon the specter of Peter's rock star—a hungry efficiency, a winning demeanor, an ability to transmute deep personal longing for order in one's world into the administration of disorder in service of capital.

Afterward I'd walked out and seen Marina, headphones on under a silk headscarf, leaping and weaving around the living room. Practice for her company's show. She popped the headphones off.

How was it?

I don't think I will be moving, to D.C. or anywhere. At least not for that job!

So as not to seem maudlin, I seasoned this with a laugh or two. The Pink House came to mind in that moment, unbidden. To be with Marina, to try to look into even a trial run of living together in a group home with my friends, while renting but cheaply (but with what money?), could justify a choice to stay in Milwaukee, keep looking for work, for at least a few months. I should, I thought, finish the damn project plan, add some realistic suggestions for how to achieve the vision incrementally, over the years.

Marina put her arms around me. I sensed something thawing in her. You can stay here as long as you need to, she said, and I knew we were both dwelling on what was not sayable—Jenny Shin's squatting, how Marina would probably like to live together for a reason more expansive than logistical ease. I smarted. Who wants to stay at their girlfriend's place on sufferance? I kissed her on her cheek. It smelled sweet and tannic.

I'm excited for you to meet Alice and Indy tomorrow, she said. They're a riot, like so funny and sweet and fun. And they can't *wait* to meet you, babe. It's been a minute since we had some fun, you and me. I want to go out with you, go to bars, *dance* with my girl—

Yay, I said, thinking of the price of drinks out, not as convincing as I could have been. And I'm excited, I murmured into her collarbone, for your show.

So you're coming.

Of course I'm coming. Do I seem like I have a particularly busy schedule?

Later that day I walked to the Public Market with Marina's credit card to replenish our wine supply for the visit. The air outside smelled like warm grass, freshly cut. Suddenly I missed Thom in a terrible and lurching way, missed, of all things, what it felt like to work to realize something with a friend, even something as objectively useless as an inbox change management plan. In front of the lobster tank I stood for a long time, watching the creatures crawl slowly over each other.

The next night, two golden numerals bobbed with a helium serenity above Marina's bookcase. On the granite counter stood what appeared to be the spoils of half a liquor store. Even with my cash infusions from Leon's, this represented more than all the money I had to my name. Good champagne, tequila, vodka, bourbon. Wine, beer, seltzer for the squares.

From Marina's bathroom I heard shared laughter, the soft roar of an expensive blow-dryer. These were the final minutes before guests would arrive. I picked up a small shot glass, chased my mortification down with a peg of something translucent and burny. In a way, her friends had been right. Never would I have thought to plan any of this, let alone its second act: bottle service at LaCage, dancing at the Pint. Even if I'd had the means. I had no idea that a person might want to be fêted that way.

I was unhappy and anxious at the party but tried not to let this on. At some point I found myself so sozzled I could barely hold a conversation. Which was immaterial, considering that nobody was talking to me. I wished for my friends, whom I had not felt right inviting, given that I'd paid for nothing. When Marina blew out the sparkler candles on her cake, I kissed her for an infinitesimal second before she vanished into the crowd. Then was relegated to piecing out the great slab of fluff and frosting. Handing out plates with an unsticky smile.

All sound seemed looping and chaotic to me, the remixes of Maxwell and Metronomy thumping away into my head. Quietly as I could, I made myself vomit.

When I walked out of the bathroom there stood Alice, her lip curling slightly. Hi! I said, brightly, stupidly, and slipped out into the hallway. Unsure of where to go after. Out into the stairwell, I decided, with its metal echo, its white secrecy. Down on a step I plonked heavily, and then, agitated by the boom of the party's sound still filtering through all these doors, fled upward. Some inhabitants of the fourteenth floor, a story above Marina's, had dragged a cracked leaner mirror to their landing.

The paleness of my own face sent an electric bolt up my spine. My cheeks were clammy from purging, my eyelashes wet, but what ran a current of shock through me was that I, in that moment, in that darkened stairwell with its tricks of light and angled mirror, seemed mistakable for white.

The party pounded below me, blessedly unheard, the party where I felt as insubstantial to the elements, as disintegratable as any of Tig's old bath bombs, where the only other brown face I'd seen was Shaka's, hovering around the fridge, surrounded by a gaggle of hungry straight girls. Farther up the stairs I walked, pushed through the door.

The roof was dark and pure and open. Around its perimeter I walked, heart calming, and then I heard Alice's voice, its bread-knife edge.

All I ask is that you don't throw your life away for some twenty-three-year-old.

In response, a strained laugh.

I peeked over the roof's edge, saw Marina's pale head nestled close to her friend's, two balconies below.

They were sharing a cigarette, I realized after a moment of terror. No silly business. Alice was saying they should leave for LaCage, Marina insisting they wait for me, or at least wait till she'd tracked me down.

Alice: I'm glad you're happy. If you're happy.

Marina: You were always most concerned with my happiness.

Alice: L.A. misses you, babe.

Marina: L.A. was bad for me. You know that.

Alice: I'm just wondering, like how much of you staying here is—her. I'm glad the job is going well. But you could, especially now, get that sort of gig a hundred places. And like, being here, after hearing Milwaukee this Milwaukee that, I truly do not get it—

Marina: Well then don't *you* live here. Don't *you* date her.

Alice: I mean, she's cute and all. I pictured you with someone different. Someone . . .

Marina: What.

Alice: Grown.

Marina: Jenny was grown—

Alice: And she's mad awkward in a group. You have to admit that—

Marina: —didn't stop you from sniffing around.

Alice: Don't put that on me. You weren't happy. You had a say in the matter.

Marina: I'm going inside.

Glass door slide. Bloom of sound. Glass door slide. Quiet.

There is a state of upset where faking sick feels not at all like an untruth. I texted an update, recaptured the bedroom from the gossiping dancers, told Marina in a whimper to have fun out, sorry about this, happy birthday baby, go wild.

From a sleep like death I woke to crashing sounds in the kitchen, identified an already-deepening hangover. The neon of the bedside clock said 1:45, the sky outside confirming the night.

Marina appeared to be cooking—something. Halved cloves of garlic were strewn about, papery skins sticking to them. In a pot, spirals of pasta lay in water resolutely unboiling, mushroom caps bobbing above like buoys. Her face was red and angry.

What the hell are you doing? I said, getting myself a glass of water, fumbling desperately on her upper shelves for Advil. On the counter, amid the strewn cups and emptied bottles, a cracked jar of oregano, a tin of turmeric, seemingly knocked down from shelves in agitation.

Mouth puckered in a lemon smile, I began to pick up the glass sections of jar. She asked me to step off. Just trying to make myself some fucking food, she said.

Let me help you. Hey, your fusilli needs to be on way higher heat.

I'm good, trust.

How was LaCage.

Shitty. Her shoulders slumped.

Why.

India broke out a bunch of coke in the bathrooms, some of the company dancers got in on it, just a mess. It just upset me. I don't like being around it, she should know that.

Because of your mom?

Butchering yellow onions with an alarming haphazardness, Marina angrily stammered, Look, I wish you'd been there. It was my *birthday*. I know you were feeling sick. I just, I needed you there.

The room suddenly felt like it was deflating. Its walls sagging in at a disorienting speed. I'm sorry, I said, as soft as Marina was loud.

I don't know! I feel like you would die for your friends. You're such a goddamn romantic about them. Sometimes it's like sweet to see and shit. But sometimes I wanna be like, Fuck off, go off with them, go live with Tig, not me! I want *something* from you, I want to know I am a priority, I want to know that I might be the person you call. That's what most people want, to know they're fucking significant to their person. All I get from you is wall after wall, like there's something I can't break through to. Sometimes you just want a door, you know?

I called you when Peter fired me.

Ah, I just assumed Tig or Thomas didn't pick up, she spat, throwing onions and potatoes into a sizzling pot and savagely grating a brick of cheddar.

What are you even making, Marina.

Pasta. Obviously. Leave me alone.

Maybe this is not working for you, I said, a familiar raw feeling climbing up the back of my throat. I wouldn't want you to *throw your life away* for *some twenty-three-year-old*.

Her eyes turned wide and fawn-like.

How did you—

Your bitch of a friend's got a carrying voice, what can I say.

I don't even— Look, she said it, not me, you shouldn't blame me.

Who said she's wrong? Why are you here? You could be in L.A., Chicago, New York, being the next Kate Jablonski or whoever you keep mentioning. Don't let *me* keep you from greatness.

I'm not saying I wanna live in Milwaukee forever! But I spent eleven years in the biggest cities in the world. Maybe I want to build something fresh somewhere new! Maybe I want to be able to afford to own a fucking home someday. Maybe I want to get married if straights ever allow it, have a kid with the right person, have a fuckin' yard.

There was a ringing silence.

Did you ever date Alice, I said.

Again the shoulder slump.

I slept with— I cheated with Alice once, she mumbled finally. I don't even remember. I was so drunk. I was back in L.A. on a job, and it happened. I was relieved, in a way. Showed me the writing on the wall. I came back, told Jenny we needed to break up, she refused to accept it, and then we were stuck for months. Anyway, I don't know how or what you heard, but yeah, Alice is totally jealous, that's definitely a contributing factor, and like, you're younger and hot and interesting in a way she's— yeah. But she's still my friend.

She seems trash to me, TBH.

Yeah so she's a tough one. But she's my friend. We've moved through a lot of time together. We were two kids in Boyle Heights finding our footing in the world, trying to become real dancers. I was a baby from the Jerz running away from my life, trying to make something decent of myself, and she took me under her wing, showed me what's up. She's always honest with me, not to say she's always right, just that I can trust her to say the thing. Alice will tell me if my drinking's gotten to be too much, like, she'll tell me what she thinks. That shit counts, not for everyone, but it does for me. I don't know.

Poor Jenny, I said acidly.

Marina covered her eyes with her right hand, turned her back to me, and burst out crying. Tightly compressed sobs ricocheted off the kitchen walls. They came harder when I wrapped my arms around her. She tried to push me away, shrug out of my hold. I didn't mean that, I said, again and again, trying to rub apology into her hot skin, dread drumming in my ears.

Finally she touched my face, wiped a streaming nose on the back of her hand. I'll be okay, she rasped. We'll be okay. I just need to eat and feel a bit sorry for myself. It was my freakin' birthday.

Yeah. Yeah. I'll clean up a bit so you can sit, I offered. Heart full of contrition.

As I set plates down on the cleared coffee table, I heard a scream. This followed by Marina shrieking, Don't look at me!

Baby, what—

Don't come here, don't look at me. I'll clean it up. Don't come here.

After seven frozen seconds of wondering whether she'd shit her pants, I disobeyed. Marina was holding an open Cento can. Its silver mouth flapping. She was shaking like a leaf. Tomato everywhere, down the fridge. On the floor. Down the front of her oxford shirt.

I'll clean it up, she said again, I don't want help, stupid thing just slipped out of my hand. Just one more thing! Cherry on top of this ice cream fuckin' sundae of a night!

Behind her the potatoes were smoking whitely. I stepped over the lakes of crushed pink flesh and turned the range off. Let me help you, I said, gently insistent, and took the yellow can from her hand, which appeared to pour tomato juice upon the floor with renewed vigor.

Yesu, I cursed softly. Guided her over to the sink, stuck her arm under the faucet's coldest gush. The tomato melted away.

And then over her forefinger, a dark ring of red bloomed, streamed a steady rivulet down her arm and into the sink.

Somewhere between walking Marina to the couch, bringing her ice and a clean towel, soothing her near-hysterical refusal to go again to the hospital, I tapped into a beatific exterior calm, even as my insides were liquefying. Apply direct pressure here, I instructed her, and then, as a black line of blood careened down her bare thigh onto the couch, I recognized I was in over my head. I excused myself, stepped out into the hallway, and called my mother.

If the cut was deep enough, Mummy told me, if it was still bleeding after five to ten minutes of pressing down on it, if its edges seemed lacy or refused to come together, then there was no help for it, and my friend should go to the hospital.

She doesn't have the money, I said, and my mother replied, in her blunt way—inadvertently reminding me that white men writing philosophy books did not invent collective thinking—Then you help her, no? She can pay you back? That is what money is for.

Otherwise, my mother said, put ice, put some Dettol—

There's no Dettol in America, Mummy, but I'll find something.

If you have mañnal root juiced or raw honey that has not been treated, you can put that after, my mother added, to help the healing. Antibacterial, also gives the cells strength to fight the infection.

The tin of turmeric, belly-up on the granite counter. Mañnal powder is okay? I asked.

Likely not, could be mixed with other things, could be abrasive. Mol, why are you and your friend doing all this koparati so late there? Mol, you call me back, okay? You tell me if the bleeding stops.

From the living room I heard Marina calling my name like a question.

As I carefully poured manuka honey into the slash ringing my girl's finger, draped it with gauze, told her she would be right as rain, I felt the terror I would come to be ever better acquainted with in the years that followed, at the fragility of bodies, the bodies of everyone I loved; we are, at the close of things, bags of meat and blood encasing what's en-souled: mercurial, flickering, holy.

As we made preparations to drop into bed, red-eyed and exhausted, my mother began to call again and again and would not stop. Out into the hallway I stepped, then elected to take mercy on Marina's neighbors. One of us softball-evicted over a noise complaint was quite enough.

From the roof I rang my mother back, prepared to tell her all was fixed, no issue, about to go to sleep now, Mummy.

Instead of this, I cried like a water balloon pricked. Like the small stupid child I knew myself to be. Said it plain. That I had been fired, that the property manager who lived below me had been after me for months, that in two weeks I would be kicked out of my apartment.

It feels so *bad* to tell you any of this, I gasped. Because of what you and Papa went through. I'm not a good child, and it's okay, I never have been, but I wanted to honor what you all did for me, Ma, I wanted to *at least* not cause you pain—

My nose dripped.

My mother asked me a few questions, her voice calm.

Okay, mollé, she said gently. Don't worry so badly. We will call in the morning. You go get sleep now.

Walking down the stairwell, I tried to remember what Marina had said once about tears. They midwifed the variegated emotions your body held, left you cleaner, open. Walking into her living room I did feel a fraction lighter. Absentmindedly I molested the Kleenex box. Blew my nose like a battle conch.

Then saw, doubled against my reflection in the French door's glass, a woman in a yellow puffer jacket, cigarette in hand, watching me from the darkness of her balcony.

Hey, baby, I said brightly, sliding the French door wide to the night. I cast around for something cursory to say about my wept-out face. Every seasoned liar knows minimalism is the key. My mendacity: the only professional-level skill I'd been left with.

How's the hand, I asked, poor muffin—

Marina was staring at me as though she had never seen me before. The back of my mouth tasted the rise of something from the region of my belly. Fear.

Who were you on the phone with? she whispered. Jaw tight. Eyes barreling toward me like a train.

Oh! Someone I—

No really, who were you speaking to—her small chin flicked upward—on my roof?

My eyes sought the curve of the Milwaukee lakeside, buried in the night. Somewhere in the June dark perched a wide pink house skirted by undulating grass, childish fantasy of an unfounded future. There was no help for it. I let out a great gasping exhale.

Heart cracking for all I knew I'd lose with the truth, I gave it up; quietly I said, My mother.

I cannot set down what came right after, other than to note that for days I dreamed nearly every night of the two of them, Marina and my mother, blurring together, wearing each other's clothes, upbraiding me for each other's grievance. To say that when I finally came back to my apartment, I knew a certain kind of bombed-out, floodlit peace, the great terror and relief of being known.

It was on this day and in this state of mind that I received a call from a number I did not recognize. A D.C. area code. As my phone continued to ring I blew my nose, watched the thin black tile vibrate.

Hello, I said thickly, picking up. This is Sneha.

Do I get to meet her? Tig asked, their eyes shining with excitement. You've met *my* mom like three times now—

We were crowded around Diana's dining table, her son's coloring pages strewn everywhere.

Yeah. Like probably. If nothing else, just show up on moving day.

Your dad coming too?

No. That pesky deportation thing, ya know?

Shit. Sorry. Sorry. Pass the wine, I'll wash down my foot.

While they took a gulp of Yellow Tail moscato, I said, Yeah, honestly I wish she wasn't insistent on coming. Super not necessary. Unfortunately she was convinced my life was falling apart.

Not anymore, bitch! You'll be on the East Coast with like a 401 account and healthcare and shit! Ayyyyyy! You have a J-O-B, and a decent one, fancy bitch!

Stoppp. Hey, Diana, thank you for all this, the borscht is *so* good, oh no thanks, I already took thirds—

So I've mostly forgiven you, Tig said on our after-dinner walk, a meandering stroll through Bay View. Mostly. The Rion project plan you sent over was sick. I don't even know how you did that budget increment shit—straight sorcery. But I wanted *you* there. I thought you were *in*. The whole point of comradeship is that it is deeper than just friendship. It is about deep intimacy, about working towards common aims. I'm *happy you have a good job*, I know it was hard looking, I know you were fucking

ALL THIS COULD BE DIFFERENT · 239

going through it, don't look at me like that, hoe. But I do have abandonment issues, you know.

Think of who you're talking to, I said, pointing to my chest. Bro, the molecules of my whole body are just carbon and abandonment issue. Look, I'm still in shock about it. This wasn't my plan. But you'll come visit. I'll come visit.

Tig and I walked down their street, turned on KK. It was the dog-walking hour. The day had been scorching, its evening cooling to a pleasantness. Tig bounded from puppy to puppy, exclaiming. I, belly uncomfortably full of borscht, was more circumspect in my affections.

With remarkable unselfconsciousness Tig began singing "I'll Be Seeing You."

Did you know he's from here, they asked, as they petted and cooed at an inky Labrador outside LuLu.

Who's from here?

Liberace!

Whoa, no way.

Yup! A flaming Pole straight from Dirty Stallis.

I thought the only *big* musician outta Sconsin was like, Bon Iver.

You so crazy. What? Son. *Garbage* came outta here. Brother Ali, hello. Les Paul—you wouldn't have Slash or Hendrix or the Who without Les, that's a Waukesha boy. Kelli Jo dad used to play sax for Al Jarreau. The Violent Femmes, they're from the Ill Mil. James Brown's drummer, he's a legend, Clyde Stubblefield, he still plays in Madison, we should've driven up sometime. Yo, so many big-name people are from here, though! Orson Welles, Spencer Tracy, *Oprah*. Lauren Ingalls Wilder or whatever her name—TBH I never read one of those books, but Diana and every whitegirl under the sun are obsessed—

Only some of these people sparked any recognition for me, but I chose to humor this. Antigone was newly sensitive to the possibility that I would turn into a snobby East Coast type, dismiss the center of the country and, with it, cities like this one.

Tig's litany of defensiveness appeared to be running out of gas. Houdini! they burst out, furrowing a brow in concentration. Georgia O'Keeffe!

One day they'll say your name, I said, smiling. Antigone Clay. Milwaukee's own.

Uh, they just might! Tig laughed and then appeared to startle. Shit, they muttered. I followed their eye line.

Right across the street, in the Boulevard Theatre's display window, were Marina and Shaka. Leotarded bodies midflight, furled like flags. *You Are Invited to an Artistic Experience*, the poster read in a brash, slightly corny font. *Shamar Dance Presents: REFRAIN*.

In silence we continued on. You gonna go? Tig asked softly.

I don't know. Like no, probably? Besides, tomorrow Thom and I are picking up my mother.

So y'all done done now?

I don't see how we come back from the shit I pulled.

Tig knelt down, retied a shoelace. Their feet are very small and delicate. Looking up at me, they asked, You feel like you're okay with it being over?

Somewhere within me a wound reopened at its lacy edges, a wild regret spurted bright and dizzying and carotid. No, I said very quietly. I mean, I'm glad the truth is out, I guess, it was always a lie I stumbled into and was so much work to maintain, and for what, I don't know now. No, I don't feel okay. I miss her. I fucked it up. Nothing to be done.

Hmmm, my friend said, and we walked in silence for a great long time, until they said, I think you can still try to see what future's there.

Don't be crazy.

Again. Not my type. Not what I'd do. If *I* was going to a new city I'd take a few months and just focus on being my best hoe self. But that's me, and you're you. You have big feelings for your lil dancer boo. And she, from the moment I first was introduced, has felt insecure cuz of her notion that she's the one with feelings, not you. All of which is to say, if you told her you want her, that might hold more weight than you think.

Yeah I'm leaving, though.

Bitch, let me introduce you to a concept called: gay people. If you haven't done yearning-filled long distance are you even a lesbian? Or just tell her you want her to come with you.

To this I said nothing. The sun dipped beyond the lake's horizon. Light cooling, water graying.

Hey, wanna go to Garibaldi? Tig asked. Feeling a beer, personally.

Bro, please no. I overdrafted my account twice in the last two months. Had to break out my CD early, pay this dumb-ass penalty, to even reserve my U-Haul box—

Ugh, like I could pay for us—

No, broke ass. You spend too much money. Let's just walk. Walking is free.

You're such an uncle. Please don't be this way in Washington.

As we passed Club Garibaldi, a high-ceilinged bar where suits and tattoo sleeves alike washed down wings with Blatz and Mudpuppy Porter, I ignored Tig's wheedling eye. We were by a large brown plaque, one I'd never noticed in the nighttime. Over the damp grass I walked to it. It said BAY VIEW'S ROLLING MILL.

Oh shit. Yeah, the Bay View Massacre happened here.

Huh, I said, and made to read it, but Tig, perhaps given their own struggles with the medium, continued.

You had people, workers all over the country then, working sixteen-hour days, six days a week. Immigrant organizers in Milwaukee. They got people to walk out of work, strike for an eight-hour workday. Literally thousands of people showed, like half the city.

Whoa.

God's truth. Strikers shut down every factory in the city 'cept this one. Fourteen thousand people out here marching, they got the National Guard out. Tried to send protestors packing! When they wouldn't leave, these motherfuckers shot at them and came after them with bayonets and shit.

Night by now was coming for us, spreading through the sky. A streetlight flickered to life, beamed down. In all my time here I had not looked at the books on Milwaukee's past. All this history unknown to me. Tig turned to me.

Their face flushed, something new and fearsome in it.

Don't you dare forget this place, they said. I think you'll eventually maybe make something of yourself out east. One reason why I'm letting you go. But don't you ever, ever, ever become one of those people nose in the air, calling all this—Tig gestured around wildly—*flyover country*. Thinking we're just about beer and cheese and serial killers and corn. Things happen here. Happened here. *This place* is part of why the rest of this stupid godforsaken nation has child labor laws and workplace safety and unemployment insurance. Why we have weekends and an eight-hour workday. We had forty years of actual socialist city government, democratically elected, here. Only city in the nation. FDR was inspired by what happened here. When he dreamed up his lil New Deal and shit. Milwaukee, baby. We have real history. Remember us right.

I'd been more afraid to tell Tig than Thom, and so had spoken to him first. But he was the one who seemed saddest I would leave. Isabel finally breaking up with him, not leaving the door open to anything besides the two of them moving on from each other, had changed him more radically than I'd understood.

What'll u do there, he'd texted, and followed it up with, thought u said you did the interview badly. typical.

I didn't get the job at the National Archives, I explained. The interviewer went with someone experienced. But they recommended me for a project associate position at the National Archives *Foundation*. A whole different deal. I'll be helping them with their internal communications, run a project plan to relocate offices. They offered $42K, with healthcare and a 3% 401K match. I told them I had a background in change management. They ate it up.

Despite his own previous struggles to find work, Thom appeared more mystified that I was leaving for something so patently unsexy. Was it the breakup? he'd asked over shrimp balls and beef pho on the South Side the day before I walked around Bay View with Tig.

Phan's is cozy, pungent, plant-studded, pink as organs. Everything in there cost less than eight dollars. I did not want to go anymore to places with expensive entrees where only the comfortable ate. I felt safe at Phan's, felt at home.

I shook my head, even though the call had come a day after I'd walked, backpack and suitcase in hand, back from Marina's apartment to my notional residence on the Hill.

Yo, I needed a job, I said, and was afraid I would never get one if I stayed here. I tried for months.

Ah. Yeah, job market is musty ballsacks right now. I don't know, my dude. It seems intense to just up and leave. Do you know anyone there?

My mother has a friend from nursing school there. I'll be staying with her for a few weeks while I find roommates and whatnot.

Huh. I'm just saying. It's a bummer, though. Tig and I were looking at the project plan for cooperative housing—thank you for putting that together, by the way. It could be this legitimately cool thing. There are *some* jobs here, if you wait it out.

Not all of us can work construction, my guy.

And you call yourself a dyke, he said, popping a shrimp ball in his mouth, shaking his head. Cheers to you, bruh.

Cheers to me.

Thom's body, once dense and soft as the custard I scooped two days a week, had turned solid, gained new tightness and definition. The Rabine effect, the twelve-hour-shift-of-physical-labor effect. Still, except when he was jovial, there was a lostness in his face I had not seen before.

He asked if I'd made any moves in getting my back pay from Peter.

Sort of. Not really. I wrote him an email to like shame him into it, but I've felt too stressed to send it.

Shame him! Let's see it.

Glasses on, his brow furrowed as he read the draft on my phone. I was rather proud of the email. It appealed to Peter's better angels, it vividly described my pain and privation, it protested his suggestion that my recorded hours were not accurate, and it requested my back pay, with the last few months of rent subtracted as concession.

Shit fire and save the matches, you are so fucking crazy, Thom said. What did I just read. Are you under the impression that Peter runs his business for some sort of *moral* afterglow? Are you trying to make him *feel bad* on your behalf?

I just think—

Son, you're so smart in so many ways, but like, please listen to me on this. Flaming Nora, I'm gonna have a heart attack. The man owes you money, money you worked for. You made him money, whatever bullshit he says to belittle you. Did you ever see the invoices Peter billed the clients? He may have paid me what he paid me and paid you what he paid you, which like, whatever, but he billed the same amount for both of us, fifty an hour. So like—

Fifty?

This is about power, my guy. Don't get it fuckin' twisted! You write this fucker a cool and clear and short email. You attach your timesheets, your proof of payment, and the amount you are still owed. And then you fucking make it clear that he can pay you or see you in court. Wage theft lawsuit, sonofabitch. He'll have to pay you the money owed *and* your legal fees. It'll be sick.

It just feels like so much, Thom, I said, hating the pleading note in my voice. It seemed like a great risk to assume that things would go my way. At seventeen I had seen the inside of a court for the first time. Had expected my father to walk free.

Thom shook his head. Don't leave money on the table! he exclaimed. It's *your* money. We need to eventually seize the means of production, obvs, make businesses worker-owned co-ops or at minimum unionize them, but until then at least take the *crumbs* that are contractually allotted to you. You have every right!

I'll think on it, I said, and he flicked my ear like a fourth grader.

Back in the car, he said, So when we picking up your mom from the airport?

Her flight gets in at ten a.m. day after tomorrow. I can be ready at nine twenty at my place or come to you. Thank you so much.

De nada. Promise me you'll learn to fucking drive on the East Coast.

D.C.'s not a big driving city. But I will do it so I can come back and visit your fool ass.

You have what you need to like pack and stuff with your mother? Boxes and tape and mattress bags and shit?

I did not have in my possession so much as a single roll of tape. Ever-obliging Thom swung us toward the hardware store. We parked by Sneha Dry Goods, its awning pink like a tongue, flapping slightly in the sun. In its window bolts of fabric, stacked boxes of nag champa and henna.

Walking back to the car, bag full of moving supplies, I looked up at the awning and grimaced.

Why d'you hate your name so much? Thom asked. He'd been watching me, leaning against the trunk of his car. Hands in sweatpant pockets.

I shook my head. Move, let me put my stuff in, I said.

What, tell me! Does it translate to like stinky pits or something in India.

Shut up, I said, feeling a floral, pistilled anger open quietly in me. This flippant fool.

Does it mean . . . hairy snatch.

Fuck. Off.

Does it mean big farty slut—

It means love! I shrieked, and punched him hard in the neck.

What the fuck, he gasped, and I hit him again, and again, suddenly light-headed with fury, the bag of moving supplies spilling at my feet. New Thom, Captain America Thom, was not having this. In minutes my hands were pinned in his. Still I continued flailing, may have tried to bite him. Summarily I was put in a headlock.

If you try whatever *that* was again, he hissed, God help you.

My whole body was trembling; I forced my lungs to take in air, my limbs to slacken. After what felt like many minutes Thom allowed me upright.

Jesus fuck, he said.

I'm sorry, I said, voice calm and appeasing. I lost control. It has not happened in a very long time, but it did. I'm sorry.

Thom massaged his neck.

That was not cool whatsoever. I was just goofing. Wasn't like trying to make a race joke, if that's what got you fucking riled—

From above the pink awning my mind floated, cool bubble on a sea of doom. A born spectator. Evaluating this absurd tableau. No, I said, channeling all my strength into putting words in relationship to other words, trying to metamorphose back into a person, civil and reasonable and contrite. No, it's not that.

What is it then?

It's complicated.

What isn't? I'd like to know. Words not fists, if you don't mind, crazy lady.

Across the street from us a couple walked, arms around each other, pecking each other at clockwork intervals. Their faces marked by adoration. A red car streamed by. I thought of kissing Pulp Fiction under a streetlight. Those early days, before the mess was visible to all.

My parents poured all their hopes into me, I finally said, in monotone, not able to look at him, thinking this was as good a place to start as any. I'm their only child. Something went wrong when I was born, like my mother had to take out her uterus after. My parents are good people. They love me so much. Everything they've done is for me. But they were always busy, always working. In our culture there is not always a big focus on, like, attention, affection, saying feelings out loud. And I think— the way I remember it, I—I was a needy little girl. Very excitable, loving, very hungry for—contact.

I swallowed hard, searching for the words. Slowly I became aware my fingers were wrapped around a warm object.

There was someone, I said, breathing hard through my nose, who paid attention to me. Made me feel special and listened to, played all kinds of games with me. This was a grown-up. He was often mean, but also he felt like my best friend. This person was not a good person. Let's just leave it at that. After he'd touch me and stuff—ugh seriously, I promise I'm okay, I'm really okay, not some small broken bird, everyone has something unpleasant to happen to them in this life and this is mine and honestly I'm over it—anyway, once I was old enough to know it was fucking not good, I would avoid him, be cold to him. He was always around, always hanging around. Anyway, he would put on this big sad act, in front of my mother. Sneha doesn't care about me, he'd say, I'm so sad because of Sneha. He'd add, What a funny thing her name is Sneha. He'd say, Do you know what Sneha means? He wouldn't stop asking me, Do you know what Sneha means.

The thing in my fingers was exerting a strange pressure upon me. I looked down. It was Thom's hand. Big and warm and pale. Squeezing mine.

My mother would say, finally, if only to have some peace, she would say to me in this cooing way, Sneha means love! Go give nice ummas—ummas, it's like kisses—go, and she'd push me towards him. I'd have no choice. He'd leave me alone for a few weeks, and the cycle would start again. And you know, it was so hard when my parents left to go back, because like, they left me, because my dad got deported and all that shit, but also because they were going back to the place where he was, like I realized I would always have to deal with *him* every time I went back to see my parents, at least while he was alive. It's hard because I am so incapable of it, of love, it feels like a weird terrible ironic rebuke, like I was never able to say it to Marina, even though—like I did—yeah. It's just weird. To feel the lack of what your own name says about you.

That's not true, Thom said very gently. I don't think you are incapable.

I don't know. Anyway. Yeah. I am sorry I lost it.

Jesus Christ on toast, Thom said under his breath.

I cleared my throat. I'm really okay, I said, conjuring up a smile from some dusty corner of my capacity. Will you drive me home?

Thom pulled me into his arms. Did not let go. Minutes rocked by. At some point I became aware I was drawing great deep ragged breaths. Not from telling the story, which was stupid and tawdry and one blessed day would wedge firmly in the dustbin of the past, never to be thought of again. It was his touch. Urgent and warm. Large arms like swaddling. The feeling of safety this lent.

tickticktick went the timepiece within me. Up I tilted my head and kissed my friend. A small moist peck. Exploratory, with a willingness to concede more ground. Our bodies pressed together. I felt him stiffen and grow against me. This seemed exciting.

Harder I pushed, opening my mouth. He retreated. Held me at arm's length. Earlier a tear had run down his face, disappeared into his beard. A thin line of wet.

I can't do it, my guy, he said. You are very cute and dope obviously, like if the timing had been different . . . maybe. But right now in my life I feel like I'd break apart into one thousand pieces. And as your friend I will be honest with you—I don't think *I'm* the one you actually want.

A sight I had never in my life pictured: Rice and rajma and coconut dal on the range, Tig laughing with my mother, both seated on newspaper. Boxes all around. Thom sawing through the meat he had grilled and driven over.

It's not my best, he told Mummy, grinning big and toothy. She laughed, jerked her head over to the stove. Said, That also is quite far from my best.

I hope in Washington, D.C., my daughter will buy and keep more than two spices in the house, she added.

She ate the rice and lentils with her hands, forming them into neat croquettes with her fingertips. Tig elected to imitate her in this, with subpar technique and outcome.

Are you *kidding*, Thom said upon first spooning the rajma into his mouth. Come *on*, ma'am. He mock-kissed the tips of his fingers. What do I have to do for this recipe? *This* is far from your best?

My mother reddened with pleasure. Actually, my best dish, she said simply, is non-veg. Take beef and fry it in a small bit of coconut oil, in a very tasty masala with onions, curry leaves, big fat chunks of coconut. The meat becomes very, very tender. With this I serve ladiesfinger and my homemade parathas, which are very flaky, very soft with ghee. That is actually my best.

Son, Thom said to me, when we going to India?!

Come anytime, my mother said with a smile, wobbling her head like a dashboard dog.

To the kitchen I went to briefly escape this love fest. As I was getting seconds of rajma, Tig gave my ass a mirthful pinch.

What a *flirt*, they whispered. Who knew he had it in him?

I shook my head, slid my eyes. It made sense enough. Once a father of a classmate in Aurora had described my mother as Julia Roberts, just short and in a sari. At least the boy was consistent. I winked at Tig. Holding the jar I had been drinking out of, I pointed below the Ball logo, to the words WIDE MOUTH.

Our laughter filled the kitchen, sound confetti, fluttering down and around us. For support I clutched the kitchen island, wheezing out my breaths. In vain Thom demanded entry to the joke.

Homie, he said in a low voice later, as I washed and he dried, you have to tell me what went down yesterday, okay? You always filling Tig in first is some essentialist shit. Every gender loves gossip. I'm hurt, my dude.

I would hardly call this *gossip*—

Right, sure, youknowwhaddimean. So, is she coming tomorrow? Are y'all . . . *back*?

In the dark theater I'd sat, feeling the crowd alive and murmuring all around me. Flowers in my hands.

I'd taken fabric scissors, walked down into Amy's plot of roses, thinking, What now, bitch. Sometimes you just want to embody karma yourself. Take the matter of comeuppance into your own hands.

As I went to make the first snip, conscience caught me, or perhaps it was the presence of my mother, who had arrived that morning and was sleeping her jet lag away. Good luck to your friend for her performance, she had said before resting her cheek on hands folded as if in prayer. I called Belle Fiori, asked them to rush a bouquet.

As I waited for the show to begin I read the program. It alternated smoothly between hip-hop, ballet, and contemporary; Vic Mensa spooning Sharon Van Etten.

Good evening, ladies and gentlepeople, thank you for coming to our show. Shaka in a red lamé blazer, spotlit, speaking what Marina had written.

> The meaning of *refrain* is split. Doubled. To refrain means to stop, to hold yourself back from something, keep yourself in check. But a refrain also points us to repetition. A song's refrain, constantly returned to. What is the thing that is remembered because it is constantly returned to? Think of the ballerina on a child's jewelry box. The refrains of our lives are the moments we revolve around, maybe the moments that were stopped too soon, stopped before we were ready, and so we are frozen, pirouetting in time, always thinking on the possibility that might have been. If only. If only.

Darkness dropped. A spotlight cleaved it. Dancers moved in parabola and wave, leaping, curving through the air as through a swimming pool. They paired up, they lifted each other into the air and moved their bodies discordantly, until the right music caught and they latched on again to perfect symmetry, moving as mirror, as clone. My chest grew cold. I watched.

As the applause faded, wiping wet from my face, I knew, for once in my stupid life, what I wished to do.

V3

Marina in the dressing room. Staring at me. My mind a sliver of Jolly Rancher on pink tongue, a metal spoon licked clean. Marina, in a marbled kimono and shiny black leggings. Her hand moved to her clavicle, tugging at the thin gold necklace resting upon it in mute agitation. Behind me I heard laughter and a striding step. In Shaka walked.

OH, he said, taking in the fact of me, looking from me to Marina. Oh okay! he went, appearing to divine something I could not from her face, whipping around and away.

Hey, I said. These are for you.

You came, Marina said, making no movement toward the bouquet.

I hope that's okay, I said. Look, it's your night, I'm sure you all have the after-parties and stuff to go to. I just wanted to come here and give you these and tell you—I felt my throat turn croaky—how *remarkable* I thought *Refrain* was. I went in knowing zero about any of, I actually went in expecting to feel like clueless and uncomfortable, like I know nothing about dance—

Believe it or not, your ambivalence was previously apparent, Marina said in icy tones. That's why when we were— That's why I asked you if you would actually come.

I came, I said, bowing my head slightly. It was incredible, what you did. It was real. It made something real happen. I don't know. I wish I could say a single smart thing about it.

She made a noise somewhere between sniff and snort.

How goes? Marina asked, staring around her dressing room, strangling herself with her gold chain.

Pretty shit, TBH, I said, taking a great deep breath. Look, it's your night. Y'all put on an insane show. Half the numbers I'm, I did not know bodies were capable of that. I'd like to talk to you some night when you're not celebrating, you should celebrate. I'll be in Milwaukee for the next two weeks, maybe we can find—

Two *weeks*, she said, finally seeming startled out of herself. You're leaving.

I am, I said. Well, I'm moving *out* two days from now and shipping my things, was going to stay with Tig for a bit, until my flight.

Like, leaving Milwaukee. And I'm hearing this now.

I am, I said. Do you think you'd be able to—talk—sometime?

Marina blinked tears away, jutted her jaw, and lit a cigarette. Taking long drags on it she said very fiercely, We can talk now, if you have something to say, say it now.

My lungs filled with air.

You are the person I want, I said softly. That has never not been true. There are all these ways in which I was scared and shut off and hedging bets all through our time together. In my own ways I am a—wounded—person, and some of the things I did, and many of the things I didn't do, are because of that. I've not been able to be honest, let someone in, tell the truth of my feelings. But I'm trying now. You are the person I want. If you don't want me back I'll understand. But I know I'll regret it all my life if I don't tell you this. You are what I want. If you were to come with me to D.C.—I would want that more than anything. I would be happy.

Marina took a terrible long pause. My skin itched with fear.

Why did you lie to me about your parents? she asked, eyes twin slits of heat.

Because I am a trash person and a coward.

She said nothing.

That's the short answer, I continued, and the language my friends had used in analyzing what had happened between us materialized in my mind, came in useful. I said, Look, please, it was an accident and a misunderstanding, at first, for real. You have to believe me. And then later it felt like a strange kind of freedom—I could pretend around you like I didn't come from parents, a culture, I don't know, that dislikes and fears people like you and me. It felt like putting on a different identity or splitting my self into two manageable halves. It felt like protection. And honestly, I have sabotaged every past relationship I've had the chance to be in, because it has felt very—difficult, like, dangerous, to be close, to be intimate, in a consistent way, without an expiration date—with anyone. It feels like an alarm is going off constantly, an alarm that only I can hear. So it was also, you could say, the most creative I'd ever gotten at self-sabotage. I'm sorry I made that choice, for lying to you. I will always regret it.

Marina turned away from me, put her head down on her arms on her dressing table, stayed that way for many minutes. Not knowing what to do, I stood where I was and waited.

Yeah so Annette is retiring from running the Brookfield studio, she said finally, voice nasal with snot. She offered the job to me to take over. It's seventy thousand dollars, good health insurance.

I tried to say congratulations. Could not speak.

In unnecessary clarification Marina added, I said yes.

We decided to decide nothing.

To See What Happens.

She would stay in Milwaukee.

I would go to D.C.

I would visit.

She might too.

We did not yet, both of us finally said after expostulation and anger, recrimination and apology, want the door between us forever closed.

Somewhere in the waning of this, Shaka had knocked very softly and then opened the door.

I don't want to interrupt nothing, ladies, he said. Eyes in the air as if we'd been caught naked. I don't want to keep y'all from y'all girlie processing, I just wanna come here and say to Marina that the after-party gonna start at Malika house, and if you want a ride I'ma head there now. I don't wanna get in the middle of anything—

Shaka baby, can you give me one minute!

She turned to me. Let out a long exhale.

Said, You want to come?

X3

Outside the house, mouth to its curb, the U-Box. Orange tarpaulin and Velcro, metal and wood, ready to be filled, then shipped to a new coast.

Aiyay, it looks too small, I said to Mummy. I should maybe just buy new furniture in D.C. Or I should only take the bedroom things.

Don't be a big sillybilly, my mother instructed me. Why waste money? Everything will fit. Where is your strong friend?

That would be me, Tig said, materializing behind us. They carried two boxes of pizza. Diana and her son walked in through my side door with liters of seltzer. Thom and KJ would arrive later in the afternoon if we needed reinforcements. From over by Wolf Peach came the sound of road jackhammering. Two seasons here, Thom had told me once: winter and construction.

Leave this to me, Tig yelled over the noise. Filled more U-Hauls than I want to think about.

That a lesbian joke or a poverty joke? Diana cracked. My mother shot a startled look at her, said nothing.

We start biggest first, all the way to the back, and pile to the ceiling, Tig called. They turned to me. Where ya bed at?

Every twenty or so minutes, I could not help but look out the window. We carried down the box spring, the dresser, the kitchen boxes. Shook and rolled the rugs. A song of dust. Diana's kid coughing hard. My mother administered a spoon of honey, said, patting him on his dark fuzzy head: Sweet boy, play outside. The plastic bear filled with golden goo back in the paper bag for St. Casimir.

Knocks and thuds. The staircase narrow. The street empty, each time I checked, save for the U-Box and Amy's small maroon truck. It was time for the couch, the tufted couch bought new, the couch that cost more than a month's rent, from a time when I thought things would go a different way. Tig was in the U-Box, playing Tetris.

It's okay, we can just take it, my mother said, directing us. We tipped the thing over. Wrapped it in furniture pads. Unscrewed the legs. Don't lift with your back, Diana said, demonstrating. My mother had the front, I the middle, Di the rear.

As we rounded the stairwell's curve, the door to the basement popped open. The Fiancé stood smiling. Amy must have deputized him. I stared at his teeth beaming anger up at us like a flashlight.

Hi! I know you're moving, but watch out about dropping the furniture and raised voices, he said to me. We can't hear ourselves think. We're nice people, we get it. Just a little courtesy is all we ask.

I could not speak. In disbelief I stared at him, bracing the couch with my hip.

While I have you, he said, appearing not to see my now-wobbling arms, Amy wanted me to tell you, don't forget to take out all the nails and fill the holes with spackle, and make sure nothing is left in the attic eaves. We will check them during the walk-through. I think you had a bunch of things nailed into the wall—

Registering a swift and enormous increase in the weight I was holding, I gasped and staggered, letting go without even realizing it. An *oh no* flew out of Di's mouth. Down the couch crashed. The Fiancé jumping out of the way with seconds to spare. His yell flying past me.

Before I could offer apology, indeed, find language, Mummy put her hand on the wrapped couch, beached like a whale.

Hello, my mother said very calmly to the man who had until now barely appeared to look at her. I am glad you were not hurt. I could not keep holding the sofa while you were talking and talking and *talking*.

The man made no reply. His face flat with astonishment, taking her in. Amy's voice from inside their apartment, calling his name like a question.

It is—peculiar—to be bothering people like this, when they are carrying heavy furniture, and moving out of a flat, Mummy said.

Look, the Fiancé began in tones of conciliation, I'm a nice person—

We are all very nice people here, my mother said, with an air of getting the nonsense out of the way. I am nicely suggesting you and your wife go work somewhere else, while we take my daughter's things out of this apartment, she appended, appearing, like Alice in the storybook, to grow large as the stairwell itself, staring her prey down with a dragon's eye until he turned and scurried back into his hole.

You want this box of stuff, girl? Diana asked me from the bathroom, shaking a dark oblong with the words NINE WEST on its lid up at me.

I took it from her, hugged it to my body. Tig's bath bombs. I'd never used them.

I'll find a place, I muttered.

The back of the U-Box was filling up, Tig having instructed us to pack everything in vertical walls, right up to the ceiling. On top of a Rubbermaid of winter clothes I wedged the bath bomb collection, went back into the house.

The future, of course, is unaccountable, antiknowable. I came to Milwaukee envisioning the life of a fledgling rock star in a blazer and hose, with three-martini lunches, steak houses and cigars, a different woman in my bed each week. All this until my youth, my allocated window of tolerated rebellion, ran its course. Instead I'd ended up with a biohazard of an apartment, a small nest of loving friends, a long wait in the line at St. Casimir. Was now leaving, bank account in tatters, to try to make good on a new coast of this strange country. I would say there is something especially American about second chances, but my father's timeline gives lie to that.

What I am trying to say is, to the extent I imagined the future of Tig's bath bombs, I'd pictured allotting myself one every few months in the new life.

A chance to wind down after a hard day's work. Conserving my friend's gift as long as it could run.

But that is not what happens. It will be a sun-drenched D.C. summer day, full of a prickling heat, when I return from the close of my first week of work in the new city and draw myself a bath. Since water is the only utility I do not pay for, I fill the tub deep. Perch the NINE WEST box on the sink's rim.

A cool lapping at my collarbone. I stretch my calves, sore from wearing my work heels on the Metro. Next to me, my phone begins to ring and ring.

Marina.

Peter has sent me a letter. Mailed it to her apartment. The last address I'd provided him. Should I open it? she asks. I, barely able to talk, choke out, Yes.

What I hear: Oh my god.

What is it, I demand, feeling crazed. Picturing a suit, a letter from a lawyer. Tell me, what is it, what did he send?

It's a check, she says.

I cannot speak a word. I'd followed Thom's advice. Sent the email, expecting nothing. Heard nothing back, all the intervening weeks.

Seventeen thousand dollars, she tells me. You got your money, whatever you sent worked. The bitch backed down.

On lifting the shoebox lid, my bath bombs explode the air with scent. When I tip them in, the whole box's worth, the chalky spheres bob in the water, harmless and bland. Fizzing slightly. Then they metamorphose. Pastel and neon and iridescent foam roars out their sides. They have names, somewhere. Intergalactic. Melusine. Sex Bomb. Twilight. Incredulously I laugh and laugh and laugh into the silence of the tiled room, beyond thought or language, ducking my head under the iridescent froth, only coming up, every part of me wild with glitter and color, once I can no longer breathe.

The U-Box was nearly full. My mother and my friends and I worked together to dismantle the remnants of residence, raising our voices over the construction's din. We wrapped the wall art. Packed the mugs. Carried down a profusion of boxes as packing tape sounds ripped the air. Off large squares of Brawny we ate pizza, the grease from the pepperoni glowing against tooth-colored cheese. With truly Herculean effort I prevented Diana from recounting a single childhood anecdote in front of my mother.

Compulsively I checked the window. My pulse sprinting. And then.

My good neighbor's maroon truck was gone. In its place, now parallel parking, a lime Kia Soul.

Hi, hi, hi! She wore white denim overalls, hair piled on top of her head, making her greetings, hugging my mother with genuine warmth. Hello, I'm Marina!

My mouth dry and oily as the pizza boxes.

When she had offered this and a conciliatory hug, avoiding my attempt at a kiss at the close of her after-party, I had not been able to say no. When she'd drawled, voice flat and bored, I'm fine with being framed as your friend, you're not the first girl I've dated who wasn't out to family, dude, I'd felt a wild, withering shame. I'd said only, Okay. Thank you. That's very kind.

So happy to meet you, you've come such a long way, Marina said to my mother. Smiling.

Betraying nothing. A dizzying grace.

What are we doing now? she asked. These boxes of clothes? Would you hold the door open for me?

My mother did. We cleaned the bathroom. Wiped down the fridge. Began to break down my desk.

Mol, I can throw away these papers, no? I heard from behind me.

Mummy, holding a stack of administrivia from Peter and the client, gesturing at a massive pile beside it. Days earlier I'd tried to look through it to see what I might need to keep. 1099s and pay stubs, timesheets and white papers. A million Excel printouts. It had felt so overwhelming I'd grown light-headed. Put it off and aside.

My mother grew cross that I had not already sorted the papers and dismantled the desk. We picked at each other. Our words smoking in the air.

Marina stepped in. I'll do a first pass at this, she said, placing a hand on my shoulder, and you can look it over. I'll keep contracts, timesheets, tax things. Sound okay?

Thank you, I whispered. Mummy smiled at Marina, her eyes crinkling at the corners. Next my mother and Tig decided to attend to the matter of the nails in the wall.

Where is your hammer, mol? You have a toolbox, my mother asked me, querulous.

My hammer—I know I have one, but I haven't seen it in months. It hasn't turned up when packing. And I don't really have anything else, besides this screwdriver—I waved the Phillips from the upturned Walmart computer desk.

Yesu, my mother muttered. And do you have this filling material?

No, I didn't think to get spackle—sorry, Ma—

Please don't live like this in Washington, D.C., okay?

Huffing in this general vein, my mother commandeered Tig to drive the two of them to the hardware store. Diana and her son decided they would take a break. A walk around the neighborhood. I stiffened, then reminded myself he was too young for anyone to email the Hill Listserv. To comment on Nextdoor, to call the police. Safe for now.

The screws from my desk went in a Ziploc bag, which I labeled with undue care. Backs to each other in the same room, Marina and I worked in silence.

This is strange, I finally said. It's so, so strange. Having you both here. It feels insane. After everything. I hope—I hope I can meet your mom someday.

Marina nodded tersely, avoiding eye contact. The extravagant warmth, a danced performance of its own, had fallen from her when everybody left. Her face was set, equal parts cold and sad.

How're you feeling? I asked timidly.

Shitty, she said, and continued working with the distinct air of not desiring conversation.

The neighborhood construction's volume picked up a hundredfold. The desk's pieces I tied up with string.

Here you go, Marina said, still not looking at me, placing a cardboard box full of colorful plastic folders on the floor next to her. My papers sorted within. As she stretched, the muscles in her back rippled. Her shoulders slumped forward. Watching her I felt as though my whole body were covered in dew.

I knew then the confession I would make to my parents before I left Milwaukee. The freedom I'd found in splitting my life like an atom was a ruinous one, and I no longer desired it. Wilhelm Meister had not had to grapple with the impossibility of return. I knew now I could not circle back after a period of freedom and adopt the profession, the compromise, the paid-for man, that I once thought I would, as payment due.

I would tell Marina too, I decided, over walks and home-cooked dinners during our sliver of remaining time in the same place, the plain facts of my life, which were not what I would have chosen, but still were my own and thus worth claiming. I traced socked feet on the honey-wood floors over to my girl.

Hey, I whispered into her ear, putting my arms around her from behind. Thank you.

I'm so sad, she murmured. I'm going to miss you. Barely audible in the din. I heard the words as sensation and outline, like the hands of small children moving beneath a bedsheet.

I closed my eyes. Dizzy with longing and fear, I said, I love you. I really do.

It was the truth.

In the face that broke away from me, spun toward me, was surprise and anger and a cratering vulnerability.

Damn it, Marina said, tears starting to her eyes. Shit. Her nose turned pink, her smoky voice wavered. Why are you saying this *now*? Now, when everything is going to end.

I leaned my face to hers. With all the ardor of a new believer, I said, It's never too late. It's never the end.

Tingle of spearmint from her gum, hint of the smoke it masked. Wet muscle of her tongue. Velvet-soft lips. A kiss extensive as a raag, tremulous as a sonata. I pulled on the harsh bones of her hips, drew her closer, my eyelids fluttering open so briefly to see her face, my girl's radiant face. It was scrunched tight, as if in ecstasy or fear.

Marina's cheeks now glazed with wet. Her lip quivering. I love you too, she whispered, voice full of sorrow.

As we broke apart I saw my mother.

Her face a mask of shock. Standing in the emptied living room of my life, watching her child, holding in one hand spackle and in the other a new hammer.

Ente Sneha, she whispered into our silence.

I took a step toward her.

Ma, I began, voice a vacant house, its only foundation terror, I—I—I want you to know who I am.

We

We chose the clock. But before that, I did. I can explain.

Five years had melted down like candle wax, melted us down with them. It was a chilly, cherry-fragrant morning in Washington, D.C., when my father sent me photographs of the riverside trees dwarfing my silver-headed mother. A tangled canopy of green and brown. She looked beautiful and a little sad in the shade I'd grown.

From the Metro's subterranean recesses I unearthed myself. For some seconds I stood by the building I worked at, tracing the photos with my fingertip, wind savaging my hair. Lovely pics, I wrote back. Going into the office. Talk soon. He messaged, Safe journey for your trip. Pls let us know when you land OK.

My mother wrote, Our blessings to your friend on his marriage.

At my desk I skimmed the news clips that pertained to asylum seekers, surveyed my meeting schedule for the day. Gingerly I sipped the sludgy coffee that powered every immigration nonprofit in this town like fossil fuels. In my peripherals the office television showed Trump and his wife entertaining the Baylor Lady Bears. Women huddled around a table groaning with McDonald's, Chick-fil-A, and Wendy's. I opened my personal Gmail. Reread the latest from Amit, the missive that had had me irritable ever since I woke to see it.

That time had arrived in our shared lives: wedding season. I was happy for Amit and Emily. Really. Sure.

My issue was *their* own clear ambivalence, their overcompensation. Antics and details arrived from Amit, drip by drip. No diamonds, no rings. The backyard yurts. Em making their own gown. Paper cranes, not flowers, which the bridespeople would be asked to fold and string together. The presence of the word *bridespeople*. I, thank goodness, had not been asked to be in the wedding party. The insistence on no gifts, only to capitulate in the prior twelve hours, a week before the wedding, to the demands of outraged family elders and send around a registry link.

(Only for those who *really* want to bring us something! Otherwise, your presence is our present!)

I took a gulp and burned my mouth. Goofy people, that was my private verdict on all this. You want to get married, simply get married. Really, the most ordinary, ancient thing imaginable. Could even be sweet, depending on how one went about it. But absolutely no need to be *quirky* here.

I felt then the old, muted twinge of pain. Three years in, and still.

I rubbed my tongue against the wet inside of my cheek. Printed and walked a communications plan to my boss, who was nice enough but old-head D.C., stymied sometimes even by G Suite. Sitting back down at my cubicle, I pulled up my conversation with my old friends. My Milwaukee friends, who would understand.

SNEHA: yeah. maybe I'm a bitter single person who knows

THOM: You would have been just as annoyed by these Extremely San Francisco nuptials if you and M were still together don't kid ya self

TIG: Listen I have a wife and two lovers on deck and *eye* think A+E are out of pocket so

THOM: I think they're trying so hard not to be bourgeois that the end effect is very bourgeois unfortunately

SNEHA: Liked "I think they're trying so hard not to be bourgeois that the end effect is very bourgeois unfortunately"

TIG: I'm just so happy this is bringing you back to MKE. It's been years hoe

THOM: To be fair, Marx was married. And quite a romantic. His letters to Jenny are real cute

TIG: I mean Marx was not a Marxist. Just like Jesus was not a Christian

TIG: Just don't get them something, they did say thats an option

SNEHA: no, I am going to. but registries are a wild American custom. my parents never had one, and they simply dealt with different relatives gifting them multiples of the same spice grinder and glass clock. wtf is an avocado slicer. bitch I'll kill u

Bed Bath & Beyond was full of brilliant light and lotion smells. Nothing on the registry registered as correct. Held any inspiration for me. I had no great desire to gift Amit and Emily a pastel toaster, rose-gold coasters, water bottles with compartments to infuse fruit. I meandered around the store aisles feeling irritable and self-righteous.

I considered texting Marina something snide and funny.

We were on good terms. But the faintest formality, a timorousness, persisted through our affection. I was shyer now about letting her see the mean, gravelly parts of me. Generous Sneha, the Sneha who would drop everything for her when she was in crisis, the Sneha who had just been promoted but was suitably modest about it, the Sneha who had many friendships of no particular depth and never appeared to be lonely—this is what I showed Marina whenever given the option. Besides, she had less reason to be cynical about romance than I did. For her, there was someone new.

We had two often-happy years. And then we ended. The fights had grown worse as my avoidance did, as Marina's drinking did, with the extension of long distance, with Marina finally moving to be with me, which didn't help nearly as much as we thought it would. With Marina driving under the influence, with my withdrawn rages, with my saying, No, you cannot come to India with me, it is just too much. It is no slouch of a thing, bitterly arguing until you can see light playing the tops of rowhouses like piano keys, then waking to see your love reaching for you like a child, her face hot and waxy from sleep. The head spin of realizing that her sweetness is not contrition, not forgiveness, but simple forgetting, a blacking out. I'm sorry I said that, she'd mumble to me, I just don't *remember*, so I don't know what to do about it, I'm really sorry—

Not to imply that what we had was not, often, so very beautiful. I can't say much more about it than that. The long letters back and forth, the perfect weekends, Marina pouring wine while I stood naked at a stove and Joan Armatrading played, the road trips, the time Marina surprised me with a long weekend's getaway to Florida and I, looking at snake-green foliage and feeling the moist heat against my face, said, Oh baby, this is what it is like, the place I'm from.

Not to imply that by the time it came, our final breakup was anything close to bearable. A condemned building experiencing its final demolition. Marina pulling the trigger, saying, face spasming with pain, I *cannot* do this anymore.

Not to gloss over the subsequent period for which my mother finally flew to D.C. and forced me to bathe and eat and go to work each day.

Nothing is implied here besides the opiate nature of time. Besides the fact that after it all went down, we had regard for each other, grudging respect, an ocean-deep understanding of the other person, and no mutual vision of romantic continuity.

At the end of the day, the worst part had not been Marina driving drunk. Her eyes turning yellow. The explosions of florid rage she would forget in the morning. What had been hardest to bear was knowing the ways in which I was responsible. Because good love can rescue a person. Pull them out of the waves. Bad love is a rip current. It can drown you.

You need help, was one of the last things I had screamed at Marina during the end, the words foreclosing the possibility that had until then existed: that the two of us could save each other.

And then Marina dated the repressed bank teller, and then the sadist postal worker, and then checked into the alcohol treatment facility in Jersey. Moved to Rhode Island with the new gf, a willowy nutritionist who tolerated my meager presence in my ex's life while making her calm dislike of me plain.

In the first two years after the end of things, Marina had called every other month or so, typically with a crisis brewing. The DUI and license suspension. Shamar Dance, her side hustle with Shaka, dissolving in financial disarray. The USPS redhead throwing all her shoes out of a tenth-floor window. Sometimes, the confessions, typically under the influence. I miss you so. I will always remember what we had. You still feel like my person and it's fucking me up.

I would drop everything, pay for the Uber, edit the resignation letter, listen to whatever needed saying.

Thom had thought this interdependence unhealthy. It's okay, Tig said in visible exhaustion, you're like, each other's emotional support dog. Emotional support ex-girlfriends.

This dynamic faded with the arrival of the nutritionist, who appeared, at least online, to be loving and not terribly maladjusted. Now I was in the group text for Marina's sobriety chip milestones. We spoke less often. We loved each other still.

For me the future was still open. That was one of the last things I said to

her during the final minutes we were, officially, together, before I had begun to cry so hard I could not speak any longer. In a possible world where
Marina could stay sober, neither of us had found lasting love, and I was
ready to open up my heart to her once again, I thought, in the months following our breakup, we could try again. For real, this time.

To think that this was almost three years ago jolted me unpleasantly. I
turned a corner. Saw the clock.

Unreal, I thought, repressing a laugh. I handled it. It said Waterford
Lismore. Neat round watch face set in a mass of glittering leaded crystal.
Cut into the shape of a diamond. A paperweight clock the size of a fledg-
ling coconut. It was classically beautiful, traditional as the *Mayflower*.
The opposite of yurts and bridespeople.

Our last one, the sales assistant told me. The floor model, so there's no
display box. Fine, I said. It was really pretty immature of me, but I
brought it to the checkout line alongside dumb fluffy dish towels from
the actual registry. No, we don't do gift wrap, the cashier said. He padded
the clock with newspaper and tape. It was hard to swaddle, its shape and
proportions senseless.

I almost missed the escalator's end, stumbled and flailed like a man on
a banana peel. The clock nearly coming to early ruin. On the Metro ride
home, I cradled the Lismore in my palm, experiencing its heaviness as
comfort.

Someone had organized a midweek birthday outing for my roommate. We ate fish crudo, drank orange wine. New acquaintances asked
each other, So what do you do? I turned down my friend V's husband's
offer to get my third glass. I'm flying out tomorrow, I said. Oh yes, he
said. The ex's wedding.

Not the ex that matters, V said, dropping into the seat next to him.
The uncomplicated ex. Here, brought you a water.

I always forget, she said, surveying me, eyes bright with interest, that
you lived in Milwaukee. Your little stopover.

2

At the airport I bought a pretzel dog, charged my phone through a fraying white cord. I realized while I chewed mouthfuls of pastry and Vienna sausage that I was so very excited. This explained my jangling nerves, in part. To see Amit married, to be reunited with two of my dearest old friends, to see the project they'd talked so much about in abstraction made real. This anticipation was layered against something else. Something like dread.

As the flight took off, I got a text from my not-quite-uncomplicated ex.

Marina wrote, hey, are you busy. I started to type back. We were far enough in the air already that my reply couldn't go through. A red exclamation mark floated. I pulled up Spotify, looked for saved playlists. While we were in the air the boss sent me four emails. As did my father. Except his were Zillow listings, forwarded on. The plane Wi-Fi was too weak to allow the pictures to load; they stayed boxy outlines.

A two-bedroom in Anacostia, a studio in Lanier Heights. A one-bedroom in Northeast D.C. My father, who with great pain and over years had finally accepted that he had a gay daughter, had since chosen to stay focused on her material advancement in the world. From two oceans away he called routinely to ask how my performance review went, whether I would negotiate a robust raise. My mother let his concerns take precedence but remained preoccupied with matters of my heart. Is there anybody? she would sometimes ask, shy and brusque at once. Three years in and she had never forgiven Marina for walking away from me.

My father rarely spoke of such things, leaving this line of questioning to her. When are you planning to go for your graduate studies, he would nudge and needle. You should own some small property by the time you are thirty, thirty-one, he reminded me time and again. Not right away, but in two, three years you can do it. You must save aggressively, Snehamol. You need to have some equity. You can always rent it out if you need to. Otherwise you are just paying someone else's mortgage only.

I walked out of arrivals and saw, waiting, in camo and leather jacket respectively, Thom and Tig.

Something broke open in my chest, valving air in. My smile so wide it could crack a face in two. I ran.

Tig lifted me off my feet, strong and laughing, kissing my face. Hair longer now and with some silver at the temples. A septum piercing acquired since I last saw them, a whole two years ago, when Tig and Diana had driven down to D.C. to protest. Stayed on the sleeper couch of my shared apartment. The crowd's singular, cellular intelligence. Diana's son holding a double-sided cardboard sign. MEN OF QUALITY RESPECT WOMEN'S EQUALITY / REVOLUTION IN OUR LIFETIME.

From the back seat of the Honda I could sense Thom sizing me up. It was three and a half years since we'd seen each other in person. If Tig had been anyone other than Tig I would have come back up at least when they married Diana. But being helplessly themselves, always and forever, they had broken their tailbone when the two of them went hiking in Utah. Decided that they were out of patience, got married at the Salt Lake City courthouse for the insurance. KJ and their mom FaceTimed in. Tig let Thom and me and Jervai know in a group text, sat on an inflatable donut for the car ride back.

Typical, Thom had messaged me separately then, adding four clown emojis.

As we drove I imagined myself through the eyes of my soft-faced friend, with his army surplus jacket and blaze-orange beanie, his skin red and flaking. How the Sneha of the present seemed.

Fatter, filled out, that's what he would notice. Speaking with a confidence he likely did not remember from me. A cropped haircut, ugly-fly, expensive. I wore a soft wool jacket, more than the unseasonably warm day required. My shoes were sensible and supportive. I smiled more than I used to, but closed-lipped, no teeth.

He turned onto the street whose name I'd heard so much.

It needs work, Tig said preemptively, midwesternly modest. They added, But what doesn't.

Thom opened my car door. For years we'd ribbed him about this sort of corny chivalry, but there was no cure.

My guy, he said. Welcome to Rion.

3

Uncharitably and against reason, staring up from the driveway, I wondered if the inside would be terrifying. Some foreclosure nest of pissed-on carpet, college furniture, rats. Because—this *house*. So much bigger than texts and phone pictures could ever let on. This would set you back cool millions in D.C. What even were mortgage costs in the Midwest?

Over the months and from a distance Thom had filled me in on the project I'd once filed away in the dusty archive of my life as the Pink House. A fantastic youthful dream. No conversation could prepare me for seeing it, far humbler, but realized.

Rion. Still a work in progress, half a year after the closing. In Harambee, not Shorewood, which had led to many mind-fucking conversations about gentrification, even though they were none of them, whatsoever, gentry. Amit backing out of the project years ago, admitting he had no intention of ever living there but wanted the vision to work out, was rooting for them. So many times in the past five years, Thom had told me, he was tempted to give up, follow convention, move out of the group flat with his savings and in with some lefty babe. As with other things, it was the disdain of his parents that kept him dogged, the middle-finger thrill of pleasure from informing them he would be copurchasing a communal house with his Black friends.

(Well, I'm sorry you feel that way. But these are *my* values. You don't have to like them.)

When they toured the Harambee property, Tig had stared around, visibly mourning their grand dream. It had vinyl siding. Only two bathrooms. An attic that Jervai and KJ heard raccoons in, set them off squealing like cartoons. The upper balcony looking perilous, rotten as a pulled tooth. Thom had taken Tig aside, talked a pragmatic line to his friend. It was the two of them who'd been the guardians of the plan, had kept the flame alive all these years.

Play the long game, he cajoled. The house had six real bedrooms and an attic. A shed. A backyard big enough: for the vegetable garden, a soaking tub, heck, even a tiny house or two. It was walking distance to the Riverwest Public House, Bremen Cafe. All this for $174,000. Less than the very down payment of the blush-colored mansion by the lake that had captured Tig's imagination so long ago.

Thom was a realist. He worked construction. Jervai bartended, Diana was a phlebotomist, Kenny a software engineer. Tig was a part-time literacy teacher for kindergartners with a bucket and a half of Alverno debt.

We can buy it nearly cash, pay this off in three years, Thom had said. Listen to me, homie. It'll appreciate, and when the day comes, if we need to, we can sell it for a dream location. Look at that space. Look at that price. Your savings, Diana's, mine, get Kelli Jo to take out a loan, see where Jervai and Kenny are at. I bet we can almost cover it.

Tig stared up at the vinyl siding, eyes full of fear and hope.

What d'you say, Thom pressed. The absolute space of it, he argued. The price unbeatable, since Tig had ruled out trying to buy cheap somewhere in rural Wisco. (We're not leaving the city, white flight ass.) Enough bedrooms and more. Guests or children. Airbnb income. Whatever they together desired.

Eventually Tig came around. Adjusted their vision. But it wasn't as though Thom had no doubts of his own. Noelle, the woman he was dating, seemed solid enough, kind, politically on point. She would be fine moving into a collective setup, though getting her equity in the house would be trickier. Maybe inadvisable. To him the future seemed endlessly uncertain.

To procreate or not. To stay committed to this woman or not, and for how long. To invest in the stock market despite its evils. To vote Democrat or Green or not at all. Sometimes he'd read articles about permafrost melt and the diseases and methane that would be released into the atmosphere and wonder: Will I get to see the world end, how do I want to live when it does?

So he pushed on. The devil of it had been tripartite: paperwork, decision-making, trust. Trying to figure out a new way in a legal and financial system made to accommodate the old. Forming the LLC, writing bylaws. He, at his mother's pleading, had written up a partnership agreement that was two-thirds dispute resolution, clauses for every contingency. Death, sickness, rifts, new additions. On top of this, Antigone giving the rest of them all these lectures on sociocracy and consensus and how conflict was best to be mediated. Are you trying to scare everybody off? he hissed at them after. They'd printed *handouts*, for god's sake.

This was when he called me.

After years of exchanging memes, texting life updates, wishing each other happy birthday, saying ghoulishly adult things like We should catch up sometime.

Ay, my dude, he'd said when I picked up the phone more than half a year ago, turns out I need A Consultant.

Despite my fears, the house was clean inside. Modest, in progress, peopled with objects found. The floor wood might have benefited from oil and stain, the kitchen tiling looked about a hundred years old. The dining table held five MacBooks laid out like place settings. I heard the stories of acquisition. The furniture was Craigslisted from the suburbs or bought at the Oak Creek IKEA. Some of these finds were kookily incredible. A 1920s mirrored armoire from Within Reason Resale, a love seat made from a claw-foot tub. Every wall was bursting with art, most of it homemade. Diana's paintings, oil and acrylic on canvas. A wall of

Post-its in Tig's writing. Thom and Jervai were the resident plant daddies; the living room was an earnest jungle. Around I walked, quietly stunned.

I longed to say, I am proud of you, but the sentiment was too small.

You must be starved, Thom said. We took the dinner out on the porch. Navy bean soup with ham. A carroty salad. Bread rubbed all over with garlic. Bowls balanced on laps. I opened the bottle I'd thought to bring, poured the gold-hued liquid out.

To reunion, Thom said.

To Rion and to what you all build, was my counteroffer, holding my glass up for a chorus of clinks.

Jervai, who appeared to be something like house administrator, said, When will you be gone for your friend's wedding shit, want to be able to plan my week.

There's a welcome high tea for everyone Friday evening, Thom said. Saturday afternoon is the ceremony, Amit says it'll be long, but not fully traditionally Hindu? KJ and Tig's gonna do some shit for the toast after the ceremony—these people are maniacs about getting their friends to do stuff. We're on the hook to bring fireworks over for the reception, it sounds like a production. I think they're inviting like three hundred people.

This wedding is doing the most, Kenny observed.

It's doing what it's supposed to, Tig said, gulping down whiskey. Romantic love is an instrument of capitalist domination. It gives people false hopes of self-actualization, ensures class division through wealth inheritance, and misdirects energy away from improving working people's material conditions. Basically love exists to market expensive fitness classes to straight people.

Laughs and groans followed this. Save it for your lil Instagram, KJ muttered next to me.

What about nonheterosexuals? Thom asked, chuckling.

Oh, we're sold Subarus.

For fuck's sake, Tig, I said, exasperated, you fully have three romantic partners. *You* are married.

Ya, I never said I was an ideologue.

At the end of the night, of the two open bedrooms, I was offered the ground-floor option. A bunk bed. Gray carpet. A rod of incense fuming in a seashell. Small spray of eucalyptus in a vase.

You want more space, I can put you in the third-floor room, Diana told me, but I waved her away. This is perfect, I said, and fell into the deepest of sleeps.

4

Coming out of the shower at six in the morning, I ran full-tilt into Antigone.

Their robe fell open. A flash of brown nipple, navel, fupa. I averted my eyes, mumbled apology. They grinned, making no motion to cover up. Chill, they said. Internet code is on the fridge door in case you need to write your little emails. See you downstairs?

I took the rest of the week off. Okay, no need to look so surprised.

And yet I am, Tig said, smirking. They considered me, fairly average by East Coast standards, a depraved workaholic. Slave to the nonprofit-industrial complex, toiling in hope of one day becoming a white-picket-fence gay. A condo-owning queer. These opinions they had let me know with candor.

I shrugged. I am here, I said simply, after literal years. I want to spend the time with you.

Tig, sleep-wrinkled, head-wrapped, a saliva crust angling out from the corner of their lip, smiled big at me in their bathroom threshold, and in that moment a whitely petalled love bloomed in my rib cage. My old friend.

I'll fix us breakfast, I said, walking down the uneven stairs. I assume you still can't cook for shit.

Tig and I had become, more than anything else, each other's counsel from afar. They advised me through the closest thing I had to an official relationship in the years after Marina. Beth was serious and compassionate, Nigerian American with a master's degree, the daughter of two law-yers. Sex with her was an earnest, earthy thing. Like gardening or proofing dough.

And I didn't wish to ask for too much credit, but Tig's most successful project so far, outside of Rion, had been my idea.

In recent years, Tig's book in progress, written in snatches of time not spent working (for the bills) and organizing (for the future), had stalled intractably at eighty-five pages. The degree of sadness this engendered in Tig shocking to everyone, most of all themself. When I think about this fat stillborn stack of pages, they told Thom and me, it feels like I'm being hit by a fucking car.

I was the one who suggested the pivot. I'd said, You want to write so that you can be read. So put it online. No, no, don't self-publish. Like, make an Instagram for it, Tig boo. Break it up into bite-sized chunks. De-sign up the quotes, make them look aesthetically good, get the zoomers and zillennials to share them. I have no doubt you'll build a following. Diana or I could probably help you do a graphics template—

@antigone_speaks was now at 45.2K followers. It had been the de-light of Tig's life, to realize that people, thousands of strangers the coun-try over, would listen to what they had to say, were hungry for guidance that they could supply.

In the kitchen I scrambled us pale-yolked eggs, heated tortillas I found squirreled away in a cabinet. Tig showed me the latest graphic in prog-ress. A gradient background. Lavender and orange and blue. Groovy font, calling to mind the 1970s.

NO CAP NONE OF THEM WANT US TO KNOW THAT WE ARE SECRETLY ALREADY FREE. YOUR FREEDOM ALREADY EXISTS, CONFISCATED IN A SAFE AND PROMISED TO YOU AFTER A SERIES OF LABORS AND COMPROMISES AND ESTATE SALES OF THE SELF, AND DURING THIS PROCESS OF

TRYING TO EARN IT YOUR BACK WILL HUMP WITH AGE AND YOU WILL BECOME FEARFUL AND FORGET YOU EVER DESIRED ANYTHING OTHER THAN THE ASSURANCE OF AN INDIVIDUATED SAFETY. BUT THE DEED OF YOUR FREEDOM IS ALREADY MADE OUT TO YOU, AND IF YOU REALIZE THIS YOU CAN RESCUE IT FROM ITS PRISON, BY WHATEVER MEANS REQUIRED.

—ANTIGONE CLAY

Tig asked to pack the food up, put coffee in to-go cups, suggested we eat outside. They wanted some privacy. Said this in a low voice. In the dewy morning we drove to the riverbank, found a bench.

Most times I feel like I have to front like we're building some utopia, they said. But not with you.

Yeah?

Tig's face twisted. It's hard, Sneha. It's often really hard.

I squeezed their hand. Don't get me wrong, they said. This ain't regret at all. But it's *work*. Our people deserve the world and dignity and thriving, but they're also people. Everyone in that house makes me crazy at least some of the time. Thom wants to bring this whitegirl Noelle in and I don't get the best vibe. Kenny acts like he's our munificent patron because he got some tech money. He's out here signing Kelli Jo up for UX boot camps and shit, trying to get my sister into his racist-ass industry. And Kelli Jo— Tig sucked their teeth.

What? I asked.

I mean, it's nothing you don't know. She's clean for a year, then uses some. Goes to clinic and church. Clean for eight months, then uses again. Goes to group, some more church. It's her own money always, far as I can tell; the second our house fund went towards it I promise you shit would hit the fan. Thom probably told you some. He offers that kind of foolishness more latitude. What I can tell you is I really don't enjoy having it in my house. And in general, I set out to be a revolutionary and philosopher and unless I watch myself I'ma end up everyone's mother.

I scooped a morsel of soft egg with tortilla. Wondered what to offer in response. In my adult life I had come to understand some things about addiction, some truths about what it meant to live as a wounded person, the past a refrain of illness within you, always summoning you back to the specter of your hunger. But I did not know how to transmute this into anything that might be useful to Tig.

So I said simply, You love her. Despite it. Maybe it'll change. Maybe it never will. Sometimes people just are that way, in perpetual recovery. But you were the one that told me, this is a commitment and a practice. You're each other's people. It won't be easy maybe ever. But we both have lived the alternative.

Lookit you turning my words against me. What about you, boo? How's your mom and pops?

Mmm. She's good, working a lot. Papa's got diabetes, we're sad about it. I told you he got promoted, right? So that's something. Their heads are above water finally. And truly who knows what will happen with this, but soon enough his no-entry ruling will be up for appeal. He might be able to at least come visit me, like they could finally come together.

Dang. I didn't know that. I'll say my inshallahs. How's dating been?

I shook my head. Maintained silence.

Like water out a stone. C'mon, son. Are you happy?

That last one is not and has never been, I said, squinting in the brightening sun, a useful question for me.

We stocked up at Aldi for the house, drove over to someone giving away a hundred Crayola markers on Craigslist. The school Tig taught at was perpetually out of supplies. They and Diana routinely bought paper, books, and stationery out of pocket. With practiced skill I held closed the floodgates of information regarding Tig's reliably intricate dynamic with

Diana and their other lovers. My primary opinion on polyamory was that it seemed like a lot of fun for logistics fetishists.

Let's get some food, Tig said. Colectivo? Would ya put these in the back seat?

Hell yes. Let me treat you.

Nah, babe, I got a gift card. That's how they pay teachers now. You can cook us dinner, though. We could pick up some nice seafood at MPM, it's technically Kelli Jo's turn to cook group dinner, y'all can team it. Make something nice? Like a little luxe? It's been a lot of greens beans sweet potato at Rion of late. I'm like what y'all doing? We deserve pleasure too. We demand bread *and* roses.

Antigone speaks, I cracked, smiling. Impulsively I cradled Tig's cheek in my hand. They closed their eyes.

It's good to have you here, Sneha, they said. I know you have your fancy life in Washington. I'm proud you're doing things, doing so well. But visit more often. Come, anytime.

At first I was thinking snapper but this is a special occasion. How y'all feel about lobster tonight? Tig asked as we sailed down Commerce.

Pretty good, I said. I'm easy.

Maybe we just do chicken, KJ suggested. Tig shot her a disdainful look. We're like ten minutes away. Public Market's got no chicken. You want chicken again, Kelli Jo? When our friend has gotten on an airplane and flown seven hundred miles to us? That's fine! Say the word, I'll turn this car around.

Nah, it's fine, KJ said, sulky and defensive. Just seems like we 'bout to blow through the house budget. To me she explained, Thom always pressed about our monthly budget. He might not even come though, so.

Tig snorted. Man's talking 'bout fixin' Noelle's bike—

Mmm. Clean Noelle pipes—

We burst out laughing. KJ was so rarely vulgar. Tig continued, Listen, I am *thee* most sex-positive person in the world, so said with respect, that girl is freaky as hell. I'm like brushing my teeth in the downstairs bathroom when she stays over last and Lord Jesus Our Savior, the things I heard through that wall. Make cam girls sound like kindergarten teachers.

Mmm, sounds like you was listening well, KJ teased. Tig reached back, swatted her. Cast eyes around as we came down Palmer Street.

Yo, they said, touching my arm and slowing, look, your old place.

It was true. A slate-gray house. Amy's porch. The rosebushes bloomless.

My skin turned cold. I saw my past self, that switch of a girl, walk her belongings up to the side door. Lie down in the slats of sun on the wooden floor.

Your awful landlord still live there, boo? KJ asked gently.

Property manager, I corrected automatically. No, I don't think so. Don't see her truck.

Holy fuck, Tig said as the car rounded the road's curve and we came up straight on Amy. Her dog straining at its leash, barking loud.

A muffled yelp flew out of my throat. Down below the window's line I flung my body, shielded my face. In the instant before I'd taken in the scene. Dog barking and Amy yelling at a dark-skinned woman in yellow sweats who was yelling back. Amy pointing, screaming. The Fit breezed past this to the next red light.

Jesus, KJ said. I raised myself upright, laughed shakily. I was mortified. Blood burning in my cheeks. I don't know what got into me, I muttered in excuse.

Tig turned to stare at me, their face twisting.

Sometimes I just want to shake you until your teeth rattle, they said. Excuse me?

They said, with near-unbearable bossiness, Hey, Kelli Jo, put ya headphones in. All but leaving out, *This is grown-folks talk.* To my own consternation KJ meekly complied.

What the hell, I said. You can't just talk to me—

Tig's eyes bulged.

You *actually* lived here, you know. You act like the things that happened didn't happen. You always have. I wanted to bite your head off when we was with you in Washington and you were complaining about how fat you are now. No, let me finish. Bitch, you were fucking starving when you lived here. You were living off scraps and air and hitting up the food pantry and telling nobody. Of *course* you gained weight later. It's how the body works.

What does this have to do—

And so yeah, I don't know where your memory has gone on holiday but *that woman terrorized you.* That actually happened. Of course seeing her is overwhelming. Of fucking course.

I was silent. Felt like a fish out of water, whacked on its head.

She needs her ass beat, Tig said. It took me a second to realize they meant Amy.

I laughed bitterly. You sound like Thomas, I said. For years, Thom, when reminded of my former property manager, had offered up gems like, I should take a shit in that woman's mailbox. Throw a brick through her window.

Aren't you *angry* about how she treated you? Tig asked.

I mostly try not to think about it, I said, truthfully. It just sucks to remember, Tig, every time I do I feel sort of cold inside, and ashamed.

Ashamed! The word exploded out of Tig.

Like, how could I have put up with that sort of treatment? My voice at a near-whisper. How did I let it happen, how did I stay?

Tig looked at me in disbelief. Glared back at the road, their nose reddening.

The light changed just as KJ said, Should we go back, like do we. Have time.

Huh? Use your words, girl, Tig snapped.

I just got mad bad vibes from that whole interaction. That dog, Amy . . . I just, I just want to check that that lady is okay. There was big calling-the-cops energy going—

I voiced agreement.

Fine, fine, Tig said. The Fit made a loop. My stomach tight. When we returned to the block of the altercation it was peaceable, empty. Only flowering trees nodding blossoms, anticipating the fruit to come.

KJ anxiously ran her thumb over her forearm, where a line of unfamiliar characters was etched.

What does your tattoo say? I asked her, once the two of us stood in line at St. Paul's. Tig circling with the car, not wanting to pay for parking. Walking in, I'd registered a shocking, almost bodily lurch of memory. The smell of oysters and ground coffee. Pink salt. A small woman with a blond ponytail climbing into a car. A woman, then a stranger.

Oh, um, KJ said, it's Hebrew. Appeared shy, tried to pull shirtsleeves down to her wrists. The crook of her arm was pocked and scratched.

What's it mean, though? I pressed, now holding the large paper bag that contained four lobsters. KJ seemed deeply engrossed in a bottle of tartar sauce. You could feel the heat of her blush. KJ too, I thought in that moment, had lost the woman she loved in the last few years. Seemed like the only other person I knew who had the same thin whine of pain in the background of her brain, some fraction of always.

It means, she said, very softly, The Lord upholds all those who fall.

Back at Rion, we set the table, poured the wine. It was deemed too early yet for dinner. We talked about the old times. Deliberated where the hot tub and sauna should go, about how much it would cost for Thom to frame up a tiny house at the garden's foot by fall. More than a couple of KJ's friends were homeless now, shuttling between cars and motels and friends' couches—it could be offered to one of them. How would we decide who? Tig asked, and this set off a firestorm of debate. I was grateful when Jervai voiced skepticism, said, I don't think any of y'all are engaging with how complex caring for any one of these people would be.

We held the lobsters down. Thanked them in advance for feeding us. KJ muttered, I'm sorry. We sliced their heads open between the eyes, which were small glassy beads of dark. Cleaned out the dark curdled tomalley.

We melted butter with coins of garlic, set a Dutch oven full of water on the stove to boil. At some point Thom ambled in with Noelle; she was attractive in a rumpled way, her hair a nest of dark brown and premature white. She held two crisp home-baked loaves. Out of the fridge someone dug leftover greens with smoked turkey.

But first, Tig told us, it was time for an inaugural house ritual. For the late spring seeds to be planted. On gray egg carton trays they had placed seeds of beets, carrots, chard, kohlrabi, turnip, and leaf lettuce. Before these went into the earth, I was informed, we were to speak our dreams over them. To say our desires—for ourselves, our loved ones, the world—into the seeds, one at a time, crouching on the patio's cracked tile.

Very frankly, I found this sort of thing unbearable. Tried to bow out. Said, Yo, I don't even live here. Was coerced by the collective will.

I crouched down by the seeds, visibly rolling my eyes.

What could I wish for? I was financially secure, professionally successful. Because I lived with some modicum of care and frugality, I would likely have enough saved for a down payment by thirty-one or thirty-two. I was insured, in good health. My parents and I had made a loving fragile peace, subject to interruptions.

I took in, once more, my friends standing in the garden around me. Tig and Diana. Thom and Noelle.

When my relationship ended, things had turned tense back home. Papa entreating me to consider at least meeting some nice boys, some NRIs they could connect me with. A lavender marriage if nothing else.

Madi, my mother had said to him with an awful finality. Madi, it will not happen the way we had hoped.

Mollé, she said to me over grainy video, we do not know what to do with all this. But we can tell you this: We do not want you to end up alone, end up by yourself. We would like to see you settled, in some way, before we die. We want you to have somebody who will take care of you, okay? Because we all are brought to our knees at some point in this life. The idea that no one will be there for you when that happens—my heart cannot take that. We want you to have family, to have somebody.

This is what I think of, staring at dark soil and egg carton, seeds pale as maggots within. I wish for health and safety for everyone I love, for my father to successfully appeal his no-entry adjudication once the ten-year mark of his deportation is crossed next year, and finally, for what my parents pray nightly.

I want to not be alone, I mutter into the earth, skin prickling with longing and shame.

KJ leads us in a halting grace; together we eat.

5

The grounds of Amit's parents' new house were flung open for the welcome tea. A white tent, cater-waiters. Sitar and pipa playing under a bower of paper cranes. Emily's mother graceful in a qipao, accepting on her child's behalf the gold-filigreed sari Amit's family presented. This was purely for tradition's sake; Em had made clear they would not wear a sari, salwar kameez, or lehenga. Still, something about the exchange, watched by all, softened Tig's snips at wedding capitalism, melted my own prickled tongue. In the golden light, people milled about in cocktail dresses and denim alike, drinking the offered cups of Darjeeling and pekoe. Emily's father—Nordic, about seven feet tall, dazzling of smile—gave a speech that left everyone alternately laughing and misty.

Timidly I approached Amit, who looked transported, incandescent with joy. You deserve every happiness, I started to say, only the slightest quaver in my voice, but Amit hugged me, ruffled my hair, peppered me with exuberant questions about my life, then before I could meaningfully answer, abruptly disappeared into the crowd.

Back at Rion that night, after watching a movie on the Craigslisted house projector, I got ready for bed. Carefully I brushed my teeth in the pink-tiled bathroom with its blackened grout. Used a brassy little stick with a rubber node to trace the outlines of my gums, massage their grooves.

Six months into living in D.C., into working at the Foundation, I'd decided it was time. Time to do adulting right and go to a dentist, get a cleaning, begin to practice good American-middle-class habits. My teeth were reasonably white, presented no pain. Better to go before there was a problem. A prattling coworker said, Oh, you must see Dr. K in Dupont. The kindest, gentlest man, Nepalese and so handsome—

It's true he was kind. He'd rubbed my shoulder gently as I heaved from sheer shock. Twelve cavities. Two large enough that he would try to fill them, but they would need root canals down the line. What's a root canal? I had asked, blinking. Trying to calculate copay and cost for twelve fillings. He'd said I had gum disease advanced enough that I'd already suffered permanent bone loss.

See how loose this one is, he noted, rattling an incisor.

It's okay, he had continued, we can cure the periodontitis. We will schedule you to come back for a root planing and scaling; it will clean out the inflammation under your gum line. But the bone loss we cannot reverse. You will have to take very good care of your teeth and gums for the rest of your life. You have, I'm afraid, started at a disadvantage.

After, I sat on a Dupont Circle park bench as snow frittered around my feet. If I'd stayed in Milwaukee, eked together odd uninsured jobs, worked as a barista, stayed scooping at Leon's, what might have happened over the years? I understood then, really only then, Marina's choice, the choice that had rankled. To try for things but stay, not move right away. Stay with the job and the money and the health insurance that would keep you from the emptied bank account and ending up at St. Casimir or on the street. Love of most kinds could not feed you, could not house you, could not protect you from permanent bone loss that would eventually cause your very teeth to fall out of your head.

Before I climbed into bed I checked my phone.

A call, hours ago during dinner, from Marina. Amid everything, I'd forgotten about her texting me. I tried her back. Nothing. Worry began to web around me, delicate, glinting.

everything okay? I texted, then added, sorry I missed your call, was flying. I'm free now, and tomorrow too. other than three-ish and the evening. amit is getting married. it's cute and shit.

Then, feeling a surge of warmth for the only woman I'd ever been in love with, I wrote her what the return to Milwaukee had been like. How it was seeing Amit about to be wed. How being back took me in lurches to the past—our shared past—with a wonder pricked with pain.

There was a universe I imagined sometimes:

1. Marina and I meet again.
2. We are happy, healthy, successful, healed.
3. This despite starting, each in our own way, at a disadvantage.
4. Life does not feel out of control for either of us.
5. Marina has not touched alcohol in years.
6. I am a loving, kind, good partner.
7. We decide to try again, and this time it sticks.

But at least for now, there was Joanna the nutritionist, and Marina had only four months of sobriety behind her, had never moved past six. It doesn't do to dwell in fantasy, even if your only fantasy is that you end up a normal boring person: wedded, safe, loving, loved.

The morning of the wedding was sun-dappled and serene. This was the weather outside Rion, mind. Inside, minor storms gathered. KJ struggled to zip into her groomsperson dress, to make sure it still fit. Tig attempted to shove her into it, prompting some sibling caterwauling. The night before, Jervai and Kenny had announced they would be taking a little couple's getaway to Chicago, claiming one of the two house cars and infinitely complicating the weekend's logistics. Tig did not sufficiently tighten the lid on the hand-me-down blender when making a smoothie, and banana and strawberry sludge spattered the ceiling. A scowling Thom brewed great vats of coffee. My nerves jangled. Never had a quiet Lanier Heights studio seemed more appealing.

Diana brought order to things. She would drop KJ off to get hair and makeup done with the rest of the wedding party, take her son to his dad's place in West Allis, and then bring the car back to Rion. Diana had plans with a friend, would get dropped off straight at the wedding, dressed for the cocktail hour that would precede the ceremony. Thom and Tig, and I, if I wanted to join, would pick up the Indiana-sourced fireworks from Thom's mother's basement. The three of us would then go to the wedding. Get ready beforehand, Diana suggested. Antigone baby, I've laid your stuff out on our bed.

Cool, Tig said. If y'all need me before like two, I'm in the study, just holler. Working on the Content.

Can I borrow an iron, please? I said.

After a lunch of leftovers, I pulled on the underskirt's drawstring, buttoned my blouse. Began to pleat and fold and pin the yards of fabric.

Raw silk with zari work. A dark, rich rose. It used to be my mother's, worn at parties and weddings. I had asked her for it as a gift for my twenty-fifth birthday. I wanted something of her here with me.

The house was different when emptier. Quiet, roomy, peaceful like a hug.

No outlet in my room appeared to function, and my sari dwarfed the stalwart little ironing board I'd been given. Over the dining table I spread the pleats, pressed the creases hot. I could see Thom working in the garden through the windows as I did this. Bent over the raised beds. Plumber's crack and sun hat.

Carrying my pinned pleats, I went out to see him. He appeared terse but only mildly so.

Hello, Thomas.

What's up, my dude? I'm just finishing. Watch your skirt thing. Just aerated that ground.

I ambled around the garden tiles, watching a blue bird hop farther down a green bough. Surveyed the house's siding. It was really quite ugly.

Would y'all ever paint the house exterior? I asked. Thom had walked up to me, sweaty of brow, smelling of yeast and onions.

He squinted at me from under the sun hat. Yeah, maybe.

To the beige siding I held up my length of hibiscus silk. Well, I think something like this would be gorgeous. And fitting. The real Pink House.

Thom winced, palmed his lower back. Things were beginning to give out for him, I sensed, bit by bit. Over the last year these had been mentioned over text: a pulled hamstring, an eroding disk. His knees popped and clicked when he bent. I'd worried out loud about this to Tig at the Aldi, experienced profound annoyance when all that materialized from the conversation was an @antigone_speaks post: THE CONSEQUENCES OF CAPITALISM ARE WRITTEN ON THE BODY. WHOSE BODY IS THRIVING? WHOSE BODY IS BREAKING DOWN?

All your ideas from the sidelines, he said. Noted for the future, bruh. Will you excuse me, I need to shower. You good to leave in forty-five for Tosa?

In the downstairs bedroom I pinned the sari to myself carefully. In my ears I slid gold hoops, old gifts from Tig. Rubbed pomade through cropped hair.

I lined my eyes. Spritz of lime perfume in the air. I packed my bag, slid in my beribboned gifts.

My room did not have a mirror and the pink-tiled bathroom's was small and smeary. I walked up the stairs, holding my sari's pleats.

On the landing of the third floor was a full-length mirror. Dusty, its neon thrift-store tag still pasted on. I surveyed myself. Found the image both hard-won and acceptable.

And then, on impulse, I nudged open the door of the unclaimed room.

Golden light poured through the windowpane. Onto a white duvet. A low bed of bleached wood. Cinder blocks as an end table. A bookshelf, empty. From the window, in the long distance you could see Brewers Hill, the river cutting by it.

An empty box. A room full of light.

I stood in the threshold, staring. I did not enter.

What would happen to us. What would happen to me.

I walked back down the stairs.

6

I don't think we would have ever tried it with Amy if not for the police.

Tig had been driving under the speed limit. Jittery about the bagged fireworks in the back seat. I always forget this shit isn't legal, they said. It's fine, they added, as reassurance, Amit got a permit.

Too well under the speed limit, it turned out. Just south of Pius XI on Seventy-Sixth, blocks from Brewski's, where Thom first kissed Isabel a hundred years ago, haunt of much past underage drinking, the cops pulled us over for driving slowly.

One white, one Black. As Tig rolled the window down, an ancient fear appeared in my friend's face.

How is this even real, I thought. I reached for my phone. Started recording. Locked my eyes on Tig. I'm here, I willed myself to communicate telepathically.

The cops demanded license, registration. Ran the registration through their database.

What's in the bags? we were asked. Long seconds of silence ticked by. Fireworks, Thom said tightly.

Out of the car, ma'am, the white officer said to Tig.

First the Breathalyzer. Tig said nothing, simply huffed, hands wrung in frustration, and for this the Black cop held them down. Face pressed against the groove where the driver's window met the car's roof. This while the other officer went through the car for drugs. Thom and I were ordered out.

All slowly, methodically. The wait of it torture. The recording now over twenty minutes. My phone informed me it was out of storage space. My chest began to hurt. I continued staring into Tig's eyes over the car's roof, trying to signal with every muscle in my face, Stay calm, don't say anything, don't rise to any bait, I need you, I need you alive.

They searched the glove compartment, checked under seats. The Macy's bags on the asphalt. Reached into with gloved hands.

These explosive devices are illegal in the state of Wisconsin, the white cop pronounced, pointing out the four mortar shells, the cluster of Roman candles.

The smoke bombs, snakes, and sparklers could stay, we were told.

We're taking these to our friend's wedding tonight, he has a permit, Thom insisted.

You have the permit on you?

No, but—

Then it don't matter, sir.

The Black cop wrote out the fine, a cool nine hundred dollars, put three of the bags in his cruiser. This was when Tig spoke, very quietly.

I really need to use the bathroom, they said.

Too bad, the cop said.

The registration search still running.

Five additional minutes passed.

I *really* need to go, Tig said again. I've been holding it for a long time. I didn't want to say anything. Can I walk over to the bushes?

No response.

Hey! Tig said, voice nearing a yell.

Shut the fuck up, the white cop said.

Thom and I stared at each other. From where I stood I watched the car's clock change, inch the minutes forward. Within me, a pulsing nausea.

Please, Thom said in a tone of perfect supplication, please, officer. Could you let my cousin go. They're—she's, she just really needs to use a restroom. She's diabetic.

More silence ticked by.

We're wrapping up. I'll walk you over, the Black cop said, appearing to relent. Hold on a bit longer, miss.

But as he began to maneuver Tig from the car, they lurched and groaned. Urine darkened the crotch of their linen slacks, spattered the gravel. An exclamation of disgust flung itself into the air.

All the way back to the house Tig was stone-faced and circumspect. Do we have anything I can sit on, they'd said, jaw tight, not meeting my eyes or Thom's, when it was finally the three of us, alone, faced with moving forward from the past hour's wreckage.

I don't think . . . Thom trailed off, combing through the trunk.

Bro, I'm just trying to not get fucking piss on the car seat, they snapped.

My heart was thrumming with its own helplessness. I reached into my bag. A single useless napkin. Here, I said, tearing the newspaper off the diamond-facsimile clock. Smoothing it down on the seat. Then giving it up, I took out the dish towels I'd bought as wedding gifts. Laid them down. Here, sit.

Even after Tig was showered, changed, shrugging into a plaid sport coat I picked out, the air was funereal. The actual ceremony now in less than an hour. Hors d'oeuvres and cocktails were being served to the first, midwesternly punctual guests. What is your ETA babes, a text from Diana pinged in. Make sure you get here before the processional pls.

Thom was beginning to pull out of the driveway when Tig said, I just can't go right now.

I cannot go there yet, they repeated. We still have time, right?

It's still the pre-ceremony mingling stuff, I guess, Thom said. So yeah, we do. A smidge.

We drove through Harambee, Riverwest, then Brewers Hill. The air in the car thick with anger.

Do you have any video? Thom asked me. We could get it on @antigone
_speaks, we could try—

I shook my head. It was too long, I said. I'm so sorry.

Putting it up would have done nothing, Tig said softly. They didn't do
anything to me, by most people's standards. Fifty thousand people would
have gotten to see me piss my pants. Raising awareness is not the answer
here.

In a faltering voice I asked if we could register some sort of complaint,
somewhere. Was met by twin stares of disbelieving contempt.

I want them to pay! I want somebody, just one of the fuckers who
have fucked with us over the years, to fucking pay, Thom finally spat out
in the silence, his cheeks red. I want to lob a mortar through the Tosa
precinct window if it didn't mean spending the next ten years in jail.
Those *pigs*.

I know what I'm finna do, Tig said, very calm. Slow down, pull up at
the corner.

We were on Palmer, approaching Vine. I saw the edge of a slate-gray
house. Rosebushes without roses.

As we pulled to a stop in front of Amy's house, Tig grabbed the remaining Macy's bag. Reached for the car door and popped the lock open.
A hot flash of understanding burst through me.

I jumped out. Wrestled Tig back into the passenger seat.

Drive, I hissed at Thom, belting myself back in. He obeyed. I grabbed
Tig's shoulder, my face suffused with the fury only family can bring
out in us.

Don't be so fucking *stupid*, I snarled. What, you were going to set off
fireworks on that woman's porch? They have a security camera, you
dumb bitch. You think you wouldn't get caught? What if that house
caught fire—

I want it to, that would be the point!

It's called arson, you absolute bloody fool! You know how much time
you would serve? You *cannot* be this *impulsive*!

Tig squeezed their eyes shut.

I'm just so tired, they said, voice small and quavering, of how everybody, every evil boss, every landlord, every capitalist, every cop, *gets away with it*. I want someone to for once not get away with it. This is Amy. Who terrorized you when you were so young and vulnerable. Who tried to put you out on the street. I just want her, any one of these people, to know that, even years later, some debts can come *due*.

I don't want to burn down her house, Tig whispered. I just want her to also know what it's like, for even one minute, to be *scared*.

The engine's hum. From the rearview mirror I could see Thom's eyes were wet, and I didn't understand why.

I stared at Tig. My darling. My old friend. Who had saved me, all those times. What injustice inflicted on them would I not bloody someone for? The years telescoped. Tig, knocking boldly on Amy's door after she'd mistreated me. Me, staring up at a copse of young manjadi trees, at what my seeds had grown. Me, reading these words in a black leather notebook in Tig's haphazard writing: *We create our lives saying one small yes to one small thing at a time. We create the world that way.*

What nobody told me when I was a very young person was that obedience, fearful toeing of every line, chasing every kind of safety, would not save you. What nobody told me growing up was that sometimes your friends do join your family, fusing care, irritation, loyalty, shared history, and affectionate contempt into a tempered love, bright and daily as steel.

All right, I said into the silent car. They both looked at me.

I put my hand on Thom's arm.

Go back, I told him. Take Commerce, loop round.

He did. I leaned forward, reached up, opened the Fit's moonroof.

Somewhere within me a juridical instinct did prickle, a voice that attempted to play the defense, noting that this sort of person was a pawn in the larger scheme of things, was not who was ultimately responsible for all that had gone wrong. But Peter, or Stacy, or the vast flickering network of finance and capital that trades on the hardship of ordinary people, these were targets too protected and diffuse for anyone to do much about. In this moment, in a lapse of the principles I'd held for most of my life, I settled for middle management.

Gun it, I told Thom as we turned onto my old street. He floored the gas. As I twisted my body between car seats, pushed through the roof, the air hit me. Cool, bracing, moving at me with great speed.

Tig did as I asked. Handed me the Lismore.

With all the force I could compel I hurled the clock through her window.

The leaded crystal sparkling in the lowering light.

Long and high and terrified, Amy's scream rang out, over the sound of breaking glass.

7

We arrived with minutes to spare. Sat on white folding chairs draped in golden tulle, adrenaline coursing through us. Our feet on freshly mown grass. Diana helped Tig fix their tie, mouthed, What happened? Next to me Noelle and Thom intertwined fingers, looked ahead into a shared sight line.

My pulse was racing still, my mind replaying the noise of a window exploding inward. Falling back down into the car as we whipped past my old home, I'd registered a jagged exhilaration. Joy cut with shame.

But if living in the nerve center of American politics had taught me anything it was that it is foolish to pretend we have no enemies. It is our enemies who have chosen us, stamped us from the beginning. Counting on nothing but continued power for their own thriving. The truth is, eventually people find targets to repay the pain inflicted upon them. That the targets are so often inaccurate is glided over, an accepted part of the way things are.

It was time.

We smiled big as KJ walked shyly down the aisle, arms sleeved in mehndi.

Em's best friend walked up to the mandap with Amit. Lifted a violin to her chin. A long, pained, gorgeous burst of sound.

And then Em appeared.

Mother and father walking them. Hair cropped to the skull. Their beauty glittering, faceted, almost painful to behold. To the shock and delight and moderate scandalization of the aunties in the crowd, they did wear something Indian after all.

They'd made their own sherwani. It was astonishingly well done. All clean masculine lines, rich, iridescent fabric poised somewhere between green and blue. They stood tall in it, jubilant, proud as anything.

Em's mother stepped forward to the mandap. At the end of her speech, this bird-boned Chinese American woman read the conclusion of Kennedy's opinion in *Obergefell*.

> No union is more profound than marriage, for it embodies the highest ideals of love, fidelity, devotion, sacrifice, and family. In forming a marital union, two people become something greater than once they were. . . . Marriage embodies a love that may endure even past death.

I remembered where we were when the news came. The scream of joy that nearly tore my eardrum. Marina flinging arms around me. The two of us absorbed into the crowd on G Street. The White House refracted into rainbow. Strangers of every age embracing each other, cheering, weeping.

A thin glitter-spattered white boy gave me a sunflower. Golden yellow with a dark core, the size of a child's skull. I'd thought, The world we knew has always been half-terrible, made as it is by the powerful, for the powerful. We were crowning a different one. Its birth would not be easy; no birth was.

I'd leaned back in my lover's arms, bumping against two older brown men, who beamed down at me. Marina's eyes blazing. Long nose red from tears. I will love you forever, she had said to me.

The prayers began. Amit tied a mangalsutra around Em's neck. They did the same for him.

As the priests chanted, Amit and Em were guided in circles around the small fire.

By the end of their final revolution, they were married.

Amit bent to be festooned with marigold and jasmine garlands. His cheeks wet with tears.

Watching, I registered a happiness licked all over with pain, a feeling gnawed down to the bone and left on the floor to trip over.

I will love you forever. A love that may endure.

But you left me, I thought with a stab of grief, as Amit kissed Em, long and slow, cradled their face in both his hands. I was too closed off for you, too withholding, too damaged. You left me, and now I'm alone. And you're not.

The crowd cheering. We watched the golden-lit newlyweds mince down an aisle of mown grass.

An arm clamped around me, drawing me close. Thom.

Are you okay? he asked.

I looked up at him, tears beading my eyelashes. In a rare honesty I shook my head.

Sneha, he said.

I shrugged.

You always have a place here with us, my dude, he said in my ear, audible under the whoops of the wedding crowd. Voice full of gruff tenderness. Whenever you are ready. You can always come back. You can bring your parents. We'd be glad to have them. You have a place here.

I clenched my teeth, bit the inside of my cheek so I did not bawl. I tried to smile. Returned his hug.

Tig, KJ, and Diana passed out glasses of orange juice and champagne, yuzu lemonade and lassi with the bridespeople. The photographer loudly snapped pictures of the newlyweds, the wedding party. The reception was soon to follow. A sumptuous meal, dancing under the oaks, the firework display by the lakefront.

We ate passed hors d'oeuvres. Greeted those around us. Smiled for pictures.

Noelle and Diana were shocked to hear about the police stop. The women clutched their beloveds close.

We sat down together to eat the wedding feast.

After, standing by myself at the open bar, I watched Em stride up to Amit on the dance floor, all iridescence and swagger, and offer their hand.

When Marina texted me midreception, formal and apologetic—no, love, enjoy yourself, we can talk later this week, I am sorry to disturb you, just have some bad news and some good news, another time is fine— I walked up to the guest bedroom, into the white marble bathroom with its Aesop soaps, closed the door, and called her back.

The words dance in me, unsaid, chaotic, alongside a new desire to renege on my long-held ultimatum about her sobriety. The notion flows from my conversation with Tig—love as a commitment, practice, a perpetual recovery. It must mean something that three years later I am still thinking about her. If we are in fact each other's person, we should simply be together, I think, watching the phone ring. Could move hand in hand through the brutal world.

She answers.

My dear, she says. It's so good to hear your voice.

When Marina tells me about the symptoms, the battery of tests, the result, I stay calm. Liver disease, she says, her voice wavering slightly before it stills, takes on a reassuring tone. As if I am the one whose feelings need soothing. She tells me statistics, the rising rates in still-young women, her confidence in her doctors. And after so many years, my uncle's face swims before my eyes.

She says her cirrhosis is not terribly advanced yet. The specialists have given her an 80 percent chance. Higher if she never drinks again.

Chance at recovery, I attempt to clarify.

Oh. Um, well. Survival. But really, babe, that's pretty high. I'm really in a good place.

My mouth floods with a metal taste. I am about to interject, offer every kind of support I can think of, money for the hospital bills if she needs it. But this is not, or not only, what she has called to say.

More than this, I wanted to tell you—because you are my dear friend, and I didn't think it was right for you to see it first on social media—well. I have good news too.

Okay?

Joanna proposed.

I touch the white tile of the bathroom wall. Close my eyes.

Marina continues, a tendril of fear in her voice. I said yes, she tells me. We are so happy. I know you will be happy for me.

Somewhere within me a planet begins to break apart, its gravitational force juddering to a halt. That is so wonderful, I use every fiber of my strength to say, lips trembling. Congratulations.

I add, Congrats to her too. Of course I'm happy for you, love. You deserve every joy.

I feel so very blessed, babe, she says, voice bright. I am very loved and supported, by you and by others, and you know, I basically am at a point where I trust a higher power, will stay sober no matter what, and plan to have a long and beautiful life. No liver disease has met this tough bitch from the Jerz, okay? I'm going to beat this, and then I'm gonna get to wedding planning!

I somehow say the right things.

Yes, she agrees, the warm smoke voice I know, I got this. I'm going to beat it.

You are, I say. Damn right! You are!

When the phone call ends I sink to the floor. The tile by the toilet is cold against my face. It smells very clean, sweetly antiseptic. Outside I hear the soft boom and crackle of fireworks. Aloneness floods me. Narcotic, alchemical. For a long time I lie there, a shocking, physical ache splitting through my chest.

Finally I reach for my phone, type a message out.

What I do not know is that at this moment Tig is helping set off the smoke bombs. The vapor, thick and cloudy, smells of sulfur and tomatoes. Here's Tig, laughing with the joyful crowd around them. Here's Tig crouched in the dark, setting off fuses and running for cover. Tig, young revolutionary in the making, showing the children how to handle the gunpowder-dipped sticks, hold fire and controlled explosion in their hands.

It is Thom who sees my message, walks up the stairs, searches the rooms, comes in. Who calls my name.

Hey, c'mon. Let's get you up, my guy. Come on, sit up with me.

I am tearless. I am quiet. I wish to vanish. To be nothing. He picks me up off the cold tiled floor and I hear his knees click, breath hiss out his nostrils from the pain. He carries me to the bed, places me down very carefully. Wraps arms around me, holds me fast.

Hey, Thom says, with indescribable gentleness.

He says my name, voice full of thorns. He says, I am so sorry.

Somewhere from a distant planet I can reconnect the words he is murmuring to meaning. You always have me, Sneha. You will always have us.

It is then that I see it flicker before me like a promise. The empty room full of light.

This is my tragedy and my great good fortune, to be the recipient of this bond, to be kept alive under its crushing warmth and weight, to be given it so freely, so much more than I have ever deserved.

The world has ended a thousand times and my name called in each new book of it.

ACKNOWLEDGMENTS

This book owes debts of gratitude to many.

To my parents, for raising me in homes where books were cherished, for the example of their courage and devotion, for the sacrifices they made, for their deep love.

To Bill, life-changer and angel; to everyone else at the Clegg Agency.

To Lindsey Schwoeri, for everything. I am so grateful. To the stellar team at Viking, including but not limited to Allie Merola, Andrea Schulz, Brian Tart, Lindsay Prevette, Mary Stone, Molly Fessenden, Sara DeLozier, Sara Leonard, Kate Stark, Jason Ramirez, Elizabeth Yaffe, Chelsea Cohen, Lucia Bernard, Claire Vaccaro, and Bridget Gilleran.

To the Whited Foundation, the Asian American Writers' Workshop, Millay Arts, and most significantly the unemployment benefits afforded by the CARES Act, which made the writing of this book materially possible.

To my teachers through the years. Ayana Mathis, Margot Livesey, Amber Dermont, Jess Walter, Ethan Canin, Sean Bishop, Ron Wallace, Emily Ruskovich, Amy Quan Barry, and Lan Samantha Chang. To Lauren Groff for that unforgettable writing workshop and every kindness after. To Deb, Jan, Sasha, and Connie. To Michael Fultz, Joshua Calhoun, and Christopher Lee for their compassion. To Gina Enk and Steven Buenning (rest in peace)—for encouragement, world-class education, care, and, quite simply, noticing the frightened new kid.

To those who read this manuscript in its adolescence, including DA Ruiz, Breanne Pemberton, Melissa Anderson, Lauren Peterson, James Frankie Thomas, Anna Lucia Feldmann, and Phillip Ortiz. Deep gratitude to C Pam

Zhang, Dawnie Walton, Steph Karp, Sanjena Sathian, Anna Polonyi, and Susan Choi for their care and support.

To my friends from Sunrise and Bed-Stuy Strong, who have shown me time and again the value of muscular optimism. To Jackson, Hanna, Chris, Alyssa, Hadass, Derek, Nia, Sky, and all the other BSS organizers who did even more while I took the time to write this.

To *Lucy* by Jamaica Kincaid, *Open City* by Teju Cole, *Here We Are* by Aarti Shahani, and *The God of Small Things* by Arundhati Roy.

To Noah Whitford, Alexandra Savilo, Katie Fischer, Meghna Rao, Praveen Fernandes, Chris Xu, and Hanna King. I've been so lucky to have you.

To Nate Sullivan, for belief in me that preceded my own, for dragging me to D— Tea in undergrad between work and classes so I would write, for painstakingly reading my drafts over the years, for unstinting grace. To Jose Cornejo, who told me to get out, told me to pause the old project and try a new one, told me there was someone I really should meet. To Shireen, best hypeman, moral support, funny guy, beloved sister.

To Phil, brilliant and caring and kind, who encouraged me to take on the risks of following my dream. Who was there through the darkest times. Who reminds me: when in doubt, go big—a hundred flyers, always. This book would not have lived without you.

at the end of the world, let there be you, my world. —Danez Smith